THE MAN WITH THE GOLDEN *TOOTH*

~ The first Gregor McAuley Book ~

JACK PARKES

Fisher King Publishing

THE MAN WITH THE GOLDEN *TOOTH*

Copyright © Jack Parkes 2023

Print ISBN 978-1-916776-03-6
Digital ISBN 978-1-916776-04-3

Published by Fisher King Publishing
www.fisherkingpublishing.co.uk

This book is dedicated to former
colleagues in HMPS.

Acknowledgements

I've often heard it said that everyone has a book in them, so during the COVID lockdowns, I thought I'd see whether this was so. 'The Man with The Golden *Tooth'* is the result and I'd like to thank Rick at Fisher King Publishing for his encouragement in bringing this project to fruition.

Primary thanks must go to my long-suffering wife Rachel for the many mental absences when I was somewhere else in my head. Thanks, too, to my friends Wayne Mallanaphy and Paddy Lafferty for lending me their names. Other than them, any similarities between anyone living or dead, is unintentional. Thanks too, to the friends who read various sections and offered constructive feedback, particularly 'no. 1 son', Kav, who mocked up the first edition and spend hours editing the final version.

I must admit that for the benefit of the plot, I played fast and loose with various lockdown dates, travel restrictions and air-bridges and I offer my apologies to any Muslim readers for having moved the date of Eid.

Prelude

Sunshine. Bright sunshine, gentle breezes and the smell of exotic flowers. Gregor McAuley had awoken to another gorgeous day of blue skies and brilliant sunshine. This city of pastel and white walls and terracotta roofs, mainly contained within its natural amphitheatre, rising up to fertile foothills with their semi-tropical greenery and furrowed terraces, was already basking in its daily heat-haze. On a day like today, when the sea was calm and still, the light played on its surface and penetrated its depths of translucent green. There was something about the feel of the place, the weather and the relaxed pace of life, which had immediately pulled him in.

The quality of light in Madeira was really quite extraordinary. It would take him a little while to acclimatise from an indifferent late English spring to these warm nights. Nevertheless, although his head was muddy, the air was clear. He sat down, somewhat warily, at a table on an otherwise deserted café terrace close to the fort of São Tiago, having walked down the narrow, winding streets from his place near the botanic gardens, ignoring the cable-car option on the basis that the exercise would do him good. He'd arrived with aching legs; steep streets were among the many things he was going to have to get used to. Given the obvious lack of clientele in his chosen café it wasn't a surprise that the waiter was particularly attentive.

"Olá, bom dia. Um café, se faz favour." He smiled

warmly as he spoke to the young man.

Did the lad look slightly disappointed? No chance to practice his English this time. Still, that at least saved him from the awkwardness of committing the most basic of hospitality faux pas, that of misidentifying his customer and addressing him in the wrong language. Not that this customer would be in a position to enter into anything other than a superficial conversation. Of course, he would need to get to grips with the language, not that he'd ever pass as a local. Before he'd arrived here, largely on a whim to keep his brain active, he'd been doing evening classes, and an online course for beginners that he could dip in and out of, mainly out of, and that had pretty much helped him make the decision about where to run away to, but it had not left him greatly equipped for deeply philosophical conversation.

How did people here always seem to know he was British? He'd eventually asked a supermarket checkout girl when she'd said, "Do you want a bag with that?"

"Well, the Scandinavian season's over, you aren't wearing walking boots so you can't be German, so you're either Dutch or British and as you both speak English I couldn't go wrong."

"What about Irish?" he'd asked.

"You're not pale enough. Anyway, there aren't direct flights."

Put like that he couldn't fault her logic.

It was only afterwards that he'd wondered what marked out the French.

This innocent exchange bothered him. He wanted to keep a low profile, mainly because of the possible risks he faced, but also because the British abroad were not always a joy to be around – well, the English primarily, but everyone got tarred with the same brush.

What he'd begun to appreciate was just how small his life had been before he came here, in contrast to the freedom he now enjoyed. The image of a hamster on its wheel had popped into his mind: the same dull journey to and from work; the same daily routine; the same faces day in and day out, most of whom he didn't care if he never saw again and some of whom he actively disliked; a dead-in-the-water social life, lived in semi-lockdown in the cramped confines of his little flat, and the misery of a relentless winter and hard spring. Now he could enjoy the feel of the sun on his skin; he could come and go as he pleased, when he pleased, and although his social circle was small, it included the most important people in his life.

He loved the island, its varied scenery and its people: in short, he felt energised and liberated, as if a weight of oppression had been lifted from his shoulders. This place was so remote, so far removed from any possibility of running into those who had threatened him. He wasn't now even sure whether those threats had been real, or just angry words, shouted in a moment of defeat, but violence had been involved and the threat of retaliation felt real at the time. The warm sunshine and quiet pace of life here had made the fear of reprisal recede somewhat, and for all he knew, his assailant's anger had cooled, but the police had told him to get away, so get away he had.

He removed his cap and scratched his head, feeling a momentary shock as he encountered only the stubble of what had once been a stylish cut. Looking blearily into the mirror first thing still took his breath away as he encountered his alternative face. This new face was him, but not him. And his beard: he felt naked without it, but the Factor 30 had done much to deal with the shaving rash and he still only had the one chin so, silver linings all round eh? He was hopeful that this mismatched complexion would even out in the coming days, but it would take him a lot longer to get used to wearing glasses again after years of contact-lens wearing. All these were reminders that he was on the run, (but without being entirely sure if anyone was actually looking for him) and these simple changes as part of this new identity were to misdirect any followers. What a good job he'd never got round to having the half-sleeve tattoo he'd been fancying for about a decade.

His legs would forever mark him out as an outsider too. He'd used to quip that he had special non-tanning legs and that the glare the international space station experienced when he was wearing shorts was simply light reflected from them.

It didn't seem quite as witty now.

He knew he needed to keep positive, and there was much here to be positive about. The sun shone for most of the year and the temperature was nearly always good enough for a T-shirt. The food was fantastic; the city, really a large town, was lovely and the scenery second to none.

What was not to like?

He noticed that the waiter wasn't bothering with a face mask. Under the circumstances who could blame him? So, he took his off. After all, who needs a two-tone suntan? That wouldn't look too great when he got home.

When he got home.

Home.

So, he was still in that default mind-set, was he?

This was now home, the country's fifth largest city, hundreds of miles from the mainland, a paradise, a floating garden they called it. Had he landed on his feet or his arse? Only time would tell, but the waters of international concerns rarely washed up on these shores. He was definitely out of the mainstream here and glad of that. This wasn't like the Greek islands where you could hop on and off regular ferries. This was the middle of the Atlantic. Well, not actually the middle, but it felt like it.

And Coronavirus of course.

Eerily empty streets and few functioning hotels, and the ocean-side boulevards now the sole preserve of the locals who seemed to be rejoicing in rediscovering their home, free of tourists – except that this was an economy based on tourism and was now in free-fall. There had been an unseemly chaos at the airport as people tried to get home and then no flights in and no cruise ships, although that suited him well enough. Even most of the elderly migrant Brits who lived here for most of the year had been panicked into going home, only to find a country lamentably ill-prepared to deal with an international pandemic, leaving behind an island which would subsequently prove to have the lowest COVID infection rate in Europe.

He let his attention wander as he thought of cruise ships, imagining what it must be like to arrive here after dark, out of the endless blackness of the night sea, to see the lights of the city twinkling ahead as if suspended like Will-O-The-Wisps and slowly growing bigger until the land materialised at the last minute. It must be truly magical.

The waiter had given up fiddling with his mobile phone and was hovering with a look of resentment, so he trawled his memory for the words.

"Para mim um bolo se faz favour, e um copo de suco de laranja."

Bolo: cake. He had a friend who'd claimed that there was no problem that couldn't be solved by cake. It was probably a good job that he'd not taken that piece of wisdom entirely to heart, and the orange juice would go some way towards reviving him. He thanked the waiter and watched bubbles rise in his drink, appreciating the condensation on the outside of the glass.

He sat, almost contented, and with the mountains behind him, did what everyone on the island did when they had a few moments to spare; he looked out at the shimmering sea, listening to the chatter of unfamiliar birdsong, and appreciating the warm breeze and the feel of the sun on his skin.

Chapter One

Flamur Vrioni turned over in bed and looked at the sleeping figure beside him. She was undoubtedly a beautiful girl, this girl from Moldova, fair haired and long-legged. She was also clever: her CV said she had graduated from a good university. He would keep her until she bore him a son who he would then send back to his mother in Albania. Even so, she was 'luckier' than the others because he kept her for himself rather than pimping her out - and she was afraid of him, which made things so much easier.

These girls and their naivety: so desperate for a better life in the west that they continued to apply for the fake jobs they saw on-line: waitress, carer, nanny, hotel domestic and so on. He knew that family apart, no one cared about missing girls any more than they cared about asylum seekers and refugees who went missing, certainly not the police it would appear: their job was hard enough without the complication of hassle from a foreign police force. Of course, once the girls had been recruited, the phone numbers and websites were discontinued, so good luck trying to track them down that way.

He looked at his watch. The next batch were due in just over an hour. Lithuanian, Romanian, Macedonian, Slovak, Bosnian, Slovenian and Ukrainian, all with their hopes and expectations about to be shattered. He looked at his sleeping partner, at the curve of her breast: did he have time? Regretfully, no. Anyway, he might have to 'induct' one of the newcomers shortly.

There was undoubtedly money to be made in the trade for fresh flesh, and he lived well, but the real money was in drugs, and he was about to make a significant move up that ladder.

Mr. Yellow.

He'd been hearing that name on the fringes of things more and more recently: a name always said with a hint of reverence as befitted someone worthy of respect and fear, but no one he knew had so far met him. He'd been told that Yellow was not a common name in the U.K. and so could be a code name. Was this a hint at Chinese Triads as others had speculated? He doubted it. Chinese gangs were very territorial, tended not to recruit outside their own communities and had not yet made inroads into the local trade. No doubt all would become clear in the fullness of time, but in the meantime, he didn't care if Mr. Yellow, (wisely in Vrioni's view), wanted to remain anonymous. As long as he paid well, he could call himself after any colour of the rainbow.

Fentanyl. This was where the good money was now – not that Vrioni knew or cared about what fentanyl was or did. He wasn't about to sample it, just distribute it.

He got up, careless of any noise he might make. Wisely, his reluctant companion chose to remain asleep. One coffee, two lines of coke and two cigarettes later, he was on his way to meet the minibus, confident that all was going smoothly. It never ceased to amaze him that these girls didn't become suspicious when they were picked up at the airport and his agents took their passports off them for 'processing.' At that point, of course, his men were all helpfulness, charm and reassurance, but they were already making their personal picks from the group.

He sat outside the hotel in his car and watched as the minibus drew up. He moved his head from side to side, feeling a clicking sound where he was sure there shouldn't be one. As he lifted his chin, the flesh on the back of his neck arranged itself into rolls. It was such a short neck that his ears virtually sat on his shoulders.

The driver of the minibus jumped down and opened the doors, chivvying the girls up with some cheerful banter as they formed a line, trailing their suitcases behind them. The hotel door was opened by a smiling man and the girls began to go in. There were about three left outside when one of the girls at the front of the line realised what they were walking into and tried to turn round. There was the sound of a shot, chaos, shouting and screaming and the last girl in the line made a break for it, running with a surprising turn of speed for a girl wearing a backpack. The girl in front of her hesitated for a fraction and that was enough for the driver to fell her with a punch to the stomach and drag her inside.

Vrioni was out of the car in a flash and on the tail of the runaway but she'd too much of a head start.

What is she? Some sort of Olympic runner?

By the time he'd made it back to the car with thoughts of pursuit that way, she'd had the wit to make for the lights of the high street and was already lost in the crowd, a crowd swollen by New Year's revellers. Vrioni cursed. He should have been out on the pavement when the minibus arrived, not sitting in his car. Out of the corner of his eye, he saw another figure hurrying away. That was all they needed, an escapee and a witness. Had things gone according to plan, the witness would have seen nothing to arouse his suspicions, just a group of girls, possibly a hen party, checking in to a cheap hotel.

The hotel was now a bust. It had been empty and on the list for redevelopment for some time and so had made a good reception centre for his girls. As they always arrived after dark, Vrioni hadn't needed to spend much to make the place look habitable from the outside, but he'd made sure the reception area looked welcoming. The normal routine was to have one of his guys, the nerdiest looking, togged up in uniform and with a name badge, process the girls one at a time and then directing them to the lounge. Once through that door, the girls would face the menacing reality of the rest of the gang and see the first girl through, held with a gun to her head. Too shocked to respond, and with a dawning reality of their situation, the girls tended to be numbed into compliance.

So, what had gone wrong this time?

The nerdy receptionist, expressing manufactured outrage in the hope of escaping blame, spragged up the rest of the gang for still being in the reception area when the girls arrived. Even the most dim-witted girl couldn't fail to realise what was going on. Vrioni was incandescent with rage, laying into the gang with fists as well as curses, and not sparing the receptionist for failing to ensure everyone had been in place. Fortunately for them, time was against him and the need to abandon the hotel in haste was now urgent.

Chapter Two

Andreja Horvat knew she'd been right to be suspicious. An investigative journalist in her native Ljubljana, she'd been working on a story about the sex-trafficking of Eastern European women to the west. There were a disturbing number of stories about young women setting off to Germany, Sweden, France and the U.K. in search of job opportunities, and dropping off the radar. She thought of these girls who had left home with dreams of a better life and ended up in saunas, pole dancing clubs and any number of other demeaning joints as sex slaves.

Against all the advice of her family, but encouraged by her editor, she'd decided to go undercover and respond to one of the ads she'd flagged up as suspicious. As English was her only other language, the choice of destination was clear cut. The ad she responded to was suspicious in her view because after BREXIT, she'd thought it unlikely that a U.K. based employment agency would still be advertising in Slovenia.

Her suspicions were raised further when on contacting the agency, she'd been advised to tell immigration on arrival that she was just visiting for a holiday.

"Just to oil the wheels of an overworked bureaucracy and avoid burdensome form filling. Are you OK with that?"

She'd said she was, and had assumed that anyone who

said they weren't, self-selected themselves off the agency's list.

Just before she set off for the airport, Oskar Petek, her editor, had given Andreja a small, gift-wrapped parcel. When she unwrapped it, she was confused to see a small jewellery gift-box. She looked at him with surprise.

"Go on, open it."

Inside was a small St. Christopher medallion on a chain. It was rather lovely too. She was deeply touched by the gesture, and rather confused.

"St. Christopher, the patron saint of travellers. My star journalist is off on a dangerous journey. I reckon she needs all the help she can get." He took the chain and fastened it around her neck and then looked embarrassed. "Good luck," he said gruffly and then gave her a tight hug. "Stay safe, you hear me?" Then he gave her a little push in the back to send her on her way. "Off you go."

Andreja didn't consider herself a religious person by any stretch of the imagination, but the gesture had been so sweet, so uncharacteristic, that she fingered the little medallion all the way to the airport.

On her flight to Manchester, and sitting several rows behind her, was Marco Erjavec, one of her paper's best photographers, in fact, one of the best in the business. He got the sorts of pictures other photographers hoped for, but rarely got. He was a useful looking man too, built like an iceberg and with biceps so big he had trouble walking with his arms by his sides. Once through passport control, she'd slipped him her genuine passport for safe keeping, confident that the false passport she knew she'd be asked to hand over would pass muster. Then she hung back to let Marco go ahead of her so that he would be able to monitor and photograph all that happened next.

In the vast arrivals hall, she'd been told to look out for a sign saying Millennium Agency. She'd dressed to look attractive: classy, not cheap but now these heels were killing her. She found airports stressful at the best of times, but this was something else.

She was greeted by a friendly young man who led her to one of the airport coffee lounges where a group of other young women were already gathered. His jeans were low on his hips, showing grey pants and half his bum.

I'm sure this isn't the image the Millennium Agency wants to project.

It was just another clue. Whoever was in charge should have given the guy some sort of corporate look. She noted without surprise, that the other girls were all pretty.

"We've just the flight from Skopje to wait for now. Shouldn't be more than half an hour. Thanks for being so patient."

Having given up her fake passport, (and expressed faux surprise at the request and then faux reassurance at the explanation), she'd tried to pump him for information, but he replied that he was only contracted to be the transport to Sheffield so couldn't tell her anything. She felt he was being evasive. He certainly looked it, despite his charm. It took her a while to spot Marco, and she felt reassured that he was getting a photographic record of everything.

She felt both excited and apprehensive. Her instincts were telling her that she was on to something.

The minibus had darkened windows which made it harder to see where they were going.

"All part of the service Ladies. We thought you might want to catch up on your sleep."

Even so, she became fairly certain after a while that they weren't heading towards Sheffield. She had opted to sit at the back and occasionally looked out of the rear window, wondering which of the cars behind them was being driven by her paper's local contact with Marco as passenger. So far, all had gone according to plan, and she was pleased with how well things were working out.

Initially the other girls had been quite chatty, but as the journey progressed, they grew quiet, and some tried to doze. Finally, they drew up in a quiet side street. The hotel didn't look much but they'd been told it was just for one night.

"OK Ladies. Welcome to sunny Sheffield. Let's be having you now. Chop chop. Form an orderly queue. There's a hot meal, a shower and a comfy bed waiting. Want a hand with that case Love?"

This was not Sheffield. Andreja knew that without a shadow of doubt, but none of the others seemed any the wiser. She hung back and was at the end of the line, a Romanian girl just ahead of her and she thought the Macedonian girl was at the front. She was on high alert, pleased that she'd slipped into her trainers on the journey.

The next thing she knew, there was a gunshot and

screams, and she was running. This was not the time to stop and ask questions. She'd almost grabbed the Romanian, but in that split second had sped off at full pelt instead without looking back. She hoped Marco had got all this. Her survival instinct had kicked in and she headed for the nearest signs of life.

The street she ran into was bright with Christmas lights and heaving with crowds of revellers. It was like a rebirth from darkness to light, from danger to safety.

Of course. It's New Year's Eve.

Once she'd burrowed her way into the crowd, trying to control her panic, she looked around to get her bearings, took out her phone and dialled Marco's number. He picked up almost at once and sounded breathless.

"Are you OK? Where are you?" She could hardly hear him for the noise of the crowd.

"I'm opposite a big store called Marks and Spencer," she shouted back, "I'm sitting at a table outside a German-style beer cellar."

"Right. Stay put. I'm on my way."

In the background a stumbling circle of people surged in and out, holding hands, laughing and chanting with more enthusiasm than tunefulness,

Should auld acquaintance be forgot...

Well, that was no stranger than throwing a shoe over her shoulder and checking its position to see whether she'd get married in the coming year. This affectionate, alcohol fuelled dance looked far more fun, she thought distractedly.

Perhaps it was inevitable that on this of all nights

there would be a heavy police presence and she saw two uniformed officers coming in her direction, one male and one female. The atmosphere was good, and they seemed quite relaxed in the crowd. She stood up and waved them over.

"Is everything alright Miss?"

She realised that what she was about to tell them was going to sound very unlikely. Things had moved quickly, and this was not something she had prepared for. Trying not to appear flustered, she got out her press card and launched into her tale, trying to sound as calm and professional as possible, which was hard as she was in complete turmoil and was on the verge of hyperventilating.

"Firstly, I need you to know that I am not drunk, and I need you to take me very seriously..."

She felt desperate, sure that shock was kicking in. She could tell the young officers were having trouble taking her story in, or at least the man was. The female officer listened more attentively and asked some pertinent questions as the crowd ebbed and flowed around them. When Andreja faltered, she prompted her gently. Then out of the crowd, Marco appeared. Andreja burst into tears and clung on to him, her hiccupping sobs a release of tension. Her tears made a dark mark on his shirt. Marco, however remained calm. His English was more rudimentary, but he had more gravitas than Andreja at that point and immediately began to show the officers the images he'd captured. The last but one image was of the Romanian girl being punched to the ground. The final image was of Andreja's back view as she fled the scene, pursued by a stocky man in a dark windcheater.

———

Under the circumstances Andreja reflected, things moved fairly quickly after that: just not quickly enough. They found themselves sitting in a comfortable interview room drinking welcome coffee, their documents checked, and their statements taken. Andreja had been offered the services of a doctor but now that she knew she was safe, she had calmed down.

Of course, the hotel was empty when an armed unit had turned up.

"Would you be willing to go back there?" a senior officer whose name they'd not taken on board had asked them.

Marco shrugged and looked at Andreja who had already been in touch with Ljubljana and was drafting her report on her laptop with nervous energy.

"Yes, if you think it will help."

It was certainly the right place. Of course, she'd not actually been inside the building, and she was surprised by how convincing the reception area looked, the area where, had she but known it, the young receptionist wearing the name badge, 'Charlie- happy to help', had had been all sweetness and light. There was even a key rack, but the lounge area was a bleak room beyond its door.

"Do you recognise this, Miss?" The senior officer held up a scarf that had been shoved down behind a seat.

Andreja didn't.

"Wait a minute." Marco got out his camera and began to flick through his pictures.

"There." They gathered around the screen.

"That's Regina," Andreja confirmed. "I think she's from Lithuania." She paused and looked around the room. "I heard a gunshot..." Her throat tightened.

"Ah, yes. This way." He led them back to the reception area and pointed at the ceiling. There was a small hole just to the right of a chandelier.

"There was no blood. We don't think anyone was hurt."

Andreja and Marco were put up in a real hotel. They had planned to return to Slovenia immediately after the police had finished with them, but their scoop was making waves in Slovenia and had been picked up by a number of European papers including in the UK. They were inundated with requests for interviews and given that the additional exposure might help the other girls, they were happy to oblige, particularly as Marco had taken good pictures of each of them which were now all over British breakfast TV. So too, were pictures of three of the gang members. Flamur Vrioni was not one of them.

"Are you able to do Loose Women?" one breathless TV researcher asked.

Andreja thought that was an unfortunate name under the circumstances but accepted. While she was enjoying the media attention, the bottom line was that she felt a passionate responsibility to the girls she'd shared the minibus with, and she involuntarily hugged herself at the thought of their fear. She hoped the families of the other girls didn't discover what had happened to their daughters via the media, but she knew the fuss the story was making internationally would ensure the issue would be taken seriously, and she took some comfort from that. Their plan to return home was put on hold. Andreja's editor wanted them to stay on for a few days in the hope that the other girls were rescued and get their stories for a follow-up splash.

Chapter Three

Up and about at the crack of a Monday's pre-dawn lull for an early shift, not that it was anywhere near dawn yet, Gregor McAuley thought that staying in bed would have been a much better option. January was an unforgiving month and today was cold, dreich and miserable. Rising at the first beep of the alarm, he wondered briefly if that made him a morning person. That was an unresolved question. He knew he wasn't a night owl. He was the only person he knew who'd choose to leave a party early and head for bed because he was tired. He thought he probably peaked at about 11.00am, then it was downhill all the way. He was sure he'd fall asleep around 4.00pm – he certainly wanted to – had it not been for the exacting work regime.

He'd not bothered with Christmas decorations. It wasn't that he was all bah-humbug about the celebrations, not at all, but it was hardly worth it for one person, although he had bought the most miniature of miniature trees to put on his windowsill to show willing.

Unlike many of his colleagues his journey to work on a good morning was a mere ten-minute drive from his flat, a flat he rented and with which he'd inherited a cat. This animal was possibly the least affectionate cat in the history of the domestication of pets, and a full-time shift pattern wasn't the best for being a pet owner in the first place, and anyway, he didn't have the right sort of hoover. It was a threadbare ginger Tom with a ragged ear, presumably from fighting. He hadn't bothered to give it a name, it wasn't as if it could speak English after all, and he was convinced that the cat, simply known as Cat, was cognitively impaired, maybe even emotionally disordered and certainly unpredictable of mood. Cat added nothing to his life, glaring malevolently at him whatever he tried to do for its comfort.

"Away wi' you then and find someone else to feed you."

Cat regarded him with malicious disdain, circled four times, seemed to lose interest, sat down, stretched and fell asleep.

It was a raw day and no mistake, and as he set off to face the wind's daily winter exfoliation, he tried to shiver off the cold. He put on Heart FM because their morning programme always made him smile and it was a good way to start the day, (although he had sworn that if he heard Slade's Merry Christmas Everybody one more time, he'd tear the radio out of the dashboard). The streets were patterned by frost, quiet and empty, at least until he hit the inner ring road, but at that time in the morning it was an easy journey as if the city was holding its breath before spitting out the commuters and a bus materialised out of the gloom, empty but with its lights shining brightly, looking (to those who, like him, had an over fertile imagination) like a ghost ship.

As he slowed at traffic lights, the Christmas lights already looked jaded, and he watched a middle-aged woman, wrapped up against the cold, her breath a plume of grey, fumbling to get a key in the lock of a florists. His mind wandered and didn't immediately come back as he wondered idly whether he would be cut out for a work routine which had sensible hours, although he couldn't see himself working in a retail or clerical role. Still, floristry: why ever not? Well, hay fever for a start. He smiled at this momentary flight of fantasy as he drew away, his long-term career aspirations still elusive. He was unsettled in his job: he liked to believe he was making a difference but, in all honesty, couldn't think of one concrete example.

These ruminations were like every unsatisfactory career interview imaginable. What do you enjoy? What are you good at? And perhaps more pertinently, what pays? In that order: music, music and not music.

Well, he'd had a job in music and one he'd loved but his career as a teacher had been something of a disappointment, burning brightly at the start and fading gradually under the inexorable workload of marking and confused government policy. He'd been a good teacher and had become Head of Department after only three years, but for all his classroom strengths, what he'd been less good at was schmoozing management and he'd had an ongoing battle of wills with one Assistant Head, a jumped-up PE type, promoted above her abilities: a woman of little intelligence and less charm. They'd argued about the cost-effectiveness of running an A Level group when Pissy Knickers had decided that courses couldn't run with less than eight students, and he'd only recruited seven.

"You want to watch out for her." the Head of RS said

on the way to registration. "If it's not English, Maths and Science, it's not important in our brave new world of education."

They'd both left at the end of that term, together with the school's only teacher of German. His leaving present was a certificate from friends:

The Member of staff most likely to say what the rest of us are thinking.

———

A rare shaft of winter sunlight reflected off the green dome of one of the city's mosques, and as he joined the queue to get into the staff car park, he tailgated the car in front thus avoiding winding down his window to flash his pass at the notoriously unreliable automated card-reader, in an attempt to keep warm for as long as possible. Then, having found a parking space near the recycling bins, with hands deep in his pockets and with his head down and his breath misting in the freezing air, he headed for the exit stairs.

Take care in winter conditions. Steps are icy.

Tell me about it.

The world was bleak in this bone-chilling cold snap and the cold had hit him like a wall. He shivered and pulled his scarf tighter around his neck as the wind nipped his ears and whipped at him with renewed force. He joined a huddle of staff waiting to get in, and by habit scanned the signs outside the main entrance as if, somehow, they would have changed their message.

It is a criminal offence to bring drugs into the prison.

Below that was the picture of a dog and a warning that sniffer dogs could detect drugs beneath the smell of perfume and soap, (and dirty nappies as dog handlers had discovered), above pictures of weeping wives and children.

And still they tried.

HMP Low Moor was situated in an area of Bradford where other premises had died a commercial death; an area ready for a redevelopment that was unlikely to happen. It was a building without any concession to architectural merit and would have looked more at home in the mountains of Transylvania, it was so formidably dark, brooding and castle-like. On reflection, McAuley doubted whether architectural aesthetics had been high on the building criteria. The place was no longer fit for purpose, Victorian, austere, crumbling and overcrowded. No doubt it was riddled with asbestos. Of course, it was all about funding.

"Yo! How you Blud?" A cheerful greeting from his friend Luke behind the window, checking staff passes as they shuffled towards the 'air lock'.

McAuley smiled. His was a disarming, ready, smile; a smile which revealed strong, white, even teeth, and one slightly crooked eye tooth.

"Aye, well enough thanks Luke. I'm in fine fettle the day. How's life in da ghetto?"

Despite his fluent use of patois when it suited him, Luke's upbringing couldn't have been further away from 'da ghetto.' His dad was a social worker from Durham and his mum a nurse from Martinique, herself part French.

Luke's real accent was pure Lancashire.

He was a joker who liked to keep the seriousness of life to a bare minimum. They'd joined the service together and had endured the ten week's training as something of a comedy duo. The Scottish Celt and the mixed-race lad from Altrincham: these were two who would not have been allowed to sit together at school - at least not twice. Being the only survivors from their intake eighteen months after joining, left them feeling vindicated, and during the time since they'd joined the service they'd grown closer, discovering a joint interest in fitness and had taken advantage of the prison gym, working with the instructors on weights and self-defence training. Luke was a very handy kickboxer. He was also a bit of a player when it came to the ladies, and he never missed a chance to give the chat.

"Watch and learn Old Son. Watch and learn. I'm shagging for England. Some days I can barely walk."

"Luke, we've talked about this..."

"You're just jealous."

"Aye, I need to be better at disguising that." He didn't wait for the comeback. He'd had antibiotics that responded quicker.

There was a kernel of truth in what Luke said, covered in numerous layers of macho exaggeration.

McAuley had once met some of Luke's university friends and it had, to Luke's discomfort, been an illuminating meeting.

"Yeah, in Fresher's week, he had three pints and threw

up all over us. He tried his first joint too and sat in the corner in a paranoid funk waiting for the police to come for him."

Not quite the legend then?

One large sliding door opened, releasing the night shift, and allowing this cohort in. Those on the way-out ought to look a lot happier than the miserable looking and exhausted bunch they actually were, he noted each time, wondering if he looked quite as defeated on his exit.

No more than eight people at one time.

He was absorbed into the space and counted fourteen: assorted officers, nurses, instructors and admin staff, most of who's behind the scenes job descriptions he could only guess at. The chance of any of them putting any physical distance between themselves and any of the others was non-existent: they were so close they could smell each other, perfume, tobacco, sweat and greasy food. They were a mixture of age, race and gender, brought together by working in jobs they probably hated. The chat and banter slowed as the first door slid painfully slowly to a close behind them and they waited for the identical door opposite to open and release them to disappear in a dozen directions to their various duties.

—

Detective Inspector Sadie Brewer was knackered and longed for a holiday she knew she'd probably never take. Chief Superintendent Murchison had called her into his office. She had been thinking of eating a sandwich, so took the summons personally. If she was lucky, Brewer would escape Murchison's habitual use of management-speak, a jargon George Orwell would surely have recognised. If she was very lucky, she wouldn't get drawn into a conversation about budgets and target setting. She crossed her fingers and leaving the sound of telephones ringing and the muted mutter of half a dozen conversations, Brewer headed for Murchison's office.

When she got there, he did not offer her coffee, which she thought was rude, and he told her he was temporarily reassigning her to the Modern Slavery and Human Trafficking Unit.

He'd recently taken up running and was in training for a marathon. For someone who was reputed to be obsessive about health and fitness, he looked distinctly unwell. This just confirmed her longstanding belief that exercise was bad for you.

"How was your last run Sir?"

She didn't actually care but felt that making polite conversation kept the channels of communication open.

"Oh, I improved on my personal best, thanks."

If I lived in Bradford, I'd run like hell to get out too.

She smiled.

"You'll have read about it in the papers or seen it on the TV. This sex trafficking case is now our number one priority. The Home Office are shitting themselves."

Now that was a disturbing image she'd be left with for the rest of the day.

She had seen it on the TV, of course. It was compelling viewing, and it didn't hurt that the young Slovene journalist was a looker, with good English and a rather attractive accent. She'd not done her career any harm. The newspapers were full of it and some soul-searching was taking place.

Is this who we are? screamed one headline in The Yorkshire Post.

Sadie was by nature a cynic and couldn't help but wonder to what extent all the sudden publicity had bumped this case up the list, given that there was sadly nothing new about sex trafficking, but instead simply asked, "Why me?"

"It's felt a woman's perspective would be helpful here and let's face it Sadie, this is right up your street - and you've nothing much else on right now, have you?"

Patronising flannel, truth and pragmatism. What a febrile combination.

"I'll need my sergeant."

Well, want rather than need, but Gill Baines was a great asset, and the pair were becoming quite a formidable double act. In addition, they were good friends. Sadie appreciated Gill for her pragmatism and unflappability. Gill Baines was also the sort of officer who could think outside the box and make connections others missed.

Murchison screwed his face into a grimace and sighed.

Do we have to go through this charade every time? Brewer found most exchanges with Murchison deeply frustrating.

This had all the hallmarks of a panicked response driven by political expediency. Helicoptering her into an existing unit was no way to do things, so she was determined she wasn't going in alone.

Murchison sighed again. "I suppose so."

There was a reason Brewer hadn't opted to move to the sex-crimes unit voluntarily. The work was, in her view, psychologically damaging. That was her bottom line. Wading through the shit of the seamiest side of society was not something she wanted for herself, and she started mentally preparing an apology for Gill Baines.

Chapter Four

There were fifteen sets of gates and doors to be painstakingly unlocked and relocked between reception and the central hub from which four wings, each with three landings, radiated. Unlocking and relocking one more gate, he entered A Wing, the wing for "vulnerable" prisoners, (also known as nonces). As McAuley approached his wing's gate there was the usual taunting and barracking of those A Wing men by men from the other wings.

"Perverts!"

"Dirty Bastards!"

"Fucking paedos!"

He sighed as he looked at the track-suited hecklers.

Stupid wee neds, he thought. *You stabbed your mother, you beat up an Asian shopkeeper for "looking at you" and you were so pished you ran over a girl cycling home from school, so let's do without the moral outrage, eh?*

He lowered the pitch of his voice. "Right yous lot. Whit d'ye think ye'r gawkin at? Oan yer bikes!" Resorting to his best Glaswegian, he waved them away. He found that the occasional judicious use of a Glaswegian accent generally had the desired effect, although there was a chance, he thought, that this approach might not embody the appropriate gravitas.

"And a happy new year to you too you Jock bastard."

The Duty Officer gave McAuley an encouraging smile

as he passed.

"Friends of yours McAuley? They seem nice."

Their targets, wilted and browbeaten in the main, had seen it all before. One or two of the younger ones, made brave by the locked gates and the wide space of the rotunda between wings, shouted abuse back, but it was empty bravado. He noted with disappointment that as usual, none of the officers on the other three wings intervened despite all the posters about fair and equal treatment and a zero tolerance of bullying, displayed everywhere.

In the wing office he exchanged the usual bantering insults with his colleagues, and they shared the usual morning rituals: complaining about the world, the universe and the meaning of life, the weather, the motorway, wondering what had died in the fridge and who the almond milk there belonged to.

"Well, I'm lactose intolerant, I heard something on Woman's Hour..." Craig Heaney responded defensively.

There was a pause.

"Of course you are. You're a fucking hypochondriac Heaney." Heaney was a nice lad, but the general view of his colleagues was that he needed to man-up a bit, and they were more than willing to help him out in that.

"What are you reading Craig?"

"Oh, One Hundred Years of Solitude by Gabriel Garcia Marquez."

"Are you enjoying it?"

"No."

"Why are you reading it then?"

"It's for my book group."

Silence.

"You live on your own Craig, don't you?"

Heaney sniffed and looked put out.

"What's in your lunchbox today McAuley?" he asked, in an attempt to change the subject. "Another Mrs. Singh special? Well, we all know what your farts are going to smell like tomorrow – same as every other day! You're a lucky sod. I wish my neighbour would cook for me."

McAuley looked a picture of health, but then he'd not been brought up with the traditional Scottish diet. Much to Luke's disappointment, he'd yet to try a deep-fried mars bar. ("I'd rather lick my own armpits.") Mrs. Singh was an elderly, lonely widow who claimed that she'd never adjusted to an empty nest once her kids had left home and who therefore had also never adjusted to the need to cook less. And boy could she cook! He knew that this much touted excuse wasn't true and he suspected that she knew he knew.

He knew. She knew he knew, and he knew she knew he knew. It was a game they played.

"We can't waste good food when there's a young worker such as yourself doing long hours and with no time to cook," she'd say in her no-nonsense style.

McAuley smiled at this memory and looked at Heaney.

"Ma guffs Craig, will as ever, smell of roses." As far as smart comebacks went, it was only a minor victory.

They settled down for the morning's hand-over from their three-striper. George Hatcher (Hatcher the hatchet, but never, ever George) was a man in his mid-fifties. He was so stereotypically Yorkshire, McAuley wondered if he had a whippet.

"Pleasant enough morning," Mr Hatcher announced, as he did every morning when the weather wasn't an actual tornado. He sucked on his teeth as he looked at his notes, much as an electrician might while appraising a particularly difficult wiring debacle. This was mesmerising because (so far as anyone could see) he only had five teeth. How someone his age had allowed his teeth to get into that state was a source of constant speculation amongst his juniors. Fighting? Dental phobia? A doing from his missus for coming home the worse for alcohol once too often? Or maybe he just didn't care. None of his one-stripers, strangely, had ever dared to broach this subject with him and no one had ever seen him eat in public, although they had opened a book on when the undoubtedly put-upon Mrs. Hatcher might trade him in for a younger version with better oral hygiene.

"Right, well, Tom's rung in sick, so we'll need to rejig things a bit today," he lisped, fingering his shoulder tabs absent-mindedly and using his most withering idiot-whisperer tone.

"He's probably taken to his bed with a nervous breakdown," Craig Heaney offered.

"Aye, well, tell him to move over and make room," McAuley sighed.

"Parson's smashed up his cell again. What's that Scottish word you use McAuley?"

McAuley's blank look was an answer of sorts.

"You know, to describe a worthless, irritating individual?"

"Aye, right. It's nyaff."

"That's the one. Well, this nyaff..." (Mr. Hatcher savoured the word.) "...is down in segregation for his own protection because he managed to rupture a water pipe. So, apart from the ongoing avalanche from the third landing and related flooding in ground floor cells, it was a hot water pipe, so no one got a shower yesterday and he's had death threats." A few eye-rolls at that.

"As if!" Officer Sharon Mills was clearly unconvinced. "A swift kicking maybe, but death threats? Come on!" There were general nods and mutters of agreement.

The Hatchet glared at them, waiting for the hubbub to subside.

"I'm the Chief Fucker, in charge of you minor fuckers, so you'll fucking listen when I speak! Don't make me say fuck again. It's bad for my blood pressure, let alone my immortal soul. Talking of which, moving on to yesterday's religious services: The C of E service was an oasis of calm as usual thanks to Fr. Leo. The Catholic service, on the other hand, was an instruction manual in chaos. Chaplaincy really needs to employ a regular priest instead of relying on volunteers. Anyway, the travellers were arseholes. The Cawleys from C Wing verses the Boswells from D Wing. I don't think they know the meaning of the word fear, but then again, they don't know the meaning of many words. Anyway, it's got to stop. We shouldn't need more than five officers in a religious service for God's sake. Of course, Madam Cynthia said she'd predicted this."

Madam Cynthia was possibly the least convincing male to female preoperative transgender candidate in the known world. She resided on A Wing in a cell that Mr. Hatcher described as looking like a Turkish brothel. In the short time she'd been incarcerated, she'd become in many ways the wing's mascot, known for her generosity of spirit and all-round kindness tempered with an ability to make grown men cry. She also had a hot-line to the spirit world. In addition, she seemed to have a thing for Mr. Hatcher, or perhaps she just liked to see him squirm, and as her cell was very close to the wing office, this was a regular occurrence.

"That man just can't leave me alone," she'd declaim loudly to anyone who'd listen, and whenever he was on the wing, she could be found lounging nonchalantly yet provocatively against her cell door, (not so much a cell as a boudoir) one hand on her hip, the other behind her head, wearing a permed wig you could go trick-or-treating in, a kaftan, slingbacks, and exuberant make up. He'd threatened to relocate her to the third landing, so she'd be out of his hair (not that he had much) but she'd managed to make a five-act drama out of that.

"Oh Mr. Hatcher, you bad man. Look he's trying to set me up in a bijou little pad off the beaten track where he can visit me on the sly."

She called Mr. Hatcher a sweetie. He called her a dirty pervert.

"Remember...," Governor O'Brien had reminded them in one of his whole staff briefings, "... we use feminine pronouns when dealing with these prisoners."

There was a loud snort from the back. No one needed to turn round to know it was George Hatcher.

As they left the office, The Hatchet noticed that someone had drawn a large ejaculating penis on the Perspex cover of the information board in indelible board marker.

"Bloody art classes!" he grumbled. "Now, why don't we... and when I say we, what I mean is you... go and do something useful? I've got one of Mrs. Hatcher's headaches coming on and she's had that headache since the second night of our honeymoon, so I don't even want to hear you fart!"

Mr. Hatcher returned to his paperwork. He didn't hear them leave.

"Blimey, he's in a bad mood today. How many swear words was that?" Heaney looked genuinely shocked.

McAuley wondered again at Heaney's naivety. "Don't look at me. I don't keep track. I'm not a fuckometer."

Heaney chose not to respond to the sarcasm.

"I'm off to change lives then," he announced as they stepped out on to the landing to begin to round the men up for workshops, education and the meds queue, and there they encountered Terry, an old jakey, busily engaged in a Forth Bridge type project, painting all the wing metalwork in institutional prison blue... over and over again. He looked pale and haggard, and there was a strong unwashed smell emanating from him. Terry shared his cell with his

B.O. and his even ranker thoughts and behaviours. Terry was so old, he'd been around at the start of evolution, but hadn't followed the trend.

"Still at it Terry? How'd you get that job by the way? Are you a painter decorator when you're not in prison?"

"No Guv. I'm a fucking thief, innit?"

It was the first time Terry had been sober since his last incarceration. He wasn't enjoying it. He hadn't been very successful at school but had discovered early on that if you hit people very hard, preferably with something solid, and repeatedly, they started to take you seriously.

"By the way, I'm told he's got a very small penis," Sharon Mills whispered to McAuley.

"Why are you telling me this?"

"Oh, I'm sorry. Is that a sensitive issue for you?"

He peered at the ceiling trying to formulate an appropriate response but before he could reply she was off, shepherding men before her.

McAuley had rarely met a prisoner who didn't try to justify his offenses in some way but reading prison records was as quick a way of seeing what was wrong with modern society as any: absent fathers, broken families, physical/sexual abuse, learning disabilities, truancy, poverty and so on – all the disabilities of the underclass. Many of these men were doomed from the moment of conception. Of course, that was no consolation if you were a victim of crime. Many of these men were beyond saving. (And was that even his job?)

"You're a prison officer not a therapist. Leave all that

to the do-gooders," he heard often enough. On the back of that he wondered if he'd ever altered any outcomes for these guys.

Working here was like living in an extended episode of the Jeremy Kyle show, which had been compulsive viewing in the prison because everyone could identify with it. It was the sort of programme which, in McAuley's jaded view, rotted both the brain and the TV. Now it had been cancelled, the whole prison seemed to be in mourning. Even so, others with the same problems coped, and some even flourished under identical circumstances without being imprisoned. Was there an innate weakness in some people, and if so, was there a way to recognise it?

Above my pay grade, he decided.

He'd like to invite an author into the prison. No one in his view wrote crime fiction that was as disturbing as his daily experience. Fiction was nothing like the reality of this world, and he was fairly sure most authors would resort to alcohol within half an hour of arrival if it was available. (Actually, it was available if you knew where to look: it's amazing what can be done with orange peel, even though yeast was a prohibited substance in the prison, and if you added soluble aspirin; well, the effervescence added something and you made a head start on the hangover, so it was win-win.)

"Guv! Can I have a word?"

This was Bruno, a gnomic looking frequent flyer, back to over-winter for a three month stretch. He was going cold turkey - from tobacco certainly, and who knew from

what else? Spice probably, from the look of him. He had
the seedy air of a flasher about him and had the stains on
his sweatshirt of things you couldn't even buy today. He
didn't just reek of piss, it seemed to seep out of him. He
really needed to see a doctor.

"Guv, am I on the list for smoking sensation? I need
something to take the edge off it." He coughed bronchially
as if to make the point and fixed McAuley with a pleading
sort of look.

Smoking sensation. By an unspoken agreement staff
had decided that they weren't going to challenge that
particular mangling of the language. Bruno had found
himself in prison again because, under the influence of
some combination of drugs and alcohol, he'd walked into a
well-known high street franchise with a starting pistol and
demanded that the rather startled receptionist give him all
the money in the till.

"I'm sorry, Love," she'd said, smoothing the crumbs of
a chocolate digestive from her blouse, "This is a Funeral
Directors."

Since the prison had become a smoke free prison, most
of the men had segued seamlessly to vaping, but a fair few
had decided to try the patches or the spray in an attempt to
kick the habit. Being a smoke free environment, however,
merely allowed other smells to be more noticeable: the
smell of men who'd given up caring. It had top-notes
of urine and loneliness. Whereas in the bad old days,
the first thing you'd notice on entering the hub was a
miasma redolent of stale cigarettes and BO, now the air

was relatively pollutant free, the B.O. mixed instead with strawberry or whatever flavour Procurement had managed to acquire on the cheap.

"Mr. McAuley! Do you have a moment Dear?"

Ah, Madam Cynthia. "We were just talking about you."

She grinned in what she must have assumed was a coquettish way.

"Nothing good I hope."

Struggling to keep his eyes off her uneven breast substitutes, he looked her in the eye, having to make a speedy choice between the blue over eye-shadowed one and the green over eye-shadowed one. Green won out.

"Actually good, as it happens. We were talking about your predictions about blood in the chapel."

"Ah well, you didn't need to have the gift to predict that one Dear, it's been brewing for weeks. Anyway, while we're on the topic of predictions I've had a premonition about you, and I'd rather like to read your tealeaves."

"We're an officer down this morning Cynthia, so I really can't afford to leave the wing, inviting as a cuppa in your cell is."

Well, not so much inviting as amazing, given that the cell was festooned with a wide variety of female apparel, and a number of items the use for which was probably best not enquired of. The upside of this was that while everyone loved her, no one wanted to share with her. McAuley had once speculated idly that this whole transgender schtick was an elaborate ruse to get a single occupancy cell.

A group of men meandered down from the second landing carrying their gym kit.

"Oy Cynthia, I've got a dick as thick as a baby's arm. Get your dentures out and we'll have some fun."

"Now, how many times have I told you Dear?" she called back cheerfully, "I don't do charity work."

The men mooched off, laughing at the victim of Cynthia's repost.

"Honestly Mr. McAuley, it's not just the cream that rises to the top, is it? The manners of young people today!"

Given that her heckler was on the older side of completely indeterminate, he decided to let it go.

"That one told me he was the man of my dreams."

McAuley looked doubtful. "What did you say?"

"Only if I eat cheese before I go to bed. Oh, the times we live in! I'll just let my chakras settle and we'll do it out here then."

Once in full flow Madam Cynthia was not one to be gainsaid and pulled rather in the slipstream of her commanding personality, he decided resistance was futile.

McAuley had never been in a Turkish brothel (or a brothel of any other nationality for that matter) but he reasoned that Mr. Hatcher, who must surely have more life experience was right, and this cell must be what one looked like.

"Of course, Earl Grey is best I find, but needs must." She tore off the corner of a tea bag and emptied it with a flourish into a prison-issue blue plastic mug. "Oh, for my bone-china tea service."

"I don't want to be difficult Cynthia, but I don't really drink tea."

"Nonsense!" She brooked no backsliding. "I can't read coffee sediment, can I? At least two good mouthfuls now, or it won't be effective."

He complied with the merest hint of a sigh, and she darted back into her cell and swished the remainder down the loo.

"Now..." (all furrowed brows and a squint) "What have we here? I see a dark man..."

McAuley rolled his eyes. "Not a tall dark stranger?"

She avoided his gaze, concentrating instead on stirring milk into her own tea. "I've a pelvic floor like a Venus fly trap you know."

He snorted tea down his nostrils at that.

"Anyway, there's no need to mock Mr. McAuley. It doesn't become you. This is not a prelude to some cheap romantic encounter, and anyway I know that sort of encounter's not your thing, if you take my meaning."

She had a far-away look in her eye.

"Not a stranger, no. Someone you already know, and he'll not be well disposed towards you. There's travel too. Over water, and a reunion with an old friend." There was a long pause as she frowned. "Do you have a pet?"

"Well, sort of. Why?" He was intrigued, despite himself.

"I'm not sure. There's an overlay of religious symbolism that I can't quite get." And then, mercurial as ever, a bright smile. "It's gone. That's it. You've a good aura by the way."

"Thanks... I think."

He decided not to press her further, concentrating on checking the length of his keychain instead.

Chapter Five

As he left work that evening, the sky had a washed out look as if the effort was too much for it, and he'd had to concede that he did in fact, look as tired, defeated and jaded as the night shift had on their departure. Escaping from the dystopian gloom of the prison into the natural gloom of a January evening, he realised he'd come to work in the dark, had spent most of the day starved of natural light and now he was going home in the dark. He was surprised more of his colleagues weren't raging depressives. On reflection, perhaps some of them were.

His conversation with Madam Cynthia was all but forgotten, overshadowed by the daily grind of prison life, and what a day it had been!

It struck McAuley again that society was very keen to bang people up but seemed to give no thought to what happened to them once they were there, and he was tired of hearing prisons described as holiday camps. Some people had no idea and no imagination.

"I've a date tonight." Heaney was looking perky.

"Blind?" Mills asked.

Heaney frowned. "What? Of course she's not."

"Blind date, dickhead."

"Oh, no. Sorry."

—

McAuley's general strategy with the men was

reasonableness and good humour. This morning had tested that mind-set: the problem was that the men were often bored, weary and exhausted from ennui, and today, Russell (aka Sprout) had climbed onto the netting that stretched over the voids between each of the landings.

Sprout had the semi-vacant look of the not-quite-all-there, with clusters of deep blackheads in the soft tissue around his eyes. Possibly the only creatures in the prison less switched on than Sprout were the pigeons that infested the place, but it would have been a close call. Sprout had climbed on the netting because, on the back of a rumour that kosher food-packs were of a higher quality than standard prison food, he'd decided he was Jewish, and was put out because the kitchen refused to provide him kosher food without the Rabbi's say so.

"Look Sprout, you can't just decide to be Jewish. It doesn't work that way."

"I am Guv. Honestly. I've got concentration camp numbers tattooed on my arm and everything."

"For fuck's sake! You're twenty-three. Get down ya wee bawbag."

"But I've got the numbers. You can see them from there."

"I can see they're biro, and just a word to the wise Sprout, the Nazis didn't use red ink. **GET DOWN NOW!**"

"YOU FUCKER SPROUT! I'VE JUST PAINTED THAT! GET OFF MY FUCKING WORK. I'LL SWING FOR YOU, YOU FUCKING ARSEHOLE!"

The art of polite conversation was not yet Terry's

strongest suit.

"Aye, thanks Terry, I think we've got this."

That wasn't strictly true. It would have been more accurate to have said that they might nearly have 'got this' prior to Terry's colourful intervention, which inevitably drew more men to what was already a crowd of bystanders who, rather like the crones who knitted at the guillotine, could scent blood in the air.

The Hatchet appeared at McAuley's elbow. When he was dischuffed, he had a look that could strip paint. Now was one of those occasions.

"For God's sake don't press the alarm. It's only Sprout. We'll deal with this ourselves. This isn't B Wing for fuck's sake. I don't want every other officer in the prison on my wing. Right Lads, get the men behind their doors."

On any other wing this would have been easier said than done, but partly by virtue of their older age profile, the A Wing men were more compliant and (eventually) shuffled off to their cells, thus avoiding the stooshie McAuley feared. O.K. there was muttering about missing the spectacle and some half-hearted posturing, but the threat of drawn batons tended to clarify the minds of the most recalcitrant. McAuley thought there was an element of touch-and-go about this and that it could turn nasty in the blink of an eye, but today the landings were cleared relatively quickly. That didn't stop the men standing at their doors and hooting derision and threats at Sprout.

"If we miss our meal because of you, knob head, you're dead meat!"

"Oi, paedo, you'd better watch your back!"

"Sprout, you nonce. We're coming for you."

A dozen or so mirrors appeared through the door flaps so that men whose site-lines were blocked could continue to watch the fun and in most cells the sound of a running commentary could be heard as the man by the door passed his observations back to his cell mate. On occasions like this, had they the time, officers could discern the pecking order of the inmates.

Only when the wing was cleared did The Hatchet notify Control and announced that his team were coping admirably and it was just a matter of talking Sprout down, and no, he absolutely did not, repeat DID NOT need the regional snatch squad in riot gear, thank you very much!

An hour and a half later there was still stalemate. McAuley was convinced that Sprout was more frightened of Terry than of any of the prison's sanctions. Governor O'Brien had appeared, presumably notified by Control, watched for a while, announced himself pleased with Mr. Hatcher's handling of events and departed.

Fr. Leo had also appeared outside the gate on the second landing, the landing where The Hatchet and McAuley were conspicuously failing to get Sprout, who was clearly only now starting to realise the depth of trouble he was in, to see reason.

"Greg! Greg, over here for a minute."

McAuley went over to the gate and the two men, heads together, conferred briefly.

He came back and spoke quietly to Sprout,

"About the Jewish thing Russell. There's an easy way to resolve this."

"There is Guv?" Hopeful.

"Aye. Drop your trousers."

"What?"

"Yeah, drop your trousers. I need to see if you're circumcised."

"But..." He threw McAuley a horrified look. So did Mr. Hatcher.

"Look, it's only what the Rabbi will ask you to do. I thought we'd just save some time here. You see..." he hurried on, looking over his shoulder at Leo, "If you're not, you know... trimmed... down there, he'll offer to do you then and there in your cell, you know, make an event of it, maybe invite a few friends as witnesses. Then you'll have to do a basic course in Hebrew and hey, who knows, by the time you're out you'll be bona fide Kosher. So, how about it? Drop your pants."

Sprout thought about it for a while.

"Circumcised? Really?" McAuley thought he looked a bit green around the gills. "O.K. Mr. McAuley, I'll come down." Which he did to the time-honoured accompaniment of wolf-whistles and banging on doors.

"Now have a bit of dignity and fuck off Sprout while I'm still in a good mood." Sprout stepped back, looking unsure. Then he stepped back again and then once more. He had, in fact, to all intents and purposes, fucked off – straight into the arms of Officers Heaney and Mills.

McAuley offered up his heartfelt thanks to the Patron

Saint of prison officers. *Was there one?*

"Well done McAuley. Played a blinder there."

McAuley felt oddly touched by this affirmation. He gave a self-deprecating shrug and tried, not entirely successfully, not to look smug.

"Thanks Mr. Hatcher, but..." He looked at the gate for Leo, but he'd gone. When he turned back, so had Mr. Hatcher.

"Come on Lads, let's get these doors open. There's a meal to get out."

After Heaney and Mills had taken Sprout down to Segregation for forty-eight hours in solitary, Sharon Mills came up to McAuley. "So, is that how it works, conversion to Judaism?"

McAuley gave her a withering look. "I doubt it very much, but the next time the Rabbi's here I'll ask him what the correct procedure is."

And so it went on, ad infinitum, "I've run out of phone credit Guv. Can you get me an emergency credit form?"

Then there was the first division footballer, in prison for under-age sex, standing there in his nice new, expensive, clean, white trainers, a group of admirers gathered around him. McAuley supposed he was good-looking, (although the prison issue sweatshirt didn't do anything for him). He'd need to ask Mills.

Then, "Have you ever killed anyone Guv?"

"No, but it's on my to-do list. Today!"

This is my life, he thought as he left work. *How desperate is that?*

Chapter Six

The Boss was right, D.S. Gill Baines reflected. She was not at all happy about transfer to the Human Trafficking Task Force. In her experience, 'temporary' in the police service was an infinitely flexible concept. Still, if it did turn out to be truly temporary, she could live with it: it would enhance her C.V. and give her a wider range of experience, all of which would help her prepare for promotion. Almost as if in consolation for the darkness of their work, the unit was housed in bright and airy offices, and Gill had settled into a desk with a window view. If she didn't look down at the car park and looked straight ahead, the view of mature gardens was a bonus.

Gill didn't see herself as a natural born cynic, but the sex-trafficking trade wasn't new by any means. It had been going on for decades, if not longer, and it offended her that it had taken a high-profile exposé of one trafficking network to cause a panic and demands for action. Crocodile tears and political expediency: the current government wanted to be seen to be tough on crime but was being reactive while pretending to be proactive.

She'd hit the ground running and had already done some homework. The name Flamur Vrioni was a name that kept cropping up. His was a thick file, and she was not at all surprised, looking at his various mugshots, to see a face that suggested a sly intelligence at the same time as showing a hard, knocked about and rather ugly countenance. Under the heading, 'Distinguishing Features', she noted that one of his incisors was a gold tooth.

Reading on, she could see why her new colleagues referred to him as Mr. Teflon. He seemed to run a rag-tag operation of Balkan muscle-for-hire, mainly Albanian, and they had a reputation for violence. She looked again at the photos the Slovene photographer had supplied, focusing on the final one. Could that man seen chasing the escapee be Vrioni? Wouldn't that be a coup? New Year's Eve: the streets had been heaving, but maybe, just maybe CCTV might come to their rescue. She jotted some notes on her to do list.

She really couldn't grasp why Vrioni wasn't already in a high security prison given his record, but nothing seemed to stick. As she read on, she put that down in large part to the services of one James Wilson, of Mainwaring, Wilson and Jones, Solicitors, based in Dewsbury. Wilson was a solicitor she'd not come across before, but the more she read, the more it seemed he was the go-to brief for the likes of Vrioni. What also intrigued her, reading between the lines, were the veiled hints that Vrioni was getting tip-offs from within the police. She'd already tried to discuss this with one of her new colleagues and had been told to leave it. It shocked her when she realised that this was because she was perceived, as a newcomer, to be a potential suspect. O.K. so she couldn't discuss this with the existing team, but she'd certainly raise it with D.I. Brewer. She wondered if Murchison was aware. She looked at her watch. Tonight, they were going on a raid.

Chapter Seven

What a day!
          He blew into his hands in the hope of thawing his fingers. This time he put on Classic FM; its music was guaranteed to sooth, and it helped him to unwind. He'd come to work in the dark and now he was going home in the dark. He really needed to get a life.

He looked up at the house. In the gloom, he could see Cat sitting on the windowsill of the landing outside his flat, looking down on him.

No change there, then.

He liked to play a game when he got home: like Madame Cynthia, Mrs Singh seemed to have the gift of foresight because however quietly he tried to get by her front door, she always heard him. One day he'd manage it, but then he'd go back and ring on her door. Their well-established evening routine was something they both enjoyed. She stood on her doorstep, wiping her hands on her pinny. She was a pensioner, but she wore her age well.

"Gregor, Putara, is that you? I'm sure you'd like a cup of coffee after your hard day. It has been a hard day, no?"

She had a lovely speaking voice, a warm contralto, and he could imagine her broadcasting on whatever the Indian version of the BBC was. He'd sometimes heard her singing in her kitchen - and not just traditional Sikh songs either: she was quite fond of Mozart which seemed strangely odd but shouldn't have been. Why couldn't an elderly Sikh lady like Mozart? He'd been so impressed with her voice that he'd asked her to consider joining his choir, the prestigious Leeds Philharmonic Chorus. She'd been delighted but had never taken him up on it.

This had become a daily ritual, a sort of Japanese tea ceremony, only Indian and with coffee. He usually stopped for about an hour or so. He'd tell her the outline of his day and ask after hers while they drank their beverages companionably, and she ladled a large helping of Goan prawn curry, or whatever, into Tupperware for his lunch tomorrow. It smelt spicy and delicious. Left to his own devices McAuley would probably have lived on ready meals. It's not that he couldn't cook or that he didn't like cooking, it was more that he took no pleasure in cooking for one. He envied Mrs. Singh's determination to be disciplined and not to give in to convenience.

It often felt like he'd been transported back to his childhood days in these moments as it always reminded him of when his mother would ask him what he'd done at school while she busied herself in the kitchen. Such memories came with a sad pang. His parents had been 'older' parents. His mother had been forty when McAuley had been born. As a child he'd thought forty was ancient. Did people live longer than that?

His parents had been enthusiastic travellers who'd liked to try whatever the local tipple was wherever they washed up. When he was eight, he'd been deemed too young to appreciate classical history, and was sent to stay with an uncle and aunt in Edinburgh while his parents jetted off to Italy. On a fateful evening in Rome, his parents had left a restaurant, and chatting happily, had looked right instead of left and walked into the path of an oncoming bus. The upside of this, if there could ever be an upside to such a tragedy, was that as an only child McAuley had inherited the lot - and there was a lot, including a substantial number of properties abroad in good locations which his guardians had arranged to go on the holiday rental market, investing the profit for him.

He preferred to identify as an Edinburgher rather than a Glaswegian. People tended to assume that if you were from Glasgow, you were dead hard, and McAuley didn't think he was hard, let alone dead hard. He could switch from one accent to another seamlessly like an actor moving in and out of role: at work he was more Glaswegian. Everywhere else he was an Edinburgher, and he did this unconsciously. A Partick Boy, he'd been taken by his father and then his uncle to Firhill Stadium every week, almost as a religious pilgrimage, but whenever a prisoner asked him who he supported, he always replied Stenhousemuir because it invariably got a blank response which made him smile.

Even as a young child growing up in the Bearsden area of Glasgow, McAuley knew theirs was a wealthy family. McAuley missed his parents of course, but the older he got and the further away they receded in his memory, the more it felt like a duty, an obligation. He could still remember his uncle Duncan, his father's brother, trying to explain in faltering but loving terms, what had happened and his own sense of bewilderment. He'd grown up fast then and had begun to realise that adulthood, disappointingly, consisted more of mowing the lawn and fighting with quilt covers than slaughtering dinosaurs or defeating aliens. It was a salutary lesson to have learnt so young.

McAuley's father had assumed, in the way fathers do, that McAuley would follow him into the family business, but when he decided to be a teacher, offered no protest from the other side, perhaps too busy spinning in his grave.

Mrs. Singh, he reflected, made an excellent alternative mother and it was clear it worked both ways. Mrs. Singh was inordinately proud of her three children, a doctor son in America, a solicitor daughter in London and an accountant son in South Africa.

"They leave me short of nothing. They are very generous."

This was why she would never hear of him paying her for all the food she cooked for him. It was not up for discussion. Still, he often did their mutual shopping.

She looked wistful. Yes, her grown up children were clearly very generous: with everything but their time. He'd met the daughter once. She'd driven up from St. John's Wood but had refused to stay the night.

"But she's so busy you know. She has a big court case to prepare for." He wasn't fooled by the excuses she made for her daughter. She'd been cut to the quick and it was obvious for anyone to see, except for the daughter, clearly.

Yes, it was an odd relationship but they both benefitted from it in ways much deeper than either of them would admit.

He liked Mrs. Singh's flat insofar as it wasn't his flat. Hers was warm and welcoming, an Aladdin's cave of family history and Indian artefacts and antiques. His, on the other hand, was spartan, functional and completely without character. The first thing that struck anyone about McAuley's flat was the predominance of magnolia. McAuley didn't actually like magnolia, but liked the idea of decorating even less, so magnolia it was, (and if it wasn't magnolia, it was beige). It was, he often thought, like living in a bowl of porridge.

McAuley could find nothing pleasurable about living in a tip just because he was a single man and had no one to nag him about it. You didn't have to be anal to keep your space clean and tidy, he reasoned. It was a matter of personal pride then, that he did keep it clean and tidy, and a balance against the chaos and disorder he sometimes encountered in the workplace, but he'd never bothered to personalise it in any way, which considering he'd been there for nearly three years, he had to concede was a bit pathetic.

It was three years since he and Molly had split up and he'd been left with no option but to move out, leaving his toddler son Sammy, the love of his life, behind. Theirs had always been a rocky relationship, only entered into because of contraceptive failure when McAuley and Molly had barely known each other. That had come as a shock, but they'd embraced it, staying up late talking and making plans for a future neither of them felt confident about.

They'd had one major row about it when McAuley had told Molly that prisons were full of young men who'd grown up without a father. He'd meant it at face value, but she'd taken it as emotional blackmail. Not that Molly was in any way awkward about McAuley seeing Sammy. Not at all, which was fortunate seeing as unmarried fathers had so few rights in law. She'd been unhappy about him leaving teaching and quickly became impatient with the family-unfriendly shift pattern of the prison officer.

"It's not as if you ever actually wanted to be a prison officer, is it Greg?"

It was an ongoing conversation in one form or another; one which was doomed to go nowhere because neither would accept the other's argument, and so they would never be free of its divisive pressure.

"No, but it's what I do now and it's important."

"It's not good for you, being with men like that."

"Look, most of those guys are ordinary guys who did something stupid. It doesn't make them evil."

"It's not them that bother me. It's the others."

It had been downhill all the way after his first assault had left him with a fractured elbow, and he wasn't well disposed to being given ultimatums. They got on so much better now that they lived apart and he knew in his heart of hearts there was no going back. In the meantime, he'd had a few romances, but they were all stillborn. He'd had colds that had lasted longer than most of them. Lots of women he'd been told, liked a man in uniform. Just not the uniform he wore, it seemed.

Mrs. Singh was knitting something McAuley doubted anyone would ever wear.

"It's for the refugees," she said vaguely.

McAuley wondered what 'it' was but decided not to ask. She persevered despite complaining about her rheumatism, but McAuley had little sympathy. He'd taken her to the doctor, and she'd come away with a list of things to do and not do, suggested changes to her diet, a Pilates exercise regime and a strong determination to ignore all of it.

"I need to live in a warmer climate," was all she'd say.

After the Channel 4 news, he reluctantly took his leave, declining Mrs. Singh's invitation to watch a new thriller together, (which he'd absolutely love to have done), and headed upstairs to his bleak attic flat. He poured himself a beer and picked up his guitar. People who didn't know him well would have been surprised to discover that he was an accomplished musician with a music degree from Edinburgh University (voice and guitar). He'd been a BBC young musician of the year finalist when he was sixteen. He'd come second and his uncle had told him off for wearing jeans. Not that he was the only graduate in the prison service by any means, but like his expensive education at Fettes College, he kept that part of his life quiet. It was a world of privilege he'd never quite come to terms with and he couldn't ever see himself in the alumni list of Old Fettesians alongside the likes of Tony Blair, Tilda Swinton and Michael Tippett, but there was still time he supposed, smiling. There was nothing he could do about his privileged upbringing, so it wasn't worth worrying about it. At the same time, he wasn't going to advertise it either. Conscious of, but not at all liking the term, 'born with a silver spoon in his mouth', he had long decided to keep his business as private as possible.

Entirely focussed, he spent the rest of the evening working on a particularly complicated piece by Haydn. As he played, the tension of the day slipped away from him. Success lifted his spirits and flushed with a sense of achievement and a concentration headache, he took himself off to bed, but with a nagging sense that he'd forgotten something.

Chapter Eight

Meanwhile, Sadie Brewer and Gill Baines were sitting in the back of an unmarked police van in a less than salubrious side street off the Leeds Road out of Huddersfield. An undercover officer had already gone into the seedy looking massage parlour they'd had under surveillance.

"You look the type," his colleagues had joked with him. There wasn't a type, of course, and they all knew it.

Again, the cynic in Gill Baines kicked in: they'd known about this place for ever it seemed, but only now had it been deemed worthy of attention.

"We must be seen to be doing something..." she muttered to herself, "... finally."

Inside, D.C. Rob Carlton was engaged in a smiling exchange with the hard-faced woman behind the counter, who was explaining the services on offer in a rough, throaty voice that suggested she was a heavy smoker. Despite his excellent physique, (he played for the police rugby union's first fifteen), Carlton wasn't the sharpest knife in the box. There really wasn't much going on upstairs. When his colleagues got to know him better, they nicknamed him Fr. Dougal, which was a bit harsh, and perplexed him. Fortunately, Carlton hadn't worked out the menu on his Sky TV handset and so had never discovered that corner of NETFLIX where old TV programmes never die. When he'd first joined the team, he confessed to being a sex-addict, which other members of the team assumed was an attempt at mordant humour; a humour that helped them cope with the dark nature of their work.

Carlton wanted to cut to the chase. There was no way this place was legit, but the woman on reception failed to mention anything overtly sexual among the services available.

"We have beautiful girls," was clearly a come on, but although Carlton expected a wink, her face never changed expression. It was after midnight and Carlton was struggling to imagine what sort of man would be sitting at home at this time of night, only to suddenly realise that what he really needed was a massage.

There was only one thing for it: he was going to have to pay for a massage and take his chances.

"I have girl from Belarus free now."

"How much?"

"Girl is freelance. She tell you." It was as he expected. Plausible deniability.

Oh, but Officer, I had no idea she was offering sexual favours. This is a respectable business.

"Sounds great. Lead on."

She handed him a towel and led him through a door to the side of the counter. As he passed through, the main door opened, and two more men came in. One, as expected, was another undercover officer, Don Griffiths. The other, a punter, who was likely to have his expectations for the night sorely disappointed.

When she returned from escorting Carlton, the madam

looked them up and down, concluded they were not likely to be trouble, smiled and said,

"Not be long. You wait."

"No problem, Magda," the second newcomer called back. The two men sat down on plastic chairs and D.C. Griffiths started to chat with his new companion. A regular was likely to be a useful source of intel, if Griffiths could win his confidence.

"So, what do you recommend?"

The other man smiled. "Well..."

———

The door closed behind Carlton, and he looked along the dimly lit corridor at three doors leading off it, and a rickety looking staircase at the end. Someone had made an effort and put a bunch of tired looking dried flowers in a vase on a side table, there were pictures on the walls, and a threadbare carpet underfoot. It was completely the wrong ambiance. There was nothing clinical about the place which Carlton would have expected in a real massage parlour. The sound of rhythmic creaking was faintly audible from behind the first door.

"This Polina's room." The woman at his shoulder knocked assertively on the second door. "Polina. New client." She unlocked the door, turned on her heel and left.

Polina was pretty, but she looked tired and offered him a wan smile. She was dressed in a white tunic, but with too many buttons undone, revealing an impressive cleavage. She'd been interrupted changing the sheet on a narrow single bed.

"You undress. This your first time?" He began to unbutton his shirt.

"No need to be shy. You want bed or chair? One rule: no kissing. Extra for no condom."

Jackpot!

She looked Carlton up and down and made a decision. Kneeling in front of him she began to unzip his trousers. She had a very unprofessional approach to issues of personal space, even for a masseuse. He needed to stop this before it got out of hand, but she was already going to work on him. He slipped his right hand into his pocket and pressed the button on his mobile.

In the reception area, Griffiths felt his own mobile vibrate.

"I'll just pop out for a smoke," he said, giving a friendly smile to the man beside him, who just nodded.

Once outside he waved to the van where backup was waiting. The doors opened and six officers piled out. Griffiths went back into the building and held up his police ID.

"Nobody move. Stay where you are. I have a warrant to search these premises."

Suddenly the small reception area was flooded with uniforms.

Magda looked decidedly put out as she surreptitiously moved her hand to press a button under the counter.

In room two, Polina was getting into the swing of things, but the sound of an alarm stopped her in her tracks.

"That's no fire. This means police."

"I know." Carlton looked down at her. "I'm sorry."

She held his gaze for a moment. "But the policeman who come here for freebies say we protected." She frowned, then to his amazement, she shrugged and carried on as if nothing had happened. Unfortunately, at that moment Griffiths came barging through the door, took one look at Carlton with his trousers round his ankles and stood goggle eyed.

"It's not what it looks like Don."

"Oh good, Robin. I thought for a moment you were getting a blow job from a tom."

"Oh, come on Don. Don't make it sound sordid."

Polina, not one to be easily distracted, ignored Griffiths and carried on.

"Miss, I'm going to have to ask you to step away from my colleague." He pulled Carlton by the shoulder, but he had a faraway look in his eye.

All over the building they could hear the sounds of doors banging, shouts and running footsteps. Someone took a tumble down the stairs. Griffiths was in a quandary, but in the end, discretion was the better part of valour, and he left room two to offer support to colleagues who needed it more than Carlton.

Outside, Bains and Brewer handed blankets to girls who had appeared in various states of undress. They were all cowed and wouldn't meet their eyes. It took a while for Brewer to notice the furtive glances that some of the girls were making at an older woman in the group, and whispered conversations that included, "Magda". Brewer thought she understood what was happening, took the woman by the arm, despite her protests, removed her from the group and put her in the back of a marked police car while Baines helped the other women into a minivan and climbed in with them.

"My name's Gill Baines. I'm a police officer. I don't want you to be frightened. I need to ask if you were being held against your will."

There was sullen silence, but one girl had more spirit.

"All of us." She had a heavy accent. "Will we be able to go home now?"

A small and dispirited group of men were confined to the reception area where their details were being taken. Griffiths noticed one man was wearing nothing but a grubby vest and one sock, his shrivelled manhood now a source of embarrassment when five minutes before it had been his pride and joy. Carlton, looking flushed, made a belated appearance.

"With me!" Griffiths said and led him back out into the hall. They started going from room to room gathering up discarded items of men's clothing.

"Where is she?"

"A window accidentally got broken. She slipped out."

Griffiths rolled his eyes. He was a conscientious and thorough copper who found being partnered with Dougal both a source of frustration and a worthy challenge, but he had no idea how to handle this situation.

"You were supposed to find out if this was a brothel," he hissed, "... not sample the goods."

"Well, you tell me how to do one without doing the other," Carlton snapped back. "It sort of got out of control. It all happened very quickly."

"Not quickly enough. If ever there was a time for premature ejaculation..."

They returned to reception and dumped the clothes in a pile. There was an unseemly free for all as the men retrieved what was theirs.

"It's not against the law you know." Now fully clothed, one of the men was feeling assertive.

"It is if the woman was being held against her will. Under those circumstances any sexual activity would be deemed to be non-consensual." Sadie Brewer had appeared in the doorway. "There could be convictions for rape."

"Every idiot knows that," Griffiths whispered to Carlton.

"I knew that."

"I rest my case."

Brewer looked around the room to gauge the reaction of the men. She was not disappointed. They looked horrified. One began to hyperventilate. "Anyway, you're free to go." She paused. "For the moment."

No one was going to follow these men up, she knew that, but the idea that these guys might lose some sleep worrying about how they would explain this when that knock came on the door, really appealed to her.

The room emptied quickly.

In the police van on the way back, there was much ribald recounting of what the officers had seen as they'd raided the rooms.

"One guy begged me to let him finish as he was nearly there." There were guffaws of amusement, but the conversation took a serious turn soon enough.

"These girls were locked in and the windows wouldn't open. They were definitely prisoners. None of them were local."

"They've started to talk," Gill joined in. "They were reluctant at first. I think they've been fed a lot of bollocks about British police, but once they started, the floodgates opened. There'll be no problem getting statements, although we may need a few translators."

"What are you two muttering about?" Sadie Brewer looked across at where Griffiths and Carlton were having a conversation in low, whispered tones.

"Well, it's like this, Gov. One of the girls told Rob here that there was a copper who used to come for free sex on the understanding that they'd be left alone."

"Is it you Don?" one of the others laughed.

"No, it's young Dougal here," Griffiths bantered back, nudging his colleague. The others laughed louder.

Carlton laughed loudly too, although he wasn't quite sure why it was funny.

—

There was an odd postscript to this event. Some weeks later, at a retirement do for one of the team, Carlton turned up with his new girlfriend.

"This is Pauline guys. She's from Minsk."

Chapter Nine

He hadn't slept well. He dozed for a while until Cat made his presence felt, demanding to be fed, and using his claws to underline the point. McAuley hid under the duvet, but Cat merely walked up the bed and sat on his face. McAuley really wasn't in the mood for this and threw back the duvet, temporarily burying Cat, then he walked into the kitchen, leaving the animal to extricate itself.

All the light seemed to have been squeezed from the world, and a mug of coffee in one hand, he hit the bathroom. His was an easy flat to keep warm, nestled as it was under the eaves and absorbing some of the heat from the lower floors, but this morning was another miserable one.

He trimmed his musketeer beard, showered (hot then cold) and twirled and then waxed the ends of his moustache. It was only then that he realised that what he'd forgotten - and had been forgetting for several days - was to put the washing machine on.

Shit!

He stood as if in a trance in front of his wardrobe. No clean uniform shirts.

Shit and double shit!

If the cursing was intended to make the situation better, it failed miserably.

He rifled through the dirty basket, found a shirt that

wasn't too creased, sniffed it under the armpits and shrugged. It would have to do - but he gave it a good spray with aftershave. When he'd finished coughing, he put a wash on, fed the cat (ungrateful bastard that it was) gulped down a lukewarm coffee, grabbed an apple and his car keys and set off for work. In this flat there was either too much food or none at all. If he didn't have an ulcer by the time he was forty, he'd be surprised.

McAuley was tall and rangy, and walked to his car, shoulders back, and with a confidence that had just the merest hint of a swagger. The morning was miserable and the communal garden, such as it was, looked more forlorn than usual as the trees dripped half-heartedly and the streetlamps were haloed in the mist. Nevertheless, there was something in him that liked this time: the air was cold and damp, but McAuley breathed it in like a man starved of fresh air, savouring the damp, earthy smell of the garden. Foxes had been at the bins again leaving a trail of torn pizza boxes and take-away cartons strewn about. He wasn't guilty on that count. Who ate that much take-away anyway, this wasn't a student area? He noticed that No. 3's dead Christmas tree from last year was still there, presumably soon to be joined by this year's. This was a battle of wills between him and the bin men who were clearly not going to take it, and Mr. Stubborn wasn't giving in. No doubt both trees would still be there next Christmas.

He stood at his car and looked back at the house. It was quite grand, a big Victorian villa in a street of big Victorian villas, now mainly subdivided into flats, although

in fairness, the conversions were tasteful, but no one cared
for the gardens. Last spring he'd had the idea of getting
together a working party of residents to get to grips with it,
but the other tenants could only have been less interested
with the aid of tranquillisers. Perhaps he could put up a
sign with pictures of interesting plants and wildlife like
they did in the national parks. Life as a forest ranger
flashed through his over-fertile and completely unrealistic
imagination. He fancied himself in a green polo shirt, cargo
shorts and big boots with a rugged outdoor look. But what
would he do between October and May?

He heard a plane going overhead long before its tell-tale
lights revealed its position. Where was this one heading?
Leeds/Bradford or Manchester? It was hard to gauge the
altitude in the dark. He'd no idea where it had come from,
but at that particular moment he wished he was there.

Behind him McAuley heard the scraping clatter of a
soft drink can as it skittered across the road, blown by a
particularly cruel gust. He sighed, unlocked his Skoda -
what a babe magnet that was - scraped the frost off the
windscreen and drove off.

What he hadn't expected – and surely that was the point
– was that this morning there would be a search of all staff
entering the prison. This was always presented as a random
event, but he knew it was intelligence led. Someone was
bringing drugs into the prison, more than could ever be
thrown over the wall or smuggled in by visitors.

"Empty your pockets Greg, into this tray, arms out, legs

apart. That's it. Put your coat and bag in that tray please. Thanks." The officer gave him a friendly smile. "You smell nice today. On a promise, are we?"

"No. You need a life for that."

This could be interesting. Like a schoolboy who never handed over his dirty sports kit at the end of the day, McAuley hadn't actually got much of an idea what he carried about in his bag, and it did look over-full. It was like a Pandora's box. Once open and delved into, who knew what would come forth? His uniform jacket took up much of the space, followed by Mrs. Singh's Tupperware. Then there was his current novel, his night-school textbook, a pair of socks, a guidebook of Valletta from two years back, a lip-salve, a pack of unopened tissues, a roll-on deodorant, the sticky remains of a packet of throat sweets and two unused disposable nappies. As he walked past the sniffer dog ("Just keep moving sir") he realised that no one had ever opened his Tupperware during one of these searches. Ever.

'... beneath the smell of the soap and the smell of the perfume'... *and the smell of the curry?*

—

"So, Trevor Kawalski's back in hospital: it was a red call."

Mick Wilson, their two-striper was standing in for The Hatchet who was on a rest day. This little group with Mr. Hatcher as the father figure was like a family, McAuley often thought, working closely together and having each other's backs. It was Wilson's malign presence that made it a dysfunctional family. Wilson could not be described as a workaholic: he pushed his copy of the Daily Star to one side. He'd been struggling with the crossword. He was a grade A dick and a poor prison officer. He was possibly the least politically correct officer in the prison service - and the competition was stiff. He had pungent B.O, halitosis and no sense of smell. The prisoners hated him: he was a sarcastic bully, and he was too quick to get physical. He was also wilfully ignorant to the point of exhibitionism. Besides being socially inept, his hobbies included nights out with the lads, fighting in clubs, pissing in the sink instead of the urinals and throwing up in taxies.

And he wore a man-bun.

Tosser!

Wilson was (probably) in his mid-thirties but had the face of a committed smoker, which together with being heavy-jowelled and paunchy, added another decade. He appeared to have shaved, but the nicks and bloodspots suggested that he needed to change his razor. He wore a garish signet ring on the little finger of his right hand, which was both incongruous and tacky. Wilson squinted at his colleagues. He should have been wearing glasses but was too vain, which was a shame as he needed all the help he could get to give the impression of even a modicum of intelligence. He tried hard to look cool. He failed miserably.

McAuley liked to believe that George Hatcher had a dartboard at home with Mick Wilson's photograph on it. The thing about Wilson was that he was universally disliked, and as such he never needed to say sorry. Similarly, 'thanks' wasn't in his vocabulary.

"The usual problem?"

Craig Heaney really didn't need to ask. It was always the usual problem with Kawalski and generally involved some very unusual and creative self-harm involving inserting objects into his urethra. Poor Kawalski. His was a single cell: his problems were such that senior staff decided he couldn't share under any circumstances – it wouldn't be fair on either party. He had a number of triggers. In descending order:

Semen - other men's

Bogies - as above

Christmas wrapping paper

Five pence pieces

Fish knives

As he was unlikely to encounter the last three in prison, but could well encounter the first two, he had to remain in a single cell, a cell he kept obsessively neat and tidy. McAuley liked Trevor Kawalski. He was articulate, well informed, easy to talk to and hospitable, always offering McAuley a coffee when things were quiet on the wing.

"Are you sure he didn't spit in it – or worse?" Wilson was all sneer and sarcasm.

"I wouldn't accept a drink from just anyone. Kawalski's O.K."

"Don't bank on it. Anyway, you're not his fucking social worker."

Like all bullies Wilson needed his acolytes for moral

support but didn't have any on A Wing which generally left him frustrated and full of bluster. McAuley wondered, not for the first time, how Wilson had earned his two stripes. It was, like the Bermuda Triangle and The Marie Celeste, one of the world's deep mysteries. McAuley had tried the greasy pole of promotion as a teacher and had no particular interest in it here, but he couldn't quite see what Wilson did that the one-stripers didn't, but then maybe Wilson wasn't the best role model. McAuley stared him down and Wilson scowled and turned away with a shrug, pretending to be absorbed in his paperwork, deep in thought.

Deep in thought? That'll be unfamiliar territory.

This wasn't really a conversation worth pursuing, but for his own self-respect McAuley was determined to have the last word.

"This really isn't the wing for you, is it? You'd be better off on B Wing."

B for Beirut, he thought. *You can strut around to your heart's content pretending to be dead hard like all the other plastic gangsters there.*

Wilson threw down his pen.

"No, you're right. I can't be doing with all these poofs and paedos, these nonces. And don't start me on political correctness. I don't do PC: life's too short and I don't give a shit."

It was so tempting to reach across the desk and punch him. McAuley already disliked Wilson, possibly more than anyone he'd ever met, and he'd worked with the notorious hard man Charles Bronson.

"Except they're not all poofs and paedos are they?"

Dan Holdsworth wasn't about to let Wilson off the hook either. Ex-navy and heavily tattooed, Holdsworth had definitely been round the block a few times – several blocks in fact. A mature entrant, straight out of training, he'd taken an instant dislike to Wilson. McAuley couldn't decide whether Holdsworth was innately liberal, or whether he just enjoyed poking Wilson.

"This wing's full of the vulnerable, Wilson, life's victims and society's poor copers. No, we're not social workers but we can still show a little compassion."

"Look, the first thing they teach you is not to trust prisoners." Wilson was looking defensive now.

"O.K. And when do you learn the rest?" Holdsworth looked at Wilson expectantly but was met with a blank look.

"What do you mean?"

Holdsworth rolled his eyes.

"It doesn't matter."

McAulay sat back, hiding the hint of a smile. His money was on Holdsworth every time: he could cut through the bullshit, and McAuley liked and respected him for that. Heaney shot the two protagonists an anxious glance and Tom Cooper found something fascinating to look at on the notice board, but Wilson knew when to back down, and he turned away before grunting noncommittally, as if he was trying to distance himself from the conversation, and returned to continue failing to crack his crossword, his face all furrowed brow.

Tom Cooper, a young officer who barely seemed to have started shaving yet, had seemed at one point to be falling under Wilson's influence, and Dan Holdsworth had taken him on one side.

"You don't want to get too close to him," Dan had warned Cooper. "He's a black hole and he'll suck you down with him. He's so stupid, he couldn't teach my arse to fart. He's no role model. And don't take any dating advice from him either. It'll definitely take more than a squirt of Lidl's own brand deodorant on your boxers, whatever he says. Trust me. And as to chat-up lines, 'Have you got any Yorkshire in you Love? No? Do you want some?' really won't cut it. Capiche?"

Cooper had got the message.

"Sorry to be late. Just dealing with a small matter of a shit projectile. Ooh, atmosphere! What did I miss?"

Sharon Mills waved her hands around distractedly. She was never one to be overly troubled by sensitivity.

Chapter Ten

The saturation level TV exposure had led to a flurry of calls to various helplines, identifying the three members of Vrioni's team. One had been pulled over on the M63 heading to Liverpool after his registration was pinged on a motorway camera, and one had been picked up at his girlfriend's house in Dewsbury. Both had given up without a fight. As a consequence, a number of saunas had been raided and a steady stream of girls rescued. Andreja had been on hand for a couple of these rescues to grab gripping testimony as these girls were escorted to police vans with blankets round their shoulders. She was distressed that none of them were the girls she'd shared the minibus journey from Manchester with.

The third gang member decided on a different approach. Following a tip-off from the proprietor, he was traced to one of the hotels that back on to Headingley Cricket ground, The Cricket Bails Hotel, basically a large converted Victorian house. He was foolish enough to wave a pistol around when he saw police officers coming up the stairs to his room. They beat a hasty retreat, closed the road and quietly evacuated the other occupied rooms: not being the cricket season, this consisted of two couples from Bristol who had come north for a family wedding. The experience certainly enhanced the father of the bride's speech the next day.

The cricket ground was only a couple of miles away

from the local BBC TV centre, and as luck would have it, one of their admin staff lived in the house opposite the hotel. Much to the annoyance of the police, led by local reporter Gloria Castle, an outside broadcast unit slipped in through the back door and set up a camera on the first floor. Then in a moment of inspiration Castle thought to contact Andreja and Marco and have them brought there.

Gloria Castle, who normally only got to cover hospital closures and local MPs opening food banks, was giddy with excitement at the prospect of an award.

Send me to cover crocheted scarecrows in Swaledale would you? Not any more you bastards.

Gloria was a lush. That's why she wasn't generally trusted with anything significant. She wasn't allowed to present the late-night local news segment because she couldn't be relied upon to remain upright, and she'd been forbidden from bantering with the weatherman at the end of the early evening programme after once developing the theme of a warm front pushing forwards. On pain of instant dismissal, she was now only allowed to read from the autocue.

"Right Aaron," the police negotiator began through his megaphone. "This is how I see things unfolding. You throw your gun out of the window, come down with your hands up, lay down in the car park, we arrest you and life goes back to normal for all these people."

"I want a helicopter, £20,000,000 and safe passage to the Maldives," he shouted from the attic bedroom window.

Gloria laughed out loud and then frowned and looked

at her sound engineer.

"We're not recording yet, are we? No? Good. A helicopter, £20,000,000 and safe passage to the Maldives? He's being a bit optimistic, isn't he?"

She stood in front of the window as her cameraman set up the shot that got her, and above, distant but clearly visible, Aaron and his gun. She paused, waiting for the handover from the studio.

And we're going live now to Gloria Castle for a report on a fast-moving situation near Headingley Cricket Ground.

Gloria assumed her most sincere/concerned look, one she knew would have the viewers eating out of her hand.

We have what appears to be an armed siege just a few steps away from Sheadingley Hopping centre...

A helicopter, £20,000,000 and safe passage to the Maldives? Where to start with that, thought the police negotiator with a sigh. *You and me both, Son. You and me both!*

"You might want to lower your expectations a bit there Aaron."

"It's pronounced Arran, Pig!"

Not with two As it's not, Matey.

"Right, Arran, that isn't going to happen. What might happen though, is that you get shot."

O.K. that wasn't strictly how these negotiations were supposed to go, but this negotiator wasn't going to pussyfoot around. He was close to retirement, was sick of dealing with arseholes and was supposed to be taking the wife out for her birthday later. On top of that, this lad had nothing to bargain with.

"Fuck off Fed! The money's now gone up to £25,000,000!"

In his safe house in Batley, Vrioni watched this unfolding on TV. He'd misjudged this kid. He wasn't just stupid, he was abusing the privilege. He settled back and opened another can, hoping that he'd be lucky, and the police would blow the kid away. He'd enjoy that. He pressed record on his fancy TV unit so he could enjoy it over and over again.

"Where are the girls?" Andreja shouted from the open window. Marco had it all on camera.

Vrioni sat up straight. This was the Slovene bitch who'd got away. He was already sick of seeing her on TV.

Andreja's intervention came as a shock to the police negotiator.

"Shut her up!" he hissed into his radio. He paused, and then just to be on the safe side, added, "And I don't mean shoot her!"

Well, you never knew, did you?

"I'll shoot her," Aaron-pronounced-Arran shouted, gesturing back into the attic room.

What? Shoot who?

There was a quick consultation with the hotel owner who was adamant that all staff and guests were accounted for.

The negotiator sighed: this was getting complicated.

Vrioni sat up straighter: this was looking better. As if in

anticipation, he rolled up a ten pound note, leant forward, put a finger over one nostril and sniffed a line of coke off his polished coffee table, then wet his finger and rubbed it through the light dusting of powder that remained, before rubbing it on his gums.

Aaron-pronounced-Arran returned to the window and pushed his luck a little further.

"Take all the time you need, but it's just gone up to £30,000,000."

"Bring whoever is with you to the window, Arran."

He dipped out of sight and reappeared holding an odd-looking young woman with his gun to her head. She looked shocked; her expression frozen. At the same time, the negotiator's concentration was further interrupted by the sound of frantic banging on the back door of the house opposite.

"Police! Open up!"

In HMP Low Moor, Terry was also glued to his TV. His cell door was open, and he shouted out to anyone who was on the landing,

"Look! It's shit-for-brains-Aaron on the news. He's in a hostage situation."

His cell filled up quickly with assorted prisoners and officers and then emptied again because of the smell. They were invited into the cell next door where Army John hospitably put the kettle on, and they all settled down on the bunks and plastic chairs to watch the unfolding spectacle.

"Bastards!" Terry muttered.

On A Wing, there was an almost carnival atmosphere.

"Anyone got any popcorn?" Officer Mills asked hopefully.

"No, but I can offer Madam an Orange Sunrise ™."

"I didn't hear that."

—

"Do not open the door," Gloria Castle shouted. "We'll pay for any damage."

Perhaps sensing that time might be against her, Andreja shouted again. **"What have you done with the girls who you brought from Manchester on Tuesday? Their parents are sick with worry!"**

Aaron-pronounced-Arran, also known as shit-for-brains-Aaron, came back to the window and waved his pistol about a bit. He was holding it sideways as a sign that he was a proper hard man. There was more hurried conferring on the ground.

"Who is she, then?"

"No idea," said the hotel owner. "Never seen her before."

"Come on Arran, you know this is a bad idea. Stop and think for a moment."

"Shut up and do as I say, and she won't get hurt."

There was a bang.

Aaron-pronounced-Arron had waved his pistol about a bit too liberally. There was a collective gasp as his hostage sort of folded in on herself.

"Firearm discharged. I repeat, firearm discharged."

Shit-for-brains-Aaron looked at his hostage and then

at his pistol with bemused surprise, before two shots fired
in quick succession effectively changed his name to no-
brains-at-all-Aaron.

Speaking about it later, several people swore blind that
they could hear the roar from HMP Low Moor.

"The poor girl looks as if she's deflating."

"Hang on. She IS deflating."

"Bugger me. She's a sex-doll!"

"Shit!"

The negotiator looked at his watch and smiled. He was
going to make it to the restaurant in good time.

All over the North of England, and soon to be picked
up by major networks around the globe (with appropriate
pixilation for the sensibilities of the squeamish), viewers
watched as no-brains-at-all-Aaron's victim hung from her
waist at the window and flapped gently in the breeze.

—

It turned out that no-brains-at-all-Aaron had not been
popular with other prisoners during his time behind bars.
The cheer at his demise had been deafening. It seemed
that pretty much everyone had been tuned to BBC local
news. Governor O'Brien had anticipated that there would
be trouble. He wasn't the only one who was surprised that
once the broadcast was over, the men simply slipped back
into their normal routines. Within a matter of minutes an
observer would have been hard put to know that anything
at all out of the ordinary had happened. To the men who
were suffering from withdrawal symptoms from the demise
of the Jeremy Kyle Show, this had been a shot in the arm.

"Of course, you wait," Governor O'Brien observed, "They'll all be coming out of the woodwork now."

'I was Aaron's best friend at school'

'Aaron once nicked my chocolate at nursery.'

'I once sat next to Aaron on a bus.'"

"He touched me up behind the cricket pavilion. He couldn't get a hard on.' That sort of thing?" The Hatchet entered into the spirit of the conversation.

O'Brien gave a mirthless smile. "That's the idea George. Isn't it amazing how the fact of his death will bring all these memories flooding back – that and the fat chequebooks of the journalists who'll pay for any old crap!"

——

Once things had calmed down, McAuley stuck his head round the door of the Chaplaincy office. He was in luck. Leo was at the desk nearest the door tapping away at his computer. It was a cramped office, too cramped for the number of people who were usually in it, but today the office's only other occupant was Errol, the Pentecostalist chaplain, who flashed him a perplexed look as if to say, "What's a uniformed officer doing in here?" He was not, it was widely acknowledged, a very good chaplain, but he had accrued some kudos in the prison by being quite stunningly rude to the Prime Minister when he had visited for a photo opportunity, and that sort of thing carried weight. (This was shortly after the men on C Wing had joined in a rousing chorus of Boris is a Cunt.)

Errol returned his gaze to his computer screen, a

position that he rarely left, and it was a standing joke in the prison that Errol was possibly the laziest prison employee. He was certainly the laziest chaplain and was rarely seen on the wings. Many of the Free Church prisoners had long since given up on him and preferred dealing with the other chaplains - any of the other chaplains - for all but the deep theological stuff, and they didn't ask much about that. Still, when you're the chaplaincy manager's best friend you can pretty much get away with anything, which probably accounted for why he was still employed, having been 'let go' for unspecified misconduct from another prison. Everyone knew this, but no one knew why, and the gossip had been a three-day wonder.

"Put the Kettle on Greg. Make yourself a drink." Leo's invitation was more than simple hospitality.

Putting the kettle on gave McAuley the chance to look over Errol's shoulder and Leo knew it.

Fantasy Football League.

Returning to Leo's desk with his coffee, McAuley innocently asked Errol what he was working on.

"Oh, just chaplaincy stuff." His tone was ingratiating.

"He's a hard worker is our Errol." Leo's face was deadpan. "He's been struggling with that problem all morning."

As if on cue they heard a rattling on the A Wing gate outside the office door.

"Chaplain Errol."

Leo and McAuley looked at Errol. Errol looked at his computer.

"Chaplain! CHAPLAIN ERROLL" (Rattle, rattle.)

Leo broke first, opened the office door and stepped onto the landing.

"Guv, is Errol in? I really need to see him. It's important but it's private."

"What's your name son?"

"Mohammed Hussain."

"Hang On." Leo stepped back into the office.

"Errol it's one for you."

"What's his name?"

"Hussain. Mohammed Hussain."

"What does he want?"

"He wants to speak to you."

"Tell him I'll see him tomorrow."

Leo stepped out again and there was a rattling of keys. Errol looked startled.

"Come on in Mohammed. He'll see you now."

Errol threw Leo a betrayed look.

"We'll give you some privacy lads. We'll go into the meeting room. Grab your stuff, Greg."

They settled in the meeting room.

"What's a Muslim lad doing with the Pentecostal chaplain?" McAuley asked him.

"No idea. I was wondering the same. It could well be about faith of course. Some people do convert you know, but it would be unusual for a Muslim to. Still, as I'm neither Muslim nor Pentecostal I don't really care."

They drank in companionable silence.

"How does he get away with it, Leo?"

"Errol? Years of practice and a complete lack of self-awareness I should think. Not giving a shit also helps. Seemingly Pentecostalists are hard to recruit to prison chaplaincy. Apparently, we're lucky to have him. Still, although we don't officially believe in Karma as such, his downfall should be spectacular when it comes."

"Why do you put up with it?" McAuley was genuinely interested: Leo was no soft touch and not at all backwards at coming forward. Assertiveness wasn't something Leo lacked.

"There are battles worth fighting Greg. This isn't one of them given that our boss will always cover for him."

Chapter Eleven

McAuley lay in that semi state between slumber and wakefulness, knowing instinctively that when he did wake up properly, he'd be feeling decidedly the worse for wear. It was all Luke's fault, (whatever "it" would turn out to be). A sober Luke was always good company. A Luke the worse for alcohol was entertaining, exhausting and the author of countless ill-advised, rash and hare-brained ideas.

"Trust me. Have I ever let you down?"

"How long have you got?"

"Anyway, I've just had this great idea..."

McAuley envied Luke's physical stamina and his ability to recover after a night out. Where McAuley was usually tired and ratty, Luke was always energised. McAuley often speculated when this might stop, when he could no longer survive a bender with self-respect: in Luke's forties perhaps or earlier. One morning he'd get up and the realisation that he couldn't do this anymore would hit him, but he'd go down fighting, in denial for as long as he could hold out.

("We've strong constitutions in my family. My grandmother ran her own knackers yard in Fort-de-France.")

McAuley fought full consciousness for as long as he could, but in the end, it was his bladder that made the decision for him. He opened his eyes, only to see the top of another head on the pillow next to him. He froze and snapped his eyes tightly shut again as his mind scrabbled for an explanation, but memory kept slipping away from him. Tricky thing, memory. Doesn't work well with alcohol.

OK. Think man! There's a woman in your bed. How did she get there? Well, that's a stupid question! You invited her obviously, unless she's a particularly niche type of cat-burglar.

So, Luke had suggested a few drinks after work with some of the others as a belated New Year's celebration and seeing that they were both on lates tomorrow – now today – he'd agreed. That much was as clear as day in his memory.

Right, good start. Then? No, nothing. Try again. OK: city centre pubs. Yes. How many? Three? No four.

He remembered thinking at some stage that it would probably be a good idea to stop drinking and go home, and then someone had appeared with a round of shots. Then beer-pong. Had he been on the winning team?

Too right he had! Yay!

Focus man!

He risked opening his eyes again in a way that might not look as if they were open to a casual observer, hoping that a visual clue might trigger something, anything.

A club! Blagging their way in with Wilson taking the lead. O Dear God, he'd actually gone drinking with Wilson? What had he been thinking? He bet he'd not paid either. Wilson was so tight, it was rumoured the queen would attend the opening of his wallet. Some memories were better left unremembered surely. Dancing? Yes, dancing – or what passed for it after (how much?) alcohol.

He wondered if he could risk farting. Ever the gentleman, he decided against it, feeling that it might spoil the moment. The mound next to him moved and a tousled head turned to him to reveal a rather pretty face. Pretty, but totally unfamiliar.

"Good morning, Tiger."

Tiger? As if this situation wasn't discombobulating enough, it came with cliches!

"Hi." He tried to sound upbeat.

"Do you know what first attracted me to you?" she asked.

"... er..."

"Your accent. I love the Irish." She played with the soft fair hair of his chest.

"Actually, I'm from Edinburgh."

"Yeah... and then that crooked tooth." She touched it. "So sweet! Have you lived here all your life?"

"Not yet."

He felt her hand on his thigh.

"Is it OK if I take the lead this time?" And, disappearing under the covers, she did.

Ah, so you're a morning person then?

———

He struggled out of bed and padded naked towards the kitchen, stumbling over a random shoe. He sat on the toilet basking in the joyful experience of an extended, very belated and much needed wee. He really needed a coffee, but on his first foray through the sitting room he'd encountered the somewhat arresting site of Luke's buttocks rising and falling in a fast, but steady rhythm, pale in the half-light.

Have I opened a bordello? O my days! I really shouldn't be allowed out without adult supervision and I don't think Luke fits the job description.

So, a refreshing shower later, he tried again more successfully this time. Luke and two surprisingly similar looking girls took quick turns in the shower and then a taxi arrived, and the girls were gone.

McAuley shooed Cat from the table and received a complaining hiss and a look of abject disapproval for his troubles. McAuley still hadn't had his first cup of coffee, which as those who knew him were aware, meant that he should be treated with considerable caution.

"Toast?" he asked.

Luke raised an eyebrow and fixed him with a rakish grin.

"Why the hell not? Here's to us!" He sat back, crossed his legs, put his hands behind his head and smiled.

McAuley sighed deeply,

Oh God, he's been on the double espresso again.

He placed the toast on the table and they both tucked in.

"When you've tried black, you don't go back," Luke volunteered.

"Oh, puleeze!"

"I can't help it if women find me devastatingly

attractive. I'm a victim of my own success. Look at me and what do you see."

"An ugly, skinny guy with a receding hairline."

"You cheeky bastard! You're a fine one to accuse anyone of being ugly and I'm not going bald. I just prefer a shaved head. What else do you see?"

"I don't think I'm allowed to comment under the conditions of the Race Relations Act."

"Funny guy!" Luke gave him a stern look. However, Luke's stern looks weren't at all stern: his default face was cheeky. He also did asleep, so it wasn't a wide repertoire.

This was, of course, the latest exchange in an infinite ritual of insults and banter. As neither man was ugly nor balding this was merely the laddish expression of friendship by two guys perfectly at ease with each other. They sat in silence for a while.

"Penny for them Greg? You're very quiet."

"I'm a bit... well... surprised... you know, about how the evening panned out."

"Surprised? What's the matter with you? You should be very pleased with yourself. Twins!"

There was a long pause.

Luke continued, "You do know, you're not technically old enough for a midlife crisis?"

"I'm never going to be allowed to forget this, am I?"

"Not for a moment... you old dog."

"Stop it."

"Not a chance."

———

93

"Of course your opinion matters, Gloria." *Just not to me*.

Gloria Castle was not appreciating the dressing down she was experiencing from her editor. His normally brash and upbeat air seemed less assured than usual. He rubbed his hands over his forehead as if to assuage a headache. Gloria assumed the headache to be largely symbolic.

"Look, I didn't shoot the little bugger, did I?" She was exasperated. "That's the risk with a live broadcast. How was I to know that the police would blow his head off?"

It was an ironic choice of words given that the smell of stale alcohol on her breath, not completely disguised by an extra-strong Trebor Mint, nearly blew his head off.

"I don't think you understand the situation we're in here, Gloria. We've had hundreds of complaints. It's not every afternoon that the country's day-time TV addicts see real blood on the carpet between Cash in the Attic and Escape to the Country. Strangely they can differentiate between Headingley and Midsomer. I'm surprised the Infirmary's not full of heart-attack victims. Upstairs is expecting a call from OFCOM any minute."

"Which leaves me overwhelmed with indifference." Gloria was not giving an inch.

He ignored her. "And God alone knows what's going down at West Yorkshire Police HQ right now. You may want to follow that up – or I could give it to Clive, and you could cover the schools under twelve's swimming gala."

She gave him a look that said, *Don't even think about it or I'll have your soft dangly bits for a necklace.*

He got the message.

She gave him a sideways look. "And our viewing figures?"

"Through the roof. That was the upside."

"We could get an award for this you know." She tried hard not to look smug but failed.

"Maybe, but which category? News or comedy?"

As they'd left McAuley's flat they'd found two Tupperware boxes on the welcome mat and a note.

I hope you enjoyed your night out boys. Here's a lunch for Luke too. Mrs. S xxx.

The boys in flat five: didn't Victoria Wood have something to say about that? McAuley wondered how Luke, a self-confessed meat and two veg man, would cope with one of Mrs. Singh's curries.

On the way downstairs the door to flat three opened. "Too much bloody noise last night!" Slam.

"Looks like a nicker-sniffer if you ask me," Luke said. "I'm sure you've had him on your wing. I bet he's got a porn collection catalogued alphabetically."

They'd left their cars in the staff car park last night, so the option was bus or cab. COVID suggested that the bus was the less good option and taxi drivers wore masks, so a cab it was. McAuley had a mask and Luke had put his scarf around his mouth. The cab driver looked ready to take him on about this but clearly thought better of it.

The power of a uniform, eh?

"You should be a Catholic," Luke told him, as he

fumbled with his mobile phone. "You've turned guilt into an art-form."

He hummed to himself as he waited for his girlfriend to pick up. McAuley was reminded again that Luke didn't see the world in the same way that he did.

"Hi , honey... yes I crashed at Greg's... Yeah, a few too many beers... No, a quiet night otherwise, a couple of games of pool, you know... Yeah, in a cab now... See you later. Love you."

McAuley wondered whether he could ever be like that. So, he should be a Catholic? Luke was, but he clearly didn't have any problem with guilt, but then he presumed Luke was a Catholic only in the sense that occasionally in life you'd need to tick a box on an official form inviting you to express a faith preference. But now, however tangentially, Luke had raised the God question, a question McAuley had been wrestling with for some time – and it had nothing to do directly with Fr. Leo's benign influence.

I'm rudderless in the ocean of life.

O my days! Stop being so melodramatic! His inner voice replied.

Excuse me! I'm having an existential crisis here!

JUST GET A FUCKING GRIP!!!

The voice sounded so much like Luke's in every sense that he threw his friend a startled glance, but Luke had snuggled down into his jacket and was in deep repose, his eyes shut, his scarf down and a contented smile on his lips.

When Luke and McAuley arrived at the prison for the late shift, they were mainlining on Fisherman's Friends because any whiff of alcohol would have had them out on their ears. It was clear someone had already been talking about the previous night's events and McAuley tried to remember who'd been there, but in the end did it matter? Luke was already filling in anyone who'd listen with the more salacious details so that genie was well and truly out of the bottle now. He went through the motions of appearing to laugh it off nonchalantly, but he wasn't comfortable. Making questionable decisions was one thing but he was at heart quite a private person and so to have those same decisions widely discussed didn't sit comfortably with him. He knew it wouldn't do his reputation any harm in what was an extremely blokey culture, but he hoped the fuss would die down soon. Who was he kidding? He sighed. This felt too much like a throwback to the immediate post-Molly period when he hadn't been all that proud of his behaviour. Too much to drink on too many occasions leading to some dodgy encounters too often played out in front of work colleagues. So he had form. 'Martini Man', Luke had called him then (and he'd had to look up the reference: "Any time, any place anywhere"), but he thought he'd moved beyond that.

I have moved beyond that for God's sake.

He may not have a perfect life, but he'd reached a contented equilibrium and now a little bit of him was unsettled. Was this the future? And at what point did you become that desperate, sad, middle-aged man out on the pull? That man that others sniggered at behind his back? OK he was only thirty, but he needed to be more... more...

well, more adult. After all, he wasn't a hormonally charged, priapic sixteen-year-old and really should know better.

—

The young footballer was looking a lot less full of himself, haunted even, McAuley noted. He had the sunken eyes of the sleep deprived and a bruise to his cheek. There were no nice, new trainers in sight either. He'd clearly been learning the hard way that prison was a great leveller and that no one liked a smart-arse. The only ones less well liked than a nonce were convicted police and prison officers.

"Mr. McAuley you do look tired. Bad night?"

"Aye, well, yes and no Cynthia. Yes and no, depending on whether or not you have standards."

"You're not one of those people who are naturally at peace with the world, are you Dear?"

Her disturbing eyeshadow was still a thing, he noticed. He'd been trying to place that elusive memory of repeats from 1970s sitcoms. Who did she remind him of? The best he'd come up with was a cross between Mrs. Slocombe (and her famous pussy) and the, "Ooh you are awful... but I like you" woman... woman? Man in drag? (The 1970s really had been another world and one best not revisited.)

"I'm from a show business family myself, you know?" she told him in a matter of fact way. "My uncle was the phone-a-friend on Who Wants To be A Millionaire. Anyway, now, have you thought any more about my reading, you know, the tea-leaves?"

"From time to time, but as yet nothing's come to mind."

"I'm sure it will Dear."

"I've got to ask you this Cynthia, what's going on with your eye make-up?"

"Lesbians, Dear."

He should, he'd realised later, have just nodded at that point and said something non-committal like, "Ah, of course," but it was too late and before he could stop himself, the word was out.

"Lesbians?"

"Yes Pet." (*Oh, a bit of Geordie slipping out there.*) "They interfere with the distribution channels."

"Oh... um... right. I... I didn't know that."

She gave him an appraising stare. "Listen to me wittering on. You've no idea what I'm on about have you?"

"Well, now that you come to mention it..."

"So, the thing is, lesbians are all so angry. All the time. When my post arrives, all those bitter women in the post room deliberately interfere with my orders."

"Right. Got it. Glad we've cleared that up then." He had no idea who worked in the post room, or even if it was called a post room, but he doubted it was a pack of marauding, angry lesbians, but what did he know?

——

"I checked the striation marks of the bullet that went through Sexy Sue and it matches the one we dug out of the ceiling in the hotel, so that's nice and neat. Same gun, so our laddo was definitely involved in the flesh trade."

Detective Chief Superintendent Murchison looked pleased. It was another piece of the jigsaw, but he wasn't sure how much further this took them.

Chapter Twelve

Maggie Fletcher was usually on C Wing and resented being away from there and being deployed in The First Night Centre because of staff shortages particularly irritated her. Her charges were the usual combination of regulars who knew the routine and who generally got on with it without fuss, the first-timers who were full of false bravado and bluster, and the first-timers who would weep into their pillows at night out of fear or shame. These were the ones who worried her the most because she would need to be on alert for acts of self-harm or bullying: she was constantly amazed by how naïve some first-timers were and was looking forward to the induction meeting later that morning which was usually fronted by trusted prisoner Ricky Clark. He'd put them right about life in Low Moor.

Ricky was an unlikely trusted prisoner: shaven-headed, tattooed and gym-muscled, he looked like something out of central casting with his big fuck-you grin, the sort of guy you might instinctively step aside to allow by, but he was a prison success story and managed to balance a persona which screamed, 'Don't mess with me,' - and very few would – with the unstinting respect of prisoners and staff alike.

"I used to be a right cunt when I was younger," he'd confided to Fr. Leo, who he'd forged a strong bond with.

Maggie sat through the hand-over from the night staff

with Luke Quarmby and Scott James who were sharing her shift. There was nothing to report. (Well, there was plenty to report, but none of it out of the ordinary.) The men had been fed and some had opted for a shower. One of the chaplains had already done his statutory rounds and Ricky had arrived and was following in his wake, going round the cells, talking to the newcomers through the door hatches, bantering and joking with them, working out who'd not yet been to an induction. He'd made his way round most of the twenty or so cells but was having trouble getting any response from cell 17. He checked his list: the name was Dale Carter and he was in the cell on his own, which was always a rare bonus in the First Night Centre which was usually packed to the gunnels. It must have been a quiet day in court yesterday.

"Dale! Come on Fella! Wakey wakey."

There was no response and Ricky could see the outline of the man on the lower bunk.

"Come on you lazy bugger, we need you up."

Ricky peered into the gloom of the cell through the hatch. He had a bad feeling about this: there was a strong smell of urine and Carter's breathing sounded laboured to him. He'd been an orderly on this job long enough to recognise the halt, lame and lazy when he encountered them, but this didn't seem right.

"Miss Fletcher!"

Maggie recognised the tone in Ricky's voice as it cut through the general hubbub of the wing and saw the look of concern on his face as she hurried over, her keys already in her hand.

"I'm not getting any response here Miss."

She unlocked the door and went in. Ricky stayed in the doorway ready to respond to her instructions and he watched her shaking the man on the bed as she called his name.

"Ricky, put the light on please."

The cell flooded with light, and they both looked at the clammy pallor of the man wrapped in his blanket. When she shook him, he was limp.

"He's well out of it," Maggie sighed.

Ricky pointed out the vomit in the sink. He was pretty sure he knew what the problem was, but he kept his thoughts to himself.

Maggie checked Carter's pulse.

"It's very slow, isn't it?" Ricky's comment was more of a statement than a question.

Maggie picked up Carter's right hand and looked at his fingernails.

"Are they blue?"

She looked over her shoulder. "Yes, they are. Go to the office and tell whoever's there to get a medic as a matter of urgency."

"Fentanyl. I'd put money on it," Ricky said to Luke, as Carter was hustled off the wing to a waiting ambulance.

"I didn't think drugs was your thing Clarky."

"It's not. No way. It's a mugs game that, but I'll be suspected."

"You and everyone else on the wing." Luke recognised

Ricky's anxiety: over a decade behind bars, now in his early forties, Ricky Clark had worked hard to get his act together while remaining his own man. With less than a year to go, his hope was to be recategorized and sent to a Category D prison on the basis of his good reputation, to a prison which would prepare him better for his release in a more relaxed environment.

"This could fuck things up for me."

"You just came on the wing Clarky. No one's going to seriously think you were involved. He probably smuggled it in up his arse crack. It wouldn't be the first time. We need one of those scanners."

Luke went to answer the office phone, leaving Ricky pondering suspension from his orderly role for the duration of the inevitable investigation. Of course, tea was the answer, so Ricky went into the wing kitchen and made two teas, taking one into the office for Luke.

"You know it could have been any of the other prisoners," Luke tried to reassure him. "Even guys passing through on their way to transfer."

"What about staff?" Ricky asked, not unreasonably. "Who came on the wing before lights out? Who was on night shift?"

Luke didn't like to consider the possibility of corrupt staff, but knew they existed. If it was a corrupt officer on the night shift, and if Security were on the ball, they might already have their suspicions, so that officer might just have handed his arse to them on a plate. Certainly, any staff who had come on the wing since this lot had been delivered from the courts was going to be looked at very carefully.

"Well, it's all conjecture. It could all be nonsense. It might be the flu." Luke offered this disclaimer with little conviction.

Ricky already had his suspicions, but again he kept his own counsel.

Chapter Thirteen

The hotel where Marco and Andreja were staying was several steps up from the Cricket Bails Hotel. As a converted terrace of elegant Georgian town houses, several flights of steps up, in fact. Theirs had been a frustrating couple of days: since the shooting of the lad who'd acted as the hotel receptionist and the release of twenty or so Eastern European girls from saunas and sex clubs all over the north of England, things had gone quiet. Granted, that series of reports had the Slovene public on the edge of their collective seats, (and, indeed, wider audiences) and their editor had been fulsome in his praise, but a day was a long time in journalism. Two days was an age, and their editor was talking about bringing them home.

Andreja had merely picked at her food that evening and following a couple of drinks and some desultory conversation, she had taken herself off for an early night. Marco had hung around for a bit longer but the young lady he'd spotted in the bar earlier and had been hoping to chat up, had simply been waiting for her boyfriend. Somewhat dispirited, he decided to follow Andreja's example.

He wasn't sure what had woken him, but he was suddenly wide awake and alert. It was dark and quiet, either very late or very early, but a sixth sense that had never let him down before, had kicked in.

Was that a noise on the corridor?

This is a hotel, man. People come and go at all hours.

That thought had barely evaporated when he was out of bed and tugging on jeans and a T-shirt. He didn't turn on his light, allowing his eyes to adjust to the dark, and held his key-card to the door. The click as the door unlocked sounded like a gunshot in the quiet. Was an unlocking door what had disturbed him? He opened his door a crack and listened intently. The corridor was in darkness, but if he stepped out of his room, he risked triggering the lights. Andreja's room was next to his. He slipped back into his room and knelt on his bed, his ear to the wall. There was muted noise, but it was a noise that didn't sound like a woman having a restless night. He knew her well enough to know that she and her fiancé were absolutely smitten with each other, so who was the man whose low voice he thought he could hear? No. Something was wrong here.

Marco scrabbled in the drawer of his bedside table for his miniature body-worn camera. He wasn't sure what British law was in relation to their use, but he'd seen cyclists wearing similar ones and his was smaller and more sophisticated.

Thank God for Japanese technology.

Anyway, at this point, he didn't care about what British law said. He clipped it on to the neck of his T-shirt and slipped into the corridor. As he'd feared, the lights burst into life, but silently, illuminating that Andreja's bedroom door was slightly ajar. That meant though, that whoever was inside, now knew that someone was outside.

Marco was usually a decisive person but now he was

wracked with indecision. If he stood outside Andreja's door, he'd be framed in the light from the corridor, but if he stood to one side, he'd have no idea what was happening within, and Andreja could be in real danger. He looked around the corridor, hoping for inspiration and the germ of an idea came to him. It wasn't much of an idea, but it was something.

He didn't have time to fully formulate a plan as Andreja's door was flung wide and Andreja was thrust out, her eyes wide with fear, her mouth taped, and a gun held to her head by a man wearing a ski mask and dressed all in black. He was not alone. The first man gestured to Marco to step back, which he did and backed up against the square box of the fire alarm. He drew his elbow back sharply and hit it with full force. The noise was deafening, but then it was supposed to be. The two men froze, looked at each other for a split second and pushed Andreja towards the emergency staircase. Marco knew immediately that these two were amateurs: they had their backs to him. He grabbed a wall-mounted fire extinguisher, took three quick paces and swung it as hard as he could at the second man's head, felling him instantly in his tracks.

The first of the doors on the corridor opened and a young couple carrying a toddler came out, looking worried. As he struggled to compose himself, Marco could hear doors opening and closing and a muted muttering from all over the building. He turned to the young couple, about to be overtaken by a tide of dressing gown clad humanity.

"There is no fire. Ring the police. Tell them there's a

violent kidnapping." They looked startled. "Please. Now! There is no time!"

They hesitated, but the man got out his phone although, hedging his bets, continued to usher his family to the stairs.

"No!" Marco shouted. "There is a man with a gun. Go back."

Confusion reigned and people simply stepped over the man Marco had taken out with the fire extinguisher. Self-preservation knocked the Good Samaritan out of the window.

Marco opened the fire doors and looked down. The stairs were crammed with a shuffling crowd of hotel guests, but there was no sign of Andreja and her captor. At some point they must have backtracked along a lower corridor. Marco pushed his way back through the stragglers and started down the main staircase. He had already worked out that the internal layout of the hotel was quirky, but would that be enough with the hotel's guests evacuating, to slow Andreja's abductor down? The main staircase was more or less clear, and it took Marco no time to get to reception where staff were directing people to the grounds.

"Where do the emergency stairs come out?" he demanded, looking around.

The young woman nearest to him, led him to the side of the building where a door was disgorging hotel guests into the cold. There was no sign of Andreja. In the distance the sound of sirens could be heard.

The hotel staff were like a well-oiled machine, calmly directing the guests who were milling about, to various assembly points, reassuring people and checking names. Most people seemed bemused and cooperative, but Marco noticed a couple of South-East Asian heritage who were quite animated. He thought how confused they must be by all the commotion.

Marco was told more than once to remain in his designated area but eventually broke away when he saw the duty manager talking to a huddle of police, firemen and paramedics.

"Sir, please return to your assembly point."

"No, you don't understand. There is no fire. I set the alarm off because my friend, she was kidnapped at gun point. I need to see the officer in charge." He knew he sounded overwrought.

"That's me. DS Humphreys. How can I help?"

Marco found himself facing a tall, smartly dressed young man who had an air of competence about him. Standing behind him was one of the officers he and Andreja had met when she had escaped from the minibus.

"Ask him. He knows me." Marco gestured to the constable. "My friend is the journalist who broke the story about sex trafficking. She's been kidnapped. It's the senior lady Officer I need to see."

The PC behind Humphreys nodded.

To give him his due, Humphreys responded quickly and got the gist of Marco's story.

"At gunpoint?" He looked alarmed. "Shit! We didn't get that part of the story."

He radioed for armed back up and grabbed a passing

constable.

"Get round to everyone. We may be dealing with an armed hostage situation. Do not engage but find out if anyone saw anything!"

A couple of minutes later the alarm stopped and the Senior Fire Officer appeared. He spoke to Humphreys and the manager.

"We're done here. You can go back into the building."

Humphreys intervened before the duty manager could draw breath. "No. I'm sorry. There may be an armed man in the building. We'll have to wait until the firearms team have cleared the hotel."

The manager took it well, Humphreys thought. He'd probably been waiting for just such an incident to put on his CV.

As the fire engines departed, the firearms unit arrived with DI Brewer.

"He must still be in the building." Marco massaged his temples.

It started to rain, and a baby began to grizzle.

"In the meantime, we need to get these people out of here." Brewer, as the senior officer took charge. She looked at the duty manager. "Is there anywhere they can go?"

He thought about it for a moment. "Well, there's a 24/7 McDonalds in the next street..."

"Great. If you could stay here with us, and your other staff can accompany the guests there with DS Humphreys."

It was not up for discussion, although Humphreys looked ready to argue. He saw this as baby-sitting and was not happy to be marginalised, but acquiesced with a poor attempt at good grace.

The duty manager gathered his staff and issued instructions. A few moments later, the group set off, looking like an ill-assorted school party in a ragged crocodile, and the armed officers headed into the building and fanned out.

It was half an hour later when Brewer took a call from Humphreys at the McDonalds.

"Guv, I have a Korean couple here, not much English, but from what I can gather, they saw a young woman being forced into a car during the evacuation. They've been trying to tell people, but language was a problem. Thank God for the translation app on my phone, eh?"

Two paramedics brought the still unconscious victim of Marco's fire extinguisher down to the ambulance.

"Fractured skull by the look of him. He's going to be out for a while."

Marco looked unrepentant and Brewer pointed to the nearest constable.

"Go with them. Make sure he's kept in isolation."

Back at the station, Marco had given his statement and handed over his camera. He didn't look forward to phoning Oskar Petek.

————

When Gill Baines arrived in the morning and had been brought up to speed, she sat down with Marco and commiserated.

"We're doing all we can Marco."

She knew it sounded hollow, however true it was.

Officers were already working with Traffic looking at CCTV for the area around the Grand Hotel, but so far had come up with nothing useful. The Korean man had described the car as red, but Gill knew that in the dark, that description was suspect. A red saloon. He'd seen it from across the car park but not close enough to be more specific and of course, there was no way the poor man could have been expected to give them a registration number.

———

Brewer was surprised when Marco, who she thought Gill had taken back to the hotel, reappeared in reception. The desk sergeant rang her office to inform her.

"He's got some news. I think he's about to burst with excitement. I can't get the full story, but the gist of it is something about a chip. I can't really understand what he's saying."

She wasn't about to put him in an interview room like some sort of a suspect.

"Have someone bring him up. Do you think you could rustle up some coffees Steve? Oh, you're a lifesaver."

Marco arrived looking flushed and held out his phone. He dialled a number. "My boss."

Sadie took the phone, unsure what to expect. "Hello?"

"Hello." A deep, heavily accented voice. "Marco tell me you the boss-lady I need to speak to."

She smiled despite herself.

"My name Oscar Petek. I am editor of Andreja and Marco. So, before they leave here, I give Andreja icon necklace. It has tracker. Top quality. Your technical people ring me OK? We sort it out."

When she heard, Gill Baines punched the air. "Yes!!!"

Chapter Fourteen

Marco and Oskar had been arguing fiercely over the phone, but Oskar's argument had won out. "Your camera footage is excellent Marco. Don't get me wrong – and we've edited out all the dead time in the car park to give it more of a sense of urgency and suspense. But, and it's a big but, we're just not showing it until we know what's happened to Andreja. Look, it's going to be part of the story one way or another and it's ready to go as soon as I say."

What he hadn't told Marco was that the paper's legal team had argued against using the footage on the paper's web pages, unless it came with the warning that viewers might find the scenes distressing. He really hoped Andreja would be fine. If the worst happened, he wouldn't use the part with her scared eyes and the tape on her mouth, but either way it was going to be a stunning story. She'd get an award, probably several. He just hoped they wouldn't be posthumous.

—

McAuley had drawn Sunday services on the deployment sheet. He usually did if he was in on a Sunday because he was generally the only officer who liked to take part in the service, and it made Detail's job easier knowing there was at least one officer who actually wanted to be there. After checking the men in and frisking them down, most officers pulled up chairs in the entrance lobby and put their feet up having picked one to sit with the vulnerable prisoners in the gallery just to make sure no one from the main wings decided to dispense a bit of extra justice. McAuley was happy to be that one, and the men appreciated that there was an officer who was willing to take communion with them on equal terms. It didn't go unnoticed, but it never occurred to him that he was gaining significant currency with those men by doing this. McAuley had learned to take his lead from Fr. Leo in his dealings with the men in chapel and it had paid dividends.

Leo had a great rapport with the men, greeting each one by name, shaking them by the hand and welcoming them in, and as the chapel filled up by wing, he worked the room in a quiet and unostentatious way. This was a man at ease and who had nothing to prove. He chatted to individuals, remembering important things like court appearances or medical appointments, or sharing a joke, always sitting with them rather than standing over them. The message was clear to some, more subtle to others but it was an effective message, "We are equal."

Over a period of time, he'd encouraged more and more of the men to read and lead prayers. When he'd first offered them the chance, they'd been either horrified or deeply sceptical. Many of the men had poor levels of literacy, often coupled with low self-esteem, but he picked his first 'volunteers' carefully from men who had some standing and influence, and he worked with them during the week, cajoling, rehearsing and encouraging. If he could get this cohort to take a lead, he hoped others would follow. And so they had. Now they were queueing up to volunteer, and if a man from the gallery spoke aloud from up there, they were listened to with respect. Sometimes McAuley could see the congregation, almost as one, willing someone stumbling over their words to succeed, and it was not unusual for a man to receive a round of applause. McAuley himself occasionally read or led prayers.

McAuley had not been brought up to be a person of faith although his uncle and aunt were nominally members of the Scottish Episcopal Church, but his uncle was also a Freemason, and he understood from Leo that membership of the two at the same time was a big no-no from the Church's perspective.

McAuley's own path to faith had nearly been blighted by over-enthusiastic members of the militant wing of the Evangelical Movement, big on judgement and condemnation but a tad lacking in the love and inclusion bit to the point where he'd begun to wonder whether it was possible to be a Christian without being a dick too.

"Maybe you wouldn't have to talk about it so much if you lived as though it meant something to you," he'd told one (soon to be ex) friend.

He'd been invited to a couple of meetings and had gone to exactly two before deciding that this wasn't for him. He had pondered whether it might be the musical snob within because his idea of Christian music wasn't a gang of smiley guys with guitars and a drum kit singing the same words on repeat, (what he'd come to consider as Jesus-is-my-boyfriend choruses) while everyone else waved their hands in the air. No. He liked a cathedral choir. And he was constantly perplexed by the obsession with speaking in tongues. The language of Heaven? Still if it floated your boat... (It not only didn't float McAuley's boat, it didn't even launch it.) There were also a lot of middle-class people talking about how Jesus had saved them from a life of sin, people he couldn't imagine doing anything worse than parking on a double-yellow line or taking a few paper-clips home from the office. He completely got the idea of surrender to God and turning over a new leaf, but did they have to lay it on so thick?

It wasn't until he'd started at the prison that he began to hear real and powerful testimonies about changed lives. Some of these men, he'd understood quite early on, had no one to talk to, really talk to, about what was eating away at their souls, unless they were in prayer. He'd found that deeply sad and strangely moving.

You had to be cautious, with scripture, Leo believed. This was a religion taken from first century Israel, (or should it be Palestine? He didn't much care.) The thing was, when you grafted it on to twenty first century England, it wasn't always a good fit, regardless of what the smiling evangelicals asserted. To McAuley's great relief, Leo didn't bang on about the book of Revelation and The Rapture all the time. In Leo's view the book shouldn't even be in the New Testament. That would certainly have saved the world from the mad predictions that the obsessed managed to extract from the book, foretelling the imminent end-times on the basis of earthquakes, plagues and questionable political alliances. What McAuley couldn't fathom was how supposedly intelligent people could be taken in by this. There had always been earthquakes, plagues and dodgy political alliances and the world managed to stagger on. He'd ventured this opinion in a phone conversation when someone had kept ranting on about the Russian threat. "Does it actually say Russia?" McAuley wasn't that hot on church history but was fairly certain that Russia wasn't even a place when the Bible was written.

"Well, not as such, but it's obvious really. It talks about the East."

"Well, OK I accept that Russia's east of here, but it wasn't written here, was it? I think east of where it was written was Syria or Persia or Babylon or somewhere like that. If you're reading it in Australia, are you terrified of the Satanic influence of New Zealand?"

He was told to fuck off and had the phone hung up on him.

Yes, let's put the fun back into fundamentalism!

Chapter Fifteen

There were eyes on the warehouse. The problem was that they were not as close as the tactical team would have liked. Setting up in someone's front bedroom is great if your target is in the house opposite. It is less good if you are watching from a back bedroom of a flat on the edge of a housing estate several hundred yards away, but you took the best that was available, and unfortunately, this was the best.

That was why Gill Baines was walking her father's dog past the warehouse. She'd used Riley as cover on more than one occasion. When she'd been a uniformed probationer, Gill Baines had learned to hate industrial estates. They seemed to be built on the same basic template and they all looked the same, were totally without character and had no real landmarks. This meant that she regularly got lost, which did little for her arrest rates. She had to admit that being here now brought back memories of frustration and disappointment. Well, now was a time to lay some ghosts.

There was nothing remarkable about the warehouse, not that she'd been expecting a neon-flashing sign announcing **Trafficked Girls Here**, but the unremarkable anonymity of the place was disheartening, its windows staring blankly back at her. Somewhere in that building, Andreja and a group of frightened girls were being kept. What had they been subjected to since they'd arrived? She shuddered involuntarily. She actually had some inkling what the possibilities were, and they were deeply unpalatable.

Two members of the gang were on remand and not talking. This of itself was a worry: their fear of the consequences of talking was greater than their fear of prosecution. A third member of the gang was dead: shot while holding a blow-up sex doll hostage. If it hadn't been so tragic it would have been funny. Actually, she found it hilarious, but decided to keep that to herself, given the amount of criticism the force had taken.

She couldn't see anything at the back of the warehouse as she slowly walked Riley, the ageing cocker spaniel: it was pretty much enclosed by a large brick wall, and the tall metal gates allowed no views either. She imagined loading bays. That's what the plans the city council had provided showed, but the area could be full of anything as most of the estate had been in mothballs for about a decade, an indication of the economic downturn. Time hadn't treated it well. Apart from a couple of small businesses at the entrance to the estate, going concerns because of their position, the place was eerily quiet where there should have been bustle and activity. The graffiti artists had been out in force, and the parking areas were littered with needles and condoms.

There was, however, one area on the estate that was busy: a large open space had been colonised by skateboarders, and while residential neighbours complained about the clanking and clattering at all hours, it had become an established feature. The firearms team had had to be particularly creative in their approach to deployment here, and the six members of the team, in ones and twos, dressed in hoodies and baggy pants and carrying skateboards, had made their way past the warehouse to take up a position in another abandoned building. Baines was heading towards that now, imagining that several armed officers were currently trying hard not to break wrists and ankles as they tried to blend in.

The pop-up skate park was out of the field of vision of the warehouse, and none of the armed officers, now changed and tooled up, were doing anything other than sitting inside their new HQ waiting for instructions, while half a dozen local kids clattered about on their makeshift apparatus. Baines hoped that someone had included them in their risk assessment. The last thing they needed was for a flock of terrified teenagers to get caught up in a shootout.

Baines stopped briefly to watch the kids as they repeatedly tried and failed to master new moves. She'd read that skateboarding was now an Olympic sport, and although she doubted that any of these would be mounting the winner's podium any time soon, she envied their determination as she started to retrace her steps.

Outside the warehouse that was soon to be the focus of a great deal of activity, she had a scary moment: right in front of the main entrance, Riley started to pull, and then squatted down to pass a very substantial poo. Steeling herself not to look at the building, but certain she was being watched, she fumbled a poo bag from her pocket and scooped up the mess.

She smiled to herself. *This is how TV extras in crowd*

-scenes, enhance their moment in front of the camera.

She could have carried on walking, holding the bag in a casual way, but she was a responsible dog-walker and looked around for a bin. There were several pushed up against the front wall, so she opened one and deposited the bag quickly. As she walked away, she could picture in her mind's eye the contents she had seen so very briefly: suitcases.

Apart from that, which was seen as very significant, and the presence of the genuine skateboarders, she had nothing to report. This meant that the operation was on.

———

In the warehouse, the guy in charge of the girls had just taken a call from Vrioni.

"No, nothing Boss, just a woman walking her dog. Took a dump right out the front. What? No, the dog."

After the call, Gary paced the room. He was bored. He oughtn't to complain, he knew. So far, this had been an easy job. His two mates were resting in the back room, Finn, nursing a black eye where the Kosovan slut had smacked him for trying it on. Since the arrival of the reporter, the girls had been more militant, working together, refusing to be split up and getting stroppier by the minute. They should have been split up at the start, but the debacle (he liked that word) at the hotel had made that impossible.

The girls had learnt some valuable lessons in the last few days and the most valuable was that there was safety in numbers. There had almost been a riot when Mitch, the Irish lad, had tried to take the Lithuanian girl for a 'debrief'. They'd fought tooth and nail as one, and Mitch had found himself with one girl clinging to his back while another scratched lumps from his face and a third kicked him hard in the bollocks.

That had clarified his mind.

A quick shag was one thing, but this trio didn't have the vicious streak the Albanians had. They'd expected the girls to be docile and compliant, and although they'd never admit it, they just didn't have the backbone or the balls. Their bravado was all talk. They were outnumbered and the hassle wasn't worth it, so after regrouping they had decided on a new strategy: they simply locked the girls away. There was now an uneasy truce. The guys had fed the girls and the girls hadn't attacked the guys again - yet.

Chapter Sixteen

The armed officers left their temporary HQ, and slipped around the side of the building, heading to the rear of the warehouse. The young skateboarders stopped and gawked. One of the officers pointed at the oldest of the lads and beckoned him over. It was touch and go whether he came, as he pointed at himself in a 'who me?' gesture, but obediently trotted over while his mates watched in fascination.

"Right son. I haven't got time to piss about here. You're not in danger now, but you need to get out of here. How do you get off the estate without using the road?"

The lad, who on closer inspection was a lass, took in the situation at once, turned and pointed to the far corner of their improvised skatepark.

"There. You can peel the wire fence back. There's a little path that leads to the flats."

"Thanks, now piss off. And if any of you phones anyone about this, I will personally come for you!"

She grinned, offered him a friendly salute and gathered her troops.

Three of the officers took up position at the rear gates. The other three evaporated into the estate, heading for pre-arranged points where they could observe the front of the warehouse.

—

They had guns, of course: they were proper gangsters

after all, but the Boss had made it very clear he didn't want the merchandise damaged, and the girls had soon worked out that the waving of guns was a bluff, and they were getting bolder. Gary knew they'd be plotting, but he hadn't passed any of this back to the Albanian. He wanted to give the impression that all was well when he was in charge. It was a matter of pride, but doubt and anxiety had been niggling away at his confidence, so he'd been greatly relieved when he'd been told that the girls were being moved tomorrow.

Gary was suffering from cabin fever. He decided to slip out for a smoke. This was strictly against the rules as well he knew, but he needed fresh air and a change of scenery. Over the last couple of days, he'd found his way around the building. That's what boredom did for you, you explored empty buildings. It might have been a nice place to work, he'd thought, but then, at twenty-four, unburdened by qualifications or talent, he'd never worked, so what would he know? What he did instead was easy money, (although he was always chasing the next big payday), and anyway, the conventional life was for losers.

He made his way to the back of the building. He knew the delivery area was enclosed so there would be no chance of his being seen. It was a surprise to him therefore, as he sparked up his lighter, to register the presence of three men in black, pointing guns at him: the sort of guns that meant serious trouble.

Fuck!

Now Gary was neither hard of hearing nor hard of

thinking, so when one of the men with guns hissed "Down" and gestured aggressively with his gun, he did as he was told.

"Where are the girls?"

It was only when he was alone, lying face down and hog-tied that he realised two things: his unlit cigarette was still in his mouth, and he'd shat himself.

———

While the officers sorted out the order for return to the wings and the other men sat and chatted amongst themselves, there would always be a group of men who stopped back to talk to Leo, to ask questions or to ask for help. If a conversation looked to be a long one, or a significant one, Leo would arrange to accompany the man concerned back to the wing himself when they'd finished.

Today the young man from A Wing who hung back was a first timer at the service. Whey-pale and unshaven, his stubble hiding a crop of pimples, and with the dark rings of the sleep deprived under his eyes, his body language was tense, and he was clearly unsure about how to proceed – or even whether to.

"I don't know if I should be doing this Father."

Leo waited. "Let's sit down." They moved to seats out of the sightline of the doors.

"I know something I wasn't meant to know, and I'm frightened."

Leo waited.

"I know you chaplains stick up for each other, but people say I can trust you Father."

Leo raised his eyebrows. There was something a bit off about that which he subconsciously filed away. He knew time was against them. The chaplaincy orderlies would soon be setting up for the Catholic service and he needed to get this lad talking quickly or he might not muster the courage to get whatever it was off his chest again. "What's your name?"

"Wayne. Wayne Mallanaphy."

"And you're from A Wing, right?"

"Yeah." Leo watched as the lad – and he was only a lad – gnawed his lower lip and fiddled with the frayed cuff of his prison sweatshirt. Leo recognised that this was going to be an issue of trust, and that this scared young man needed reassurance and support.

"My cell-mate, right? It's about drugs."

"O.K. Go on."

A set of wing gates clanged open and a group of the R.C. men started to queue up outside the chapel. Wayne looked stricken and half-rose to his feet. "I have to go. Please..."

It was obvious by his jumpy response that Wayne didn't want to be seen by other prisoners. Most of the men in the prison had perfected the art of selective vision and hearing: see no evil and hear no evil – and most certainly speak no evil, unless you wanted someone coming after you with three billiard balls in a sock, so Leo took him out through the vestry and the scenic route back to the wings, letting him into the central hub where he could slip anonymously into A Wing. Wayne had said nothing else all the way back and Leo was frustrated, but content to allow the lad to choose his own time and place to resume this conversation.

In the meantime, the men continued to assemble for Catholic Mass, but there would be no chaos this time. Sister Mary Clodagh, all five foot one of her in her nun's flat shoes, had been drafted in by the Bishop.

"How old do you think she is?" McAuley asked.

"About a thousand I'd say," quipped Pete Brown from B Wing.

She surveyed the gathered group, officers to her left and prisoners to her right. She smiled pleasantly and opened her mouth. "MY NAME'S SISTER MARY CLODAGH. YOU! YES YOU. STAND STILL MAN. DO YOU NEED THE TOILET OR WHAT?" The smile had gone, and although shocked into silent immobility by Sister Mary Clodagh's diatribe, they nevertheless huddled together emotionally.

"I put it to you that she is Irish," Pete whispered.

"Never trust anyone with too many letters in their name," Maggie Fletcher whispered back and touched the side of her nose knowingly.

"GET IN LINE NOW! YES YOU. I'M TALKING TO YOU MAN. ARE YOU DEAF OR IS IT OUTSIDE YOUR BAND-WIDTH? DON'T MAKE ME USE MY POKING FINGER. NOW, LET'S GET SOMETHING CLEAR. YOU'LL ALL DO AS YOU'RE TOLD THE FIRST TIME YOU'RE TOLD AND THERE'LL BE NO ARGUING OR YOU'LL BE BACK TO YOUR CELL AND YOUR FEET WON'T TOUCH THE GROUND."

A stunned silence descended on the men, and they shuffled into a line.

"CALL THAT A LINE? I'VE SEEN BETTER ORGANISED PLATES OF SPAGHETTI. THE GENERAL CONVENTION IS TO JOIN A LINE AT THE END. WHO BROUGHT YOU UP? YOU: BALD MAN, BLUE T-SHIRT. ARE YOU LAUGHING? THIS IS NO LAUGHING MATTER. THIS IS THE LORD'S HOLY SACRAMENT!"

Maggie Fletcher looked on in awe, "Can we get her in for staff training?"

Sister Mary Clodagh rounded on the officers. "AND DON'T YOU LOT THINK YOU'RE GOING TO BE SITTING OUT HERE ON YOUR ARSES DRINKING COFFEE. YOU'VE A JOB TO DO. I WANT YOU UPSTAIRS, (pointing at Maggie) YOU TWO STANDING AT THE BACK AND YOU TWO SITTING AT THE SIDES. CLEAR? GOOD! RIGHT, INSIDE. NO LOITERING. I'M SORRY? ARE YOU STILL HERE?"

"I think she's from the Sisters of Mercy."

And just like that, a cowed group of men and officers filed into the chapel in silence, and it was only at that point that anyone noticed a young man in a dog-collar, his thick-lensed glasses smeared with fingerprints, standing to one side and looking like a rabbit caught in the headlights. He'd arrived without noticeably adding anything to the dynamic.

"I'm Father Stephen."

"Straight out of seminary, saint's preserve us," Sister

Mary Clodagh muttered as she passed him.

—

Catching the officers on their way back to their normal duties, Leo asked if they could spare Greg for five minutes. Still in shock from Sister Mary Clodagh's new regime, they had no resistance left in them.

Leo handed McAuley a coffee and Sister Mary Clodagh waved a box of butter shortbread in his direction with an encouraging smile.

"Fair play to you," she said when he took one. Her smile was one of genuine piety. He'd never understand nuns. She was absolutely delightful when she was off duty, chatting quietly in her Irish lilt to Fr. Stephen and the orderlies and making them laugh.

"I need to ask your advice," Leo said, manoeuvring McAuley into a corner.

"I had a very strange conversation with one of your lads, or more accurately I nearly did. It was going to be about drugs but then he got spooked and clammed up. There's almost nothing to go on. Do I pass it on to Security?" He outlined the conversation, such as it had been, and McAuley frowned.

"I think you have to. I know it doesn't sound much but it could be a small piece of a bigger picture that makes sense to someone. Aye, go for it. Do you want me to do it?"

"No. I think it has to come from me. They won't call him in, will they?"

"On that? Doubtful, but there's bound to be a bit more attention paid to A Wing as a result."

Mo Hussain sat on the toilet in his cell, lamenting that cells on other wings had separate cubicles. All A Wing had was a modesty board at standing waist height between the toilet and the end of bunks. Hussain thought about his cell mate. He couldn't be sure what if anything he'd heard from the illicit phone call he'd made on the mobile he kept blu-takked to the underside of his sink. They could have their cell spun at any time, so he hoped it would be safe there, not that there were many other options for concealment. If it was found, he'd start by blaming pretty-boy and denying all knowledge of it, although he doubted anyone would buy that, but if ownership couldn't be proved they'd both be punished and that might even involve a transfer which would be very inconvenient. Something needed to be done.

Hussain had been furious when he'd found out that the lad had asked to change cells and had marched him straight down to the wing office to retract the request. They'd stood in front of the officer's desk, Hussain's arm around the other lad's shoulder, like twins in their matching grey sweatshirts with HMP Low Moor printed on the back. "Go on. Tell him."

"I made a mistake," Mallanaphy mumbled, almost imperceptibly. "I don't want to change cells." Any other officer would have read coercion in every move, but Mick Wilson just nodded and went back to the complex business of cleaning his nails with a paper clip.

"OK. Leave it with me."

Wilson didn't give this request, or the circumstances

behind it, a lot of deep thought. He didn't give many things a lot of deep thought. As it happened, he didn't give many things a lot of perfunctory thought either. "It's on my list," he said.

He didn't have a list.

"What was that all about?" Tom Cooper came into the office and scrabbled in the filing cabinet for a master copy of the form needed to bring clothes in from home. "How do we get through so many of these?"

"It's the craze for origami." Wilson pointed at an impressive paper swan on the shelf.

"Well, I wish they'd stop."

"Look, anything that keeps them quiet Mate."

Hussain and Mallanaphy were forgotten.

The prison was quiet now that lunch had been served. The men were behind their doors and the officers were either in the office, the staff mess or off-site having a smoke. Hussain's cell-mate lay on the bottom bunk, curled up in a foetal position facing the wall. He'd just returned from chapel – and that was a new thing that needed to be nipped in the bud. He was crying again, weeping silent tears. Well, that's another lesson he won't need to learn again. The thought of punishment aroused him, and he lay on the bottom bunk behind the lad, slipped down the lad's joggers, then his own, and began to inflict the latest round of punishment.

Chapter Seventeen

In the small, windowless room where the girls were being kept, their plan was ready. All it needed now was for one of the idiots who'd been left to guard them to open the door to bring them something. A few steps away from the door, the Bosnian girl lay prone with the Ukrainian by her side holding her head. It looked to Andreja to be quite convincing. It only needed to convince the moron (who would surely be carrying a tray) for a couple of seconds, before the others mobbed him. He'd be hemmed in in a moment.

Since they had been reunited, Andreja had been pleased to discover that the others hadn't been passive and had already brainstormed the layout of the warehouse from the memories of when they'd arrived. They knew exactly where to go once they were out of the room, and now their captors had taken to coming singly, and not stopping any longer than they had to. It was clear that the girls were intimidating which had emboldened them, but Andreja realised that their power was unfocused and needed a direct plan.

This was it.

———

In what had probably been a staffroom, now smelling of unwashed youth and marijuana, Mitch nudged Finn.

"Your turn."

"Fuck off. It's Gary's turn. I'm watching the match."

Mitch looked around theatrically. "No. Not seeing any Gary. So, still your turn, Pal."

Finn sighed. "It's not fucking fair!"

Mitch kicked him. "What are you? Twelve? Get on with it."

Finn put down his tablet, went to the sink, filled a large jug with water and dug around in a carrier bag for a couple of packets of biscuits.

"This won't last long you know. We're running low."

"It won't need to. Gary said the boss rang and the girls are being collected tomorrow."

"Fucking wicked! I'm sick of this."

"Are you sick of the money?"

Finn didn't reply.

___

Following Gary's directions, which had been delivered in a high-pitched, tremulous voice, the three armed officers crept through the warehouse like mist and up the rear staircase. As they turned a corner they stopped suddenly and fell back, as a spotty youth in a baggy sweatshirt came up the front stairs carrying a tray. In their briefing they'd been told not to engage unless it was unavoidable. It would have been a moment's work to take this lad out, but they knew not to depart from their instructions. It was unclear how many men were guarding the girls and they couldn't afford to take chances.

It was obvious where this lad was going, and they decided to give him the opportunity to get clear before they went for the girls. The plan, if it worked as it should, was to get the girls out without alerting the bulk of their guards. The one they'd disabled so far had put up no fight, and by the looks of this one, neither would he. Perhaps these were the gofers, and the real men were watching the football. They could hear the tinny sound of the commentary from somewhere downstairs. Careless.

The lad hadn't returned. This was a complication but the longer they waited the more chance there was that they'd be discovered. Leaving one covering the staircase, the other two headed along the corridor. There was only one door, and it was partly open.

These were men not generally given to being taken off guard, but the scene that met them was completely unexpected.

Spreadeagled on the ground in a puddle of water and being hit repeatedly around the head with a metal tray, was the lad they'd just seen, surrounded by a group of dishevelled looking young women, landing kicks with a focused ferocity. One officer covered the corridor and as the other watched open-mouthed, one of the women hit the lad with a stiletto heel. The officer winced. Apart from the sounds of the assault, the room was eerily quiet.

He coughed politely.

One of the girls looked up, saw the officer, gasped, nudged her neighbour and set off a chain reaction. In a couple of seconds, they all stood silently, facing their rescuers. The lead officer raised a finger to his mouth in a shushing gesture, stood back and motioned the girls to follow his partner. In seconds the room was empty (apart from Finn).

——

As Mitch continued to watch the football, the girls were crossing the rear loading bay, taking it in turns to stop and kick Gary as they passed. The rear gates had been opened with a bolt cutter and the girls were ushered out. Much to their surprise, a gaggle of teenagers joined the troupe and escorted them through a gap in a fence and along a path away from the warehouse.

They met Gloria Castle and Marco coming the other way. Andreja rushed into Marco's arms. Their reunion, sweet as it was, was brief.

"Fuck's sake! How did you know we were here?" The senior officer was exasperated.

Gloria gestured back to the flats. "No secrets here Sweetheart."

"Do not film!" he warned her.

Gloria was almost sober. She pulled herself up to her full height, fixed him with an icy stare and declaimed in her most authoritative voice.

"Freedom of the press occifer. You've heard of that, I assume?"

Marco, who had grown up in an environment where freedom of the press was new and fragile, stepped in.

"We aren't broadcasting. We only want to record. We just talk to the girls."

He received a curt nod in reply, and the little posse moved on. Marco stepped back to let the group pass as he fiddled with his camera. Now at the rear of the column, he took some surreptitious footage of their back view and then once they were out of sight, looked both ways, made a quick decision and nipped back across the open space. He stuck his head around the partly opened gate to get some background context and got some great footage of Gary lying on the ground. He quietly closed the gates and headed off after Gloria.

—

It occurred to Mitch suddenly that Garry and Finn had not returned.

Arseholes! Are they getting a sly leg-over without me? Bastards!

He stubbed out his joint, got up slightly unsteadily, and went in search of his mates.

As he stood in the doorway of the girls' room, his brain was playing catch-up as it struggled to make sense of what he was seeing.

"Finn, mate. What the fuck?"

"They hurt me." He certainly looked like he'd taken a beating. His nose was off-centre, there was blood on his sweatshirt, and one eye was swollen closed. Mitch suddenly realised that Finn was crying. He was appalled; he was actually crying.

"They hurt me, Mitch." Mitch sneered at him. He wanted to take him by the throat and shout at him for being so pathetic. Then, through his fogged brain, the seriousness of their situation began to dawn.

"You let them go? **You let them go!** We're fucked now. We're dead meat." He looked around. "Jesus, where's

Gary?"

He didn't wait for Finn as he fled the room. **"Gary! Gary! Where the fuck are you, you cunt? They've gone."**

The last place he expected to find Gary was in the yard. Mitch just stood there. "Shit Gary! Shit! You let the girls do this?"

"Untie me you gobshite! It was the police!"

Finn appeared, clutching his ribs and limping.

"Jesus Gary, you stink"

"And that's what's important is it? Jesus Christ! Untie me you morons!"

Finn pulled his sweatshirt over his nose. "Phew, you tramp. I'm gipping here!"

Garry rubbed his wrists as the pins and needles kicked in, grimacing.

Mitch hit his forehead repeatedly with a balled fist. "Police? Police!" He looked around. "Where?"

Gary pointed to the gate. "Well, they've gone now, haven't they?"

"Let's go then!"

Gary looked at them pityingly. "Oh, great idea. Let's go out of that gate, straight into the arms of the police. Back inside. We need to think."

They made a sad little trio as they supported each other back inside.

"Jesus, man. You smell."

―

"Make them sweat," the senior firearms officer said.

"They must be bricking it. We've got the girls now."

The girls were being debriefed by Baines and Brewer, and Brewer had some information that she needed to pass on. She radioed the senior officer on site.

"There are only three of them and they're definitely third division. The girls disabled one, and your guys got another."

"Ah, well, unfortunately, he wasn't a priority. We went back for him, but he'd gone, back inside we guess because he didn't come out the back. We were told not to engage because the hostages were safe, and at that stage we didn't know how many men were inside."

"What? And they've not come out?"

"Not so far."

"What are they up to?"

"Panicking, I'd guess. I don't think they're very bright. Maybe they think we've just gone away."

"So, what are you going to do?"

"Nothing. We wait until told otherwise."

—

Inside, Mitch was looking at Finn's injuries. He was just going through the motions really, as he had no first-aid experience, and there was only so much he could do with a bowl of cold water and a pack of tissues. They'd sent Gary away to clean himself up. It hadn't been a success. He still smelt of shit.

"What are we going to do, man?"

Mitch was rapidly tiring of Finn's whining. He was looking through the blinds at the empty area outside.

"We're going to walk out of here." He sounded decisive. More decisive than he felt.

"But the police."

Mitch grabbed Finn and pulled him to the window. "Look." He pushed his face against the blinds. "Who can you see?"

"Jesus man. Chill." Finn thought Mitch was going to hit him. Mitch wanted to.

—

"Some activity detected from a ground floor front window, a movement of the blinds. Someone checking out the lay of the land. Stand by for possible breakout." The senior officer was hopeful that this would all be wrapped up soon. Keeping a firearms unit on indefinite standby did not sit well with him, but the men inside the warehouse were armed and therefore a potential danger to the public. His headset crackled.

"Van approaching. I repeat, van approaching."

This was unexpected. Had the men inside the warehouse called for back-up?

The door to the warehouse opened and three young men came out, trying to look casual.

—

Gloria's outside broadcast team was getting this all from the balcony of a fifteenth-floor flat. The wind blew her hair over her face as she struggled to maintain composure talking about the atmosphere on the estate. Then it blew her scarf over her face, muffling her speech, and a cutaway to the studio revealed a smirking presenter.

"Gloria seems to be having a problem with wind today. Now, over to Clive for the weather."

In HMP Low Moor, Trevor Kawalski had been watching the sport's news. When it was over, he thought about turning it off, but his attention was grabbed by the breaking news logo along the bottom of the screen.

"Look guys. It's that arsehole Gary on the BBC." Acoustics and the prison grapevine being what they were, the majority of prisoners were tuned to local BBC in a matter of moments.

"Has he wet himself?" Dan Holdsworth was looking at the state of Gary's trousers.

At that moment a white minibus with tinted windows, screeched to a halt outside the warehouse. Four men got out. Two were Asian, one was white, and one was black.

"Who the fuck are they?" Despite himself George Hatcher, standing in Kawalski's doorway, was allowing himself to be drawn in.

Chapter Eighteen

"Who the fuck are they?" Mitch looked around at Finn and Gary. Both looked wide eyed, partly because they'd clocked the weaponry the newcomers were packing. They certainly looked menacing enough. They didn't need to try to be hard. They were hard. There was no bravado about them. This was the genuine article.

"We've come for the girls," the Asian in the baseball cap announced, conversationally. Wearing sunglasses on a miserable English winter's day, it was unlikely that he suffered from light sensitivity. He had the look of a man who didn't accept criticism easily.

Finn found his voice. "You're a day early." He was doing a very good impression of not understanding what was going on.

Baseball cap, who seemed to be the spokesman, laughed and turned to his crew, who dutifully joined in.

"I don't think you understand little boy. We're moving in and taking over. If you know what's good for you, you'll do as you're fucking told." He laughed as if he'd said something funny.

"We don't scare easy." Mitch's voice was more threatening than he felt, but the white guy held his gaze and raised one eyebrow in a dismissive way, then pointed his shotgun and smiled.

Gary, who didn't appreciate having a shotgun poked in his face, immediately voided his bowels again.

"You two..." Baseball cap pointed at Finn and Gary. "... on the ground. "You..." he pointed at Mitch, "... take us to the girls."

"They aren't here." Mitch's tone was flat.

"Do I look fucking stupid? We know they're here."

"The Feds came and took them away." As he said it, Mitch knew how lame that sounded.

Baseball cap looked around and snarled. "They took the girls and left you here? Nice of them."

That's when Armageddon happened.

"Armed police. Drop your weapons now."

Three of the armed squad appeared with that distinctive crablike scuttle and took up offensive positions. If the newcomers thought that the odds were in their favour, they'd not factored in the possibility that there might be three other armed officers already in position out of sight.

Baseball cap's crew, of course, did the exact opposite, and guns appeared from all directions.

(Viewers to BBC local news were thoroughly enjoying the scene. This really wasn't what you expected on a Yorkshire industrial estate, and Sunday morning TV had been as bad as ever so far. Things were most definitely looking up now.)

Shotgun swung his gun towards Mitch and was immediately flung backwards by two shots from somewhere to the right. As he fell to the ground, some reflex in his trigger finger set off his shotgun which shattered the window of the minibus and set off its alarm. Mitch was surprised to find himself still alive, if suddenly deaf, but had the presence of mind to fling himself to the floor from where he could see red laser-dots appear on the bodies of the three remaining gunmen. Baseball cap, however, unaware of the targets on him, was determined not to go quietly: that was not at all his style. He pointed his gun at the nearest officer who in turn had no hesitation in firing first, two shots: one to the body and one to the head. Baseball cap was dead before he hit the ground. Unfortunately, he landed on top of Finn, who finally appreciating that he might not be cut out for this sort of thing, promptly burst into tears.

The remaining gang members dropped their guns. They'd clearly been through this routine before because they put their hands behind their heads and lay face down on the floor.

Soon after, a convoy of police vehicles arrived and Mitch, Gary, Finn and the remaining gang members were taken away.

"Man, you stink," the Asian lad said to Gary.

———

It was several days later when Mr. Hatcher, picking thoughtfully at his tombstone teeth, announced that the governor had ordered a full staff meeting to talk about COVID.

"Yay!" Cooper said unenthusiastically, punching the air in a half-hearted way. "Another meeting that would be better as an email, no doubt."

Wilson leant back precariously in his chair, dusting crisp crumbs from his lap, and McAuley tried to calculate the angle that would be the point of no return, hoping someone would 'accidentally' knock into it. Wilson had a look about him that said, 'piss off or else!' McAuley looked around the dark and cramped office at the dirty windows, the grubby carpet tiles, the institutional cream paintwork, at the chipped table and dented filing cabinet and then back at Wilson. The whole place was not fit for purpose, not for prisoners, not for staff. The heating system was Victorian and arbitrary: one side of the wing was always sweltering and the other freezing while mysterious draughts eddied around the landings.

"Right, no unlock and skeleton staff." The Hatchet looked around the small office. "Holdsworth and Wilson that's you today. The rest with me." Wilson eased himself out from behind the desk, delighted to be missing the meeting but dischuffed and resentful to be paired with Holdsworth, who he knew he couldn't push around, and who wouldn't let him sit in the office while Holdsworth did all the work, so he grunted and looked like a dog that had been neutered. He shifted on the seat and broke wind ostentatiously.

"Magnificent! That's better out than in."

He wafted his hand around.

"Jesus! Maybe not."

The others looked appalled and fell over each other in their rush to leave the office.

His movement from behind the desk dislodged some of the liberal sprinkling of dandruff from the shoulders of Wilson's uniform jacket as he joined them.

As they left the office, they heard Wilson talking to Holdsworth. No one enjoyed his own 'jokes' more than Mick Wilson. Hoping for stimulating deep conversation, a person would be better off talking to someone else. Anyone else.

"Did I tell you about the Paki I caught wanking?"

Wilson was his own target audience.

"Great!" Holdsworth could be heard to mutter, with all the distaste he could muster. He stood up and started to undo his belt.

Wilson looked startled. "What are you doing?"

"I'm dropping my pants so you can kiss my arse."

McAuley didn't know what made Wilson so stupid, but whatever it was, it was clearly working. McAuley had ear wax smarter than Wilson, and he mentally added casual racism to the indictment against him. During lockdown, he realised, he'd spent so long in this place, with this odd assortment of misfits and the socially inept, that he worried he'd forgotten how to behave in normal society.

Chapter Nineteen

He'd watched it all unfold on TV with a sense of déjà vu. Anger didn't do justice to Vrioni's current mood: blind rage would be nearer the mark, but he was a pragmatist. The Slovene bitch had been all over the TV again, and now those girls were all in a five-star spa hotel near Ripon, because some bleeding-heart liberal thought they needed a break after their trauma, and as if that wasn't enough, job offers were coming in from all over. None of this would have happened if it hadn't been for him. He should be getting more credit.

He laughed at the idea.

O.K. the journalist had helped to destroy what had been a very lucrative period and had decimated his network, but then he'd been the one responsible for putting the three amigos in charge of the warehouse, not that he'd had much choice as his team was significantly depleted, and the outcome would probably have been the same, only with more blood. Looked at a different way, Vrioni was still free and by no means out of pocket. The thing was, Vrioni was a criminal. He'd always been a criminal and had never considered being anything else. If people thought he was a criminal, then why should he give a shit? They were right. What mattered was that he stayed ahead of the game, consolidated and moved on. Anyway, he'd always believed in diversification, and it was clearly time to move on. That another gang had tried to muscle in on his territory was all the incentive he needed, particularly as he'd no inkling who this new consortium was.

The mysterious Mr. Yellow had made some tentative offers which the Albanian knew to be test projects which he'd passed with flying colours. Anyway, when it came to choices, what were the options? To wallow in angry self-pity or to move on to new and better projects? Still, he had a long memory, and there were certain people who'd better hope they never crossed his path again.

———

"Hi Greg, come on in." Molly lent in to receive a kiss on the cheek and gave him a hug. It was a friendly and affectionate hug, but one which still felt to McAuley as if it had acres of physical space between them. Still, things were so much better than they had been when they'd first decided to split up and McAuley had nowhere else to go, and they'd carried on living together but lived totally separate lives in the same house for a couple of weeks. They'd become like housemates circling around each other in a space that now felt too confined, sitting and pretending to watch TV together as they ate from trays on their laps, rather than sit together at the table and worry because they had no conversation. The only thing they had in common now was Sammy. McAuley could have afforded to buy a place of his own, but he'd decided that he couldn't commit to anything in the medium to long-term and decided to rent instead. It was a huge relief to them both when he moved out. At one point, for the briefest of moments, he'd considered returning to Scotland, but that felt like an admission of failure, and anyway, he'd fallen in love with Yorkshire, and he wanted to be close to Sammy.

McAuley stepped back and looked at her. "New haircut?"

Molly kept her blond hair short. The tomboy look suited her elfin face. Molly, with her head often too full of Thomas the Tank Engine and nappies, had often expressed the view that she'd forgotten how to function as an adult, and of an evening could barely string a sentence together. She was very pleased indeed to be back at work.

"Daddy!" Sammy came steaming down the hall at full pelt into McAuley's legs before being gathered up in his father's arms and thrown, squealing with delight into the air. "Again Daddy. Again."

"Well, this could go on all day" he smiled.

"I think someone might be sick before too long if you carry on like that." Molly stepped back, put her hands on her hips and smiled.

"Look at you two." Sammy was nestling his head on McAuley's shoulder, thumb in mouth, feigning shyness.

McAuley tried to hand Sammy over, but he wasn't having any of it and clung, limpet-like to his dad's neck, giggling loudly as Molly took him under the arms. She led the way back down the hall.

"How's Luke?"

"Ha! Luke is Luke. No change there."

"Yes, they broke the mould when they made Luke. Probably a good thing."

Molly liked Luke, (everyone liked Luke), but she was

under no illusions about him. She also didn't know how Sonia put up with him.

"Yes, he's seen me through some tough times."

McAuley sensed he was heading towards difficult ground; ground he didn't want to cover again. He'd been invited for a baby-sitting day, not another post-mortem about the failure of their relationship.

"You shouldn't let him dominate you, you know." she chided gently.

"He doesn't dominate me. He just talks louder."

"Yes, and you can always tell what he's thinking. He thinks very loudly too."

The thing about Luke was that he led a charmed life. His world was quite a simple world: he arranged it around himself in the way he believed things should be, with him at the centre. It was nothing short of the natural order of things and it was entirely unconscious.

Molly's phone call had sounded slightly panicked.

"The nursery's closed because of Corona virus. I don't suppose there's any way you could have Sammy for a few hours?"

McAuley was on a rest day, but his body clock had woken him at the usual time much to his annoyance and he'd no plan as to how he was going to fill his day now that their freedoms were so curtailed. The prospect of a domestic day really hadn't appealed as he ate his Weetabix and eyed his Facebook feed with a jaded eye, so this came as a very welcome diversion. Time with Sammy was very precious and always a delight. "I'll be there before you set off."

They sat at Molly's kitchen table drinking coffee as Sammy ate his breakfast.

"Mrs. Singh's bored to tears since the Gurdwara told all the old ladies to stay at home."

Poor Mrs. Singh had been devastated. She'd lost her complete social network and her raison d'être in one blow. What was she going to do all day if she couldn't sit gossiping with her friends while they made pakoras and samosas?

"Can we be a bubble at the same time?" he asked Molly. Molly had clearly been thinking about this.

"I've been all over the INTERNET. As I understand it, shared parental responsibility allows us some leeway, so yes. Anyway, we'll talk about that when I get in. There's pizza in the fridge and I've made up Sammy's snacks. Give me your car keys and I'll strap in his booster seat on my way out."

Having done that, she picked up her keys and looked in the mirror, frowning.

I can't use this mirror. People look fat in it!

She ran her fingers through her hair, checked her makeup and grabbed her bag.

"Not too much TV! Have fun you two. Bye," and she was gone, gone to the family business of funeral directors where she was receptionist and administrator.

"I'm strictly front-of-house," she'd said when they first met and McAuley had shown a real interest in knowing how it all worked. Possibly too much interest on reflection:

having seen a few bodies through his work, the dead held no particular fear for him. He'd had to backtrack a little, after all he didn't want her to think he was a weirdo when things were looking so promising.

"Right Sammy, coat on. We're going to the park."

The departure was delayed for about ten minutes as Sammy appeared only to have odd shoes and McAuley had to wrack his brains to think where a four-year-old might hide stuff as he certainly wasn't going to tell. He just sat there smiling inscrutably.

In his bed.

Of course. Why not?

It didn't matter how many books you read, there were lots of things they didn't tell you about being a parent.

The big disappointment was that the children's playground was closed, and they joined a despondent group of the COVID-disenfranchised at the padlocked gates. McAuley had no intention of getting into a debate about the fascism displayed by the Town Hall in making that decision, so he shepherded Sammy off for a little kick about on the grass.

When it clouded over, they headed back to Molly's via a diversion to have tea and cake with Mrs. Singh. McAuley lost count of the number of times they sang The Wheels on the Bus on the way home.

As he parked on the road to allow Molly to get onto her own drive, he looked around the cul-de-sac which was beginning to have a slightly abandoned feel to it: only the five houses, with four of the gardens running wild. One house was empty with a For Rent sign at a slight angle in the garden and two were usually occupied by students, so were also empty as they'd decided to go home during the lockdown. (On-line teaching was better when your parents pay the bills and feed you, it seems.) The final house was owned by an elderly widower who was deaf and had mobility problems but was resisting his children's attempts to encourage him to move into residential care. He didn't care about the students because he couldn't hear them, but Molly was enjoying the relative quiet that COVID 19 had brought to her street. It wasn't that the students were particularly anti-social, but the houses were rammed full and there was a constant coming and going at all hours.

By the time Molly got home Sammy was happily eating fish fingers and beans and some of Mrs. Singh's best was in the oven.

"Dinner for two Madam?" Then he saw her face. "What's wrong?"

"It's been a rough day," and she burst into tears. He gave her a hug and waited until the sobs subsided and the story emerged. There'd been a pile up on the ring road and her company were taking care of the bodies of a family of four, including two small children. "It's so upsetting when children are involved. Will you stay for a while and keep me company?"

McAuley failed to see the chasm opening up before him. "Aye, of course I will. Don't be daft." He squeezed her hand.

"I think I'll be able to take Sammy to work with me

tomorrow. It's not ideal but Dad says he can play in the office."

Ah, Mr. Woodruff, who would rather let hell freeze over than have anything to do with McAuley, the man who had so casually impregnated his daughter and then, in his view, abandoned her.

"Actually, I've got a suggestion on that front."

She raised her eyebrows. "Go on then."

"Would you consider letting Mrs. Singh look after him? She's great grandmother material. That's "great" as in wonderful by the way. Not "great" as in great-grandmother."

He realised he was gabbling. "It doesn't seem like she'll ever be a grandmother. Her son in Chicago bats for the other team and her daughter, and her daughter-in-law in Johannesburg are so career focused there's not even a gleam in anyone's eye."

That's more detail than she needs to know, he thought. *Cut to the chase.* "That's a sort of long-winded way of saying I've sounded her out but made it clear that the final decision's yours. What do you think?"

"I think it's great. Let me work out the practicalities and I'll ring her. But there's one condition. She doesn't drive him anywhere. I've seen her reversing and I've also noticed that she never gets out of second gear. You can break that news to her." She frowned for a moment. "God alone knows where that leaves us with our COVID bubbles, but at this point I've lost the will to live with it all."

They watched a bit of TV and after three hundred bedtime stories, or so it seemed to McAuley, one very tired and over-excited little boy finally fell asleep.

They watched a bit more TV, then Molly's tears began to flow again. McAuley was caught off guard as the tears turned to sobs and it was an instinctive reaction when he put his arms round her. She buried her face in his chest, and he rubbed her back murmuring soft reassurances, and then to McAuley's utter amazement, Molly cupped his head in her hands and pulled him towards her.

"I'm probably not thinking clearly now but please stay with me tonight. No strings. No change to how things are between us, but after the day I've had, I need to do something life affirming."

He kissed her back tentatively at first, but then with growing enthusiasm as they rediscovered each other after so long. McAuley allowed himself to be led upstairs.

So much for integrity and self-control, he thought, not entirely comfortable with the idea of having been used as a sex object.

Chapter Twenty

I hate night duty. I hate night duty. I hate night duty. Maybe if I put that to a tune? He tried. *No, I'll still hate night duty.*

He'd arrived for that shift to see the new COVID regime in action. All staff were wearing facemasks, mainly hastily constructed bits of cloth, but a few had the proper medical type. (The effect was spoilt to some extent by those who were wearing theirs as chin-warmers.) On top of that, all staff were using the same entrance, so in order to maintain physical distancing the line was hundreds of yards long and it was raining. Once in, McAuley encountered the only sanitised-gel dispenser currently on the premises. It was on the Governor's corridor, and it was empty. McAuley had already dug around in his bathroom cabinet and to his surprise, had found some that was still within date. This, he decided, was to be kept well out of sight.

Night shifts were generally tedious and dull. Apart from statutory duties, night shifts were what individual staff members made of them. Many brought in books or puzzles, one wrote song lyrics, some occupied themselves with the new colouring-in for grown-ups' craze. One officer was heavily into crochet. McAuley caught up with coursework. It wasn't as if night duties were particularly onerous: now they were in lockdown, once the men had been fed, (door to door using a trolley was the current preferred method) that was pretty much it.

"By the way, Madam Cynthia's been released," Dan told him. "She went this morning. I thought you'd like to know. Apparently Mr. Hatcher's going to throw a celebration party."

They sat at their desks and worked out which of the most vulnerable of the vulnerable they'd have to see during the night and at what intervals before writing themselves a schedule. Lockdown had caused a spike in mental health problems and so there were more than normal.

"So, my role is to shine a light into the faces of men who are already suffering from mental health problems at regular intervals during the night to check on their mental health, and write down that I was told to 'fuck off and let me sleep.'" Dan was still learning how things were done and this was his first night shift.

"That seems to be the long and short of it." As someone who could turn sleeping into an Olympic sport, McAuley disliked this part of the routine immensely and sympathised with the men, but the risk of acts of self-harm in the dark hours of the morning made it vital.

He took out his notebook and textbook. It was half past midnight and he'd just finished his latest rounds. There were still a very few subdued conversations behind the doors. Being locked up for twenty-three hours a day probably meant that you weren't very tired, but most of the TVs were off now. He tried to concentrate on the latest exercise.

Dan was curious. "What are you reading McAuley?"

"The Girl with the Dragon Tattoo and the Death of

Anyone Who Interrupts Me." He smiled up at Dan.

"Joking." He ran his fingers through his hair. "I don't know about you, but I need to keep my brain active but learn something practical at the same time. It was this or car maintenance and I didn't want to put Skoda out of business. It's a personal discipline I suppose."

Dan looked over McAuley's shoulder.

"That's a bit niche, isn't it? Still, everyone speaks English now, don't they? I was rubbish at languages at school, but I did get German GCSE."

"And how is your German now?"

"Comme ci comme ça."

The night dragged by slowly. He massaged the back of his neck: too much time sitting in front of his textbook on an unsuitable chair was taking its toll. He yawned, checked his watch and pushed his chair back. All was silent but for the gentle (and not so gentle) sound of snoring as he passed doors, and at 4.00 in the morning, he was on his rounds again.

He'd set his camera to record. Weary didn't sum it up! He opened the next door on his schedule: Wayne Mallanaphy – the documentation said depression and anxiety. This was his fifth scheduled visit to this cell, and all had been well at 2.00am. Trying to open the cell door as quietly as possible, he knew instantly that something was wrong. There was resistance and he had to shoulder barge the door to get it open, and then, Narnia-like, he entered another world: not one of snow-covered magic, but one of darkness and death.

It took a second for his eyes to adjust to the pre-dawn dim light, but he knew that what he was seeing was all wrong and snapped on the light. Neither bed was occupied and hanging by a sheet from the window fitment high-up by the ceiling, was one of the occupants while the other was holding him round the legs.

"Jesus!" (On reflection McAuley decided that had been a prayer rather than a curse.)

"Help me Guv. I'm trying to hold him up!" Hussain looked like a rabbit caught in the headlights.

McAuley reached for his belt and fumbled out his cut-down tool, a tool he always carried but hoped he'd never have to use.

"Don't move. Keep him there," he shouted to the other lad as he clambered onto the bunk and started slashing at the sheet with the curved blade of the knife. "Help me get him down."

They laid him on the floor and McAuley tore off his mask and started on mouth-to-mouth. In the back of his mind his illogical voice was telling him he'd probably die of COVID now.

"Mr. Holdsworth's on this landing. Go now and tell him it's a code blue call. Don't just stand there GO. IT'S AN EMERGENCY." He could hear the panic in his own voice.

The other lad took one last glance at the scene and fled. McAuley carried on with mouth to mouth and then tried chest compressions. From somewhere he could hear his desperate voice repeating , "NO NO NO NO NO NO," and the sound of blood pounding in his ears so loud he was convinced the whole wing could hear it. He felt as though he was about to fall through the floor, and he was having trouble focusing. Was he about to pass out? He tried desperately to think clearly through his panic.

"I've radioed it in." Dan Holdsworth knelt beside him. "Dear God!"

Below they could hear the sound of gates opening and running footsteps.

"Step back Greg." Paddy was a nurse McAuley knew well and he calmly took over.

"He's still warm Paddy but I can't find a pulse."

"Thanks. Step out of the cell please both of you."

McAuley, feeling strangely light-headed and other worldly was assisted out by Dan and was vaguely aware of the sound of the defibrillator behind him.

"I think you need to sit down Greg." He looked at Dan blankly and nodded, too frightened to speak at first in case he was sick.

"Sit down Mate." Dan had his hand on McAuley's shoulder. He slid down the wall and sat with his head between his legs, his face an unhealthy colour.

He tried to string a few words together to explain. They wouldn't come. "Not my finest hour, eh?"

"Don't be silly. You've been a fucking hero."

At some point paramedics arrived and it was clear that the whole wing was now awake. Mirrors were poking out of door slits everywhere, but the place was eerily quiet.

Paddy came and knelt in front of McAuley. He was still sitting with his head in his hands, trying to control his breathing.

"How are you doing Greg?"

He was starting to calm down, but the blood was still rushing in his ears and his heart was still trying to escape his rib cage. "How is...?"

"Never mind about him. I want to know how you are. Are you OK?"

"No... but I will be." The enormity of what he'd just been through was starting to sink in, but at the same time the sense of shock and powerlessness was starting to recede a bit."

"He's dead, isn't he?"

"Just been pronounced by the paramedics. He was what? Nineteen? Well, he's not going to get any older now, the poor little bugger. What a waste. There was nothing you could have done Greg. Why didn't the other lad press his bell?"

McAuley shook his head. "No idea. Panic?"

Dan had his arm round McAuley's shoulders as they descended the stairs to their office, McAuley somewhat wobbly around the knees, leaving the fuss and bustle around Wayne Mallanaphy's cell behind. His cellmate had been examined by the medics, given an initial debrief and taken to the health care wing where a bed had been found for him in a cell with an experienced Listener. Now that Wayne had been declared dead it was as if the natural order of things had been restored. Efficiency took over. A death in custody: there was a protocol for that, and various things would swing inexorably into place. His body would be left in situ until the forensics people had been and the cell would be locked and sealed. The coroner would be informed as soon as his office opened and the governor or one of his deputies would visit Wayne's family that morning with a Family Liaison Officer and one of the chaplains to break the news. McAuley, Dan, Paddy and Wayne's cellmate would be interviewed and McAuley's camera footage analysed, his visit notes studied and Wayne's history with Health Care looked into. All this would be part of the investigation that would follow as seamlessly as night followed day.

Suddenly the office seemed the most reassuring place ever. Someone, he didn't know who, made him a coffee. He smiled his thanks, not willing to trust his voice. Other staff came into the office, but understanding some unspoken message disappeared again. He'd heard them talking outside the office in subdued tones and wondered what they were saying. The Duty Officer suggested gently that if McAuley felt up to it, it might be a good idea to start writing his statement while things were fresh in his mind.

Fresh in his mind?

It would always be fresh in his mind. It was like a film played in slow motion, on a perpetual loop on the inside of his eyelids. The D.O. sent Dan into a neighbouring office to type his up: they shouldn't be seen to be conferring.

He spent some time analysing whether there was anything he could have done differently in his earlier visits to Mallanaphy's cell. He finally concluded that there hadn't been, but that familiar feeling of guilt hung around his neck like a millstone. Perhaps he should give in to it after all and follow Luke's advice and join the Mother Church. But then again, perhaps not.

Before he started typing, McAuley found some scrap paper and started writing random things down as they occurred to him, linking them by arrows to make a timeline. His mind had come out of its fog and was working overtime now, but it was like a jigsaw with too many missing pieces. He looked at the scribblings and the arrows. Something wasn't making sense, but he couldn't see it set out like this. He sat resolutely in front of the keyboard, adjusted his seat, flexed his fingers and began typing.

———

He read the finished article for the third time and sat back. He was happy that what he'd typed was accurate, but now he could see inconsistencies. He badly needed to talk to Dan and Paddy, and he really wanted to see his camera footage. Indeed, at this particular moment, he'd sell his soul to see the forensic photos. He knew he'd be questioned closely on this statement in the coming days, but as it stood his statement was implying something between the lines that was disturbing. He could believe Wayne Mallanaphy had hung himself. He could - if he tried really, really hard. A wave of fatigue washed over him: his shift was long-since over, but he was surprised at how quickly time had passed.

Deputy Governor Hirst arrived, pulled Dan back into the main office, and sat with them for a while.

"I've had a quick look in the cell. I wanted to see for myself before I read your reports, otherwise I'd be pre-programmed to see what you saw. Just tell me the outline lads. I just need to know the basics. The rest will come later."

Dan and McAuley talked freely, and the governor listened intently, asking some pertinent questions. While they talked, his frown deepened.

He thinks it's dodgy too, McAuley realised with a jolt.

"Look lads, you really need to go home. I don't want to see either of you for the next twenty-four hours and if you need it, you know we can provide support. You've had a rough time so don't minimise it and don't pretend to be coping if you're not. And... thanks for what you did last night."

Having dismissed the pair, Hirst picked up their accounts and started to read.

Last night?

Time had little meaning just now for McAuley.

As they left, Dan shared some of his own misgivings which chimed with McAuley's.

"There's something not right about this." Dan paused to light a cigarette. "But my brain's scrambled and I need sleep." A long exhale. "Will you be OK Greg? You had the worst of it."

"Sex offenders are my thing – so to speak, not suicide. I'm a bit out of my depth. I need a shower, a beer and bed. Whether or not I'll sleep's another matter. You got someone at home?"

"Yeah. I'll be fine. I've already rung the wife. You?"

McAuley was tempted to lie and be all blasé but instead just said a quiet no.

"That's tough. Sorry. Look, you take care, right? You did well tonight."

In that moment they understood each other through the trauma they'd shared, as significant yet as subtle as a breath. Dan headed for his car and flicked his cigarette away. McAuley watched it bounce off the tarmac in a shower of sparks.

He clicked his remote, the car's indicators flashed and he climbed in. It wasn't often that he was confronted by the full ugliness that was always a potential in the world he inhabited at work, and he was not one who generally took work home with him. Today would be different. As he sat in his car, before he could even put the key in the ignition, he let his head fall onto the wheel, and with his shoulders shaking, wept silent, angry tears.

Chapter Twenty-One

As McAuley had approached the house, he could see from the road that many of the lights were on. Most people seemed to be at home. It should have been a welcoming sight, but this morning it wasn't. McAuley didn't want to be here, but then he didn't really want to be anywhere else.

At about the same time that McAuley was driving home, Leo was sitting in the back of Deputy Governor Hirst's car on the ring road. When he'd arrived that morning he'd expected a normal day, not that any day could be described as normal in prison, but he'd expected a day which could at least be reasonably predictable. What he'd not expected was to have been met on arrival and taken to the Control Centre. When he'd asked the officer escorting him what was going on, she said that all she knew was there'd been a death in custody and guessed that was what it was about.

He wasn't sure he knew the names or the exact roles of most of those who worked in this part of the prison, other than Deputy Governor Hirst, who he liked and respected, so when he was ushered into the conference room, he felt on the back foot. He didn't get over here very often.

"Thanks for coming Leo." Peter Hirst sighed and rubbed his eyes. "Look, there's been a death on A Wing, a suicide, and we'd like you to come with us to notify the family - not that we know what their faith position is, so you may or may not be redundant. I know these occasions can be a bit exposing for the chaplain and I'm sorry for that, but I'd appreciate the moral support. I've spoken to Imam Khan, and he says that the team can cover anything that would've come your way today. I'll fill you in on the details as we go."

Leo hated funeral visits, but at least at those the family had begun to get used to the idea of death. This was going to be something quite different, and he didn't relish it. It wasn't his first such visit, of course, so he had a fairly clear idea how it was going to go. Leo was good with the recently bereaved, but it was always a strain, and it took it out of him emotionally. To be one of those who notified the death was to face unexpected responses, particularly among the families of prisoners: grief, but not always, sometimes indifference; shock; denial; calm acceptance; occasional rejoicing or deep satisfaction. Taking prisoners' funerals was also occasionally fraught.

"No one wants to do the eulogy (occasionally urology) Vicar because he was a bastard, we all hated him, and we're pleased he's dead. I hope he suffered."

That's the thing about funerals of course, they're often about hypocrisy.

Yes, indeed, funerals and the preparation for them were great opportunities for studying family dynamics and human nature, as was the wake, and Leo smiled as he remembered with amused affection his own mother, who after a few gins, could be relied upon to tell a few home truths.

Leo pondered these and many other thoughts as they

drove to meet Mallanaphy's mother.

"How well did you know this lad, Leo?"

"Barely at all. He came to chapel once. I put in an intelligence report. Did you see it?"

"Not personally, but all the strands will be drawn together in the investigation. Do you think it's relevant?"

Leo weighed this up for a moment. When he'd first heard who the death in custody was, he'd wondered if it was linked in some way to their brief conversation.

Poor lad. How desperate do you have to be to kill yourself?

"It's hard to know: he hardly said anything but he was frightened. It was something to do with his cellmate and overhearing something about drugs. Then he clammed up." A pause for breath, then, "Do you have some doubts about this Peter?"

"I do, actually. It was McAuley and Holdsworth who found the body and their accounts don't add up."

"What? You think they're lying?"

"No, no, not at all." Their eyes met in the mirror. "What I mean is that the circumstances don't add up, not the reports. I think the lads did exactly what they should've done, and I believe what they told me, no question about it."

"So, what's your hunch then?"

"Well, it is only a hunch at this stage, but I don't think it was suicide, particularly on the basis of what the lads said, especially McAuley, who was the one who found the body. Of course, we don't mention any of this to the family, but we do need to find out from them what he may have written to them about. We'll also need to review his phone-calls. I don't think we've had cause to listen to any of them, but we'll need to know what they knew about his state of mind or what had been going on with him and Hussain. It may help us with the investigation."

"Hussain? Mohammed Hussain? The kitchen worker? He was the cell-mate?"

"You know him?"

"Not directly, but he's been to the chaplaincy office."

"Really? Why?"

"I don't really know. Errol was dealing with him."

"O.K. I just wondered."

"I'm sure you'll tell me in your own time."

Hirst gave him a searching look in the mirror and smiled.

———

As it happened, McAuley had slept and slept deeply. Emotional as well as physical exhaustion had ensured that he had, but he had woken bathed in sweat, and with pins and needles in his arm where he'd lain on it. Staying cocooned in his duvet was a huge temptation, and he was reluctant to leave, but he stumbled out of bed, woolly headed, his groggy mind failing to engage fully, but it was good that he had slept through because lack of sleep was when the mind got things badly out of proportion. That would normally be in the dark hours of the morning, but he had slept through the day, and the evening sunlight seemed to him to be casting disturbing shadows around the room.

He'd so far managed to shut that door in his mind that he knew would lead to nightmares: he wasn't yet ready to free those monsters. As he stood in the doorway between rooms, had he but known it, the light cast his face into shadow, highlighting his bone structure and leaving his eyes in pools of shadow like a skull.

He allowed himself to think about Mallanaphy for a little while: the boy who would never now have his release from prison party and be welcomed home and hugged by his family; who would never again settle in front of the TV for a good film; never again drive a car or go for a beer with friends; never jump on a plane for a holiday in the sun; never have a girlfriend, maybe marry and have children. All that and more had been stolen from him and it saddened McAuley deeply.

He threw on whatever clothes came to hand. The tie-dye T shirt he'd picked up in a vintage shop was an aberration of colour in the otherwise uniformly neutral palette of the flat. He turned on his phone and picked up texts and voicemails from Luke and Leo. He didn't really want to talk to anyone, so he fired off a couple of "I'm fine" texts. He wasn't, of course. He knew that.

For a long time, he'd been used to being emotionally self-sufficient, but now he felt like a lost child as he pondered the day ahead – or the evening and night as it now was. The cat sashayed by, aloof as ever and McAuley ignored him. The mug of coffee on the floor at his feet, had long since gone cold, and he disconsolately logged on to his e-mails. Just the three phishing attempts today, one each allegedly from HMRC, TV licensing and a bank he didn't have an account with, all of which he deleted. There was some information about music from the choir and a CORONA VIRUS update from the city council. They would all have to wait until his head was in a position to function. If this selection was some sort of commentary on his life, he'd really need to up his game.

With Governor Hirst's "I don't want to see you for 24 hours" ringing in his ears, and in a frame of mind that was oscillating between odd, and distinctly odd, he knew that today would be unproductive, but the problem with being alone was that he was likely to dwell on yesterday's events and his mind shied away from that: he already felt bad for wishing Dan had visited the cell first instead of him. Neither did he want to self-medicate. That way madness lay, not that he kept much alcohol in the flat at the best of times. Alternatively, he could turn on the TV, find the catch- up option and keep fit with Joe Wicks. Strangely, that didn't appeal.

For a while he couldn't stop pacing backwards and forwards and recognised that this was a response to stress. In the end, in frustration with himself, he dragged his fingers through his hair and flopped on to the sofa. He wasn't himself, but he was near enough to face the world. He was suddenly acutely aware of the silence and turned on the radio, more for distraction and company than anything else. Noise leeched into the room. The PM was waffling on about keeping the NHS safe.

Well, there are distractions and then there are

distractions.

He switched it off. Somewhere outside a child kicked a ball against a wall – repeatedly. The dull thud, thud, thud got under McAuley's skin.

For God's sake! Where's the pleasure in that? It's just mindless. Give it a rest.

He was actually considering heading outside to remonstrate with the kid when he realised that he was being unreasonable. Yes, it was irritating. Yes, it was mindless. Yes, it was pointless, but it was just a kid. He knew this mood was just a reaction to his current situation, and chewing off some poor youngster for playing with his ball wasn't the answer.

A plan of action was needed, but a plan of action required discipline and in order to be disciplined you needed to be motivated, and that was something he most definitely wasn't just now. Meanwhile, as McAuley sat in his jogging bottoms and T-shirt with the front of his feet stuffed in his trainers and the backs trodden down, life went on in the outside world: a train passed in the distance, full no doubt of ordinary people doing ordinary things, and in countless sitting rooms families sat and shared their days with each other.

But not a day like his.

For a while he sat and looked out of the window, but he saw nothing: his thoughts were turned inwards, and he didn't like the way Cat followed him with his eyes while his tail swished from side to side.

A bit of TV news distracted him for a while, but it did

nothing to lift his spirits. He supposed he ought to eat and drink something, but he wasn't about to go downstairs and sponge off Mrs. Singh. He wondered if he had the energy to pop to the Sainsbury's Local. He decided that he hadn't. The content of the fridge was infinitely dispiriting but nevertheless he managed a three-course meal: cheese on toast followed by spaghetti-hoops on toast and a well past its best banana. It did the trick though, and as he wiped away the ring his plate had left on the work surface, Cat proceeded to lick the plate, but McAuley couldn't summons the energy to remonstrate with him so left him to it.

He felt his energy levels begin to rise to the extent that he considered getting out of his joggers and maybe, who knew, even having a shower.

It wasn't called the smallest room for nothing: when McAuley sat on the loo, he rested his forehead on the bathroom cabinet. He found it strangely comforting. He didn't need to look in the mirror to know that he looked shit, and when he did have a shower, a cold shower, it seemed to take forever for it to bring him back to some semblance of life. Attic living was great for keeping the heating bills down, but today McAuley felt the oppression of the low ceilings as if they'd conspire to press down and flatten him.

Chapter Twenty-Two

The visit to Wayne Mallanaphy's family home was as awful as could have been predicted. Wayne's mother, who barely looked older than her son, and his younger sister, Kirsty, were at home when the bearers of bad news, the worst possible news, arrived. Kirsty was wearing a threadbare sweatshirt several sizes too big, Wayne's probably, and she held her arms across her body, holding her elbows, in a defensive position. The likeness between her and Wayne was clear.

Leo sat glumly in the back seat on the return journey going over bits of the conversation in his mind while Gov. Hirst and the Family Liaison Officer, who Leo didn't recognise and whose name he hadn't caught, chatted disconsolately. Mrs. Mallanaphy had sat in her armchair in her down-at-heel living room, rocking backwards and forwards and wringing her hands. 'Hand-wringing' was a term Leo knew well, but he also now knew that he'd never actually seen it before today. The poor woman had been rendered so numb with shock as to be virtually speechless, but Kirsty had rallied her and had kept her focused enough for them to realise she had little information to offer. Yes, she knew Wayne would struggle in prison, and yes, she knew that he was being bullied by his cellmate, but what could she do? No, Wayne was not a druggie (toxicology would ultimately vindicate that belief) but he was a good lad, and so on.

"He was never going to cope well in prison," Mallanaphy's sister lamented. Leo, who remembered the tired, pasty features, the frayed cuffs and the almost pathological determination to be invisible, knew this to be a sad truth.

"He asked to change cells, but nothing happened," Kirsty offered. None of the visitors said anything, but they exchanged glances, and the FLO wrote it down. Leo knew Hirst would follow it up. Gov. Hirst had offered his condolences, and Leo had sat quietly holding Mrs. Mallanaphy's hand, which she seemed to find comforting.

"Did you know him?" She'd looked up at Leo imploringly.

"He'd just started to come to chapel, and we'd begun to chat." This was factually accurate, but Leo felt the weight of his omissions.

"I'm glad," she'd said. "Will you be doing the funeral?" Suddenly she'd seemed very anxious, and Leo recognised, not for the first time in his ministry, the beginnings of a dawning of the practical implications of a death. Sometimes the need to be busy gave the grief-stricken a project through which to sublimate their grief, a project they would cling on to like a lifejacket.

"If you'd like me to, I'd consider it a privilege, but that's something you don't need to worry about now." This was the prompt for the FLO to begin to talk about how the prison would handle all the arrangements, and then abruptly there was nothing else to be said and they sat in awkward silence. Kirsty broke the silence by offering them tea, the British panacea for all woes, which they declined, mumbling about how they needed to get back, and then they were on their feet. Kirsty showed them out. As they left they heard a chilling, keening howl of grief from behind them.

———

"Why didn't you ring me?" Molly was annoyed with him.

"Look. This is me ringing you." This call had been a bad idea he reflected. "But it's not as if you could've done anything. I just felt you ought to know."

"I can listen" she'd replied, and she did, and far from feeling that he didn't want to talk to anyone, he now discovered that he did, so much so that as soon as he'd put the phone down, he'd rung Luke, who in time honoured best-friend mode, had arrived about twenty minutes later with a Chinese and a multipack of cans.

———

About ten minutes into the journey back, Gov. Hirst had asked, with a lightness of tone that immediately made Leo wary, "How do you get on with Imam Khan?"

Leo narrowed his eyes. He needed to be careful how he phrased his answer as the Chaplaincy Manager had senior management status and sat in meetings with Gov. Hirst. Leo found the Imam to be a perfectly pleasant young man but not, in Leo's view, really management material in that he didn't really direct his team and largely left them to get on with things while he did management-type stuff. He was also guilty of assuming that his staff knew things he hadn't told them but should have, and rarely disseminated information from all the meetings he attended. What really annoyed Leo though, and most of the rest of the team, was how he let Errol get away with being lazy.

"Well, he's a Haji." he said, playing for time. Even in these days of easy travel around the global village, going on the pilgrimage was no mean feat.

"He takes his faith very seriously," he added as if by way of further commentary. "He's OK. We get on well enough but I'm not often in the office."

Whilst not being an answer in the sense that Peter Hirst wanted, it had the advantage of being true, and Hirst acknowledged the answer with a slight nod of the head. In Leo's view, the chaplains were a dysfunctional team, and he didn't need to be in the office much to do his job, so he stayed away as much as possible, preferring to spend his time on the wings with the men and eat his lunch in the staff mess. So, what had led to this 'innocent' question? Surely, he didn't think the Imam was somehow involved.

—

"So, how are you doing Greg?" Peter Hirst was a good manager and McAuley knew it was meant kindly - and he appreciated it, he really did, but if one more person asked him, ever so nicely, "How are you?" (How *are* you?) or, "Are you OK?" (*Are* you OK?) he felt he might snap. Of course, if he did that would just confirm what people suspected and what was behind all the solicitous enquiries. They wanted to know if he was coping.

"Thanks for asking. I'm doing fine, thanks. I'm getting

there." He felt that had the right casual tone and he smiled cheerfully.

"Good. I'm pleased."

He'd been offered counselling, of course. He wasn't averse to the idea at all and would certainly take advantage of the offer if he felt he wasn't coping, but he'd seen death and experienced shock before: there hadn't been flashbacks, he was sleeping and eating well, he wasn't self-medicating and he was in good spirits. In his book that was as good a definition of coping as he could envisage. Anyway, there was no prison officer who had never plumbed the emotional depths. If you couldn't cope with that you were in the wrong job. McAuley, of course, thought he was in the wrong job, just not for that reason.

He was hoping this shift would be a lot less shitty than the last one. On A Wing, things were the same as ever. His colleagues had got the message about not asking him how he felt about finding Mallanaphy's body, (They were not a group likely to stray into the dangerous territory of feelings and emotions, so it was a relief to them that they didn't need to).

As to the prisoners, some were genuinely upset and some had jumped on the bandwagon and had made the most of the drama, although by the time McAuley returned it was already yesterday's news.

Chapter Twenty-Three

"Well, this is all a bit cloak and dagger," said Paddy as he entered the room. "Notes delivered in sealed envelopes - it's all a bit old-school. Did I miss the instruction to eat after reading?" He looked around the room. "I didn't know this place existed. I'm not even sure I can find my way back to Health Care."

Already in the room were Dan Holdsworth, Gov. Hirst, McAuley and Leo.

"Do you know what's going on?" Paddy asked Dan as he slipped into a chair beside him.

"It's been years since I knew what was going on," Dan grinned.

"I'm sorry about all this, lads. I'm just being cautious." Hirst looked around at the group as Paddy took a seat. "There might be no need, but just in the short-term I'd like you all to keep what we discuss - even the fact that we've been meeting - to yourselves. So, firstly, it seems some of the drugs we've been finding are fentanyl. Now that's deeply scary stuff because it's significantly stronger than most of the street drugs we usually encounter. Even a small dose can be fatal. We'd have been looking at a spate of overdoses."

"Now that's just by way of information, what I really want to discuss is Mallanaphy's suicide and to what extent it may be linked to our drugs problem."

He looked around at the group and began. "This is what

we know so far. Just after 4.00am Officer McAuley was conducting statutory visits on A Wing. When he reached the cell shared by Muhammad Hussain and Wayne Mallanaphy, he was unable to gain entry without the use of force. On entering the cell, he noticed the plastic bucket chair had been partially wedged under the sink, obstructing the door."

Hirst looked at McAuley, who just nodded.

"On turning on the light he saw Mallanaphy hanging by a ligature made from sheets from the window fitment and Hussain appearing to hold him up to allow him to breathe. The cell bell had not been pressed. Officer McAuley cut Mallanaphy down and started mouth-to-mouth, having sent Hussain to find Officer Holdsworth, who in turn, notified Control of the situation and a blue call protocol was initiated. Officer Holdsworth then attended the cell."

Dan nodded.

"On or about 4.12am, Nurse Paddy Lafferty attended the scene and applied a defibrillator. At 4.27am paramedics arrived and pronounced death. Before the cell was sealed it was noted that there was evidence which suggested that a struggle had taken place. Bruising to Hussain's body seemed inconsistent with his account of events." He paused for breath. "I'm happy for people to chip in ideas as we go along: all contributions welcomed. Now, the cell's been swabbed so we'll know soon enough if there's any drugs residue. A mobile phone was found. First of all, then, is there any evidence that Hussain is a user?"

"I don't think so. He's not on one of our programmes.

It's not my area but I checked with the drugs and alcohol team." Paddy looked alert. "Why, what's your hunch?"

"I just wondered if he might have been off his head. I know it's unlikely: you couldn't keep that a secret here, not for long anyway. Any suspicions and he'd have been tested. I just thought it might be worth flagging up."

"What about Mallanaphy?" Leo asked.

"Clean unless the post-mortem tells us otherwise."

There was a pause while they digested this.

Hirst changed tack. "Now I know everyone here has misgivings, and while I don't want to jump the gun with a post-mortem and a coroner's findings pending, I'd like us to try and work through some credible scenarios. Paddy, can I start with you? What can you tell us about Mohammed Hussain when he was taken off to Health Care?"

Paddy took out a small notebook. "He seemed genuinely upset but what I found odd was that he had defensive wounds..."

Hirst was jotting down notes. "Hang on, sorry? Defensive wounds? As in the sort you'd get if you'd been fighting?"

"That's right. They were on his arms and wrists, quite heavy bruising that suggested he'd been held by the wrists at some point. There were bruises to his torso and legs too, as if he'd been punched or kicked. None of these were very clear to start with, but over the next few hours they developed nicely. We've photographed them."

Hirst looked more attentive and tapped his pencil on his notebook. "What's your hunch Paddy?"

"I'm not sure. He said he got the bruises when he was trying to help Mallanaphy. He said he was flailing about."

"But you aren't sure?"

"I'm a nurse. Forensics isn't my area. What he said could be true, but I've tended a few fights over the years. The post-mortem should tell us what we need to know, but what we can be sure of is that there was a struggle at some point. Can I ask a question?"

Everyone nodded.

"It's for Greg and Dan really. There was blood on the floor where the body was laid down, under his head, and the back of his T-shirt had blood around his neck and shoulders. I noticed it on your hands Greg. Once you'd cut him down how did you put him on the floor?"

"We... that is Hussain and I... we laid him down."

"Gently?"

"Absolutely."

"So, there was no chance he banged his head then?"

"No." McAuley shook his head.

"Dan?"

"I wasn't there at that point. I arrived later, but I did notice the blood."

"The thing is, from the point of view of nurses, we didn't need to examine the body," Paddy said. "I just checked for life signs and there weren't any. The paramedics confirmed what we already knew: the lad was dead. There was nothing more for us to do, so no reason to. If he'd still been alive, we'd have triaged his wounds, but he wasn't, so we didn't - and the blood could be misleading: scalp wounds are notorious bleeders even when they aren't serious."

McAuley was staring into the middle distance, transported back to those few moments. "Did anyone see any blood on the wall, where he might have hurt himself while he was swinging?"

Dan and Paddy looked at each other. Dan shrugged. "Sorry, no."

Paddy shook his head.

"There was," said Hirst. "Not much, but it was there. Now, I may have been watching too much CSI, but if he'd banged his head hard enough to have caused that much bleeding, wouldn't there have been spatter, and if there was no spatter was it just transfer? If he'd banged his head while he was struggling, wouldn't he have hit the wall more than once?"

He looked at them.

"Just rhetorical questions. I don't expect clinician level answers, I'm just trying to picture what went on, but if there was no spatter on the wall and he hit his head, where is the blood? We'll have to wait for the forensics report for the answer I'm afraid, but I think where that wound happened could be important."

"Was he popular?" Hirst again.

"He might as well have been invisible," Dan answered. "I think the only person who knew him was Hussain. He was doing basic literacy and numeracy. Education say he was quiet, not very bright but no bother, kept himself to himself."

Hirst made a face. "Not much to go on."

Leo raised his hand. "Was there a note? I know there isn't always, but the absence of a note looks iffy to me."

The others around the table shook their heads.

"He didn't have that long left to serve either," Dan offered. "Three months, which is interesting. You don't top yourself when you're so close to the end of your stretch. He'd only been in for six months so it's not as if the prospect of leaving held any terrors, surely? It's not as if he was institutionalised."

"Are we suggesting that the head wound had nothing to do with the hanging itself then?" Hirst looked around. "Because, if we are, we're suggesting that there was a fight and Hussain hit Mallanaphy and he fought back. Are we also saying that following a gash to the scalp – or worse, it remains to be seen - that Mallanaphy went on to hang himself?

"Without Hussain noticing?" Dan looked doubtful. "If you've been in a fight, you're too wired to just go straight to sleep. He must've watched while the kid did it."

"Or he helped the kid to do it, voluntarily or involuntarily."

"McAuley, I'm sorry. If you want to stop, say so. You too Dan." Hirst's tone was sympathetic.

"Thanks, but now we've started..." McAuley looked at Dan who nodded.

"Tell us about the chair Greg. I know that worried you."

"Well, it was blocking the door. Not just in front of the door but in such a way that it was stopping me getting in.

I had to give it a good shove."

"So, what are you thinking?"

"It's only guesswork, but if the lad stood on it before kicking it out of the way, could he have booted it twelve feet across the cell with such force that it got wedged under the sink? Plastic bucket-chairs don't weigh much. Where was it when you arrived Dan?"

"Just inside the door."

"Right then. The scenario we're piecing together here suggests a fight and then the hanging and then the chair being wedged against the door." Hirst was scribbling notes again. "Obvious question, but why block the door?"

"To stop someone getting in."

"That was never going to work for more than a few seconds," Dan said.

"An early warning then? A delaying tactic?"

"Hussain said he was trying to hold Mallanaphy up." Hirst was looking at his notes again. "Could he have been doing the opposite? Could he have been pulling him down?"

There was silence in the room and then McAuley spoke.

"He could have. Yes, but what I don't understand is, if he did do that, why he timed it to coincide with my visit. I visited that cell every two hours from 8pm, so why wait until just before the 4am visit was due?"

There was another pause while they thought about this.

"Could this have been an assault that went wrong, a sexual assault perhaps?" They looked at Dan. "Hussain was gay, wasn't he? That's why none of the other Muslim lads would share with him. What about Mallanaphy?"

"I don't think so." Hirst was writing again. "He was on A Wing because he was vulnerable to being bullied. He had victim written all over him. He wasn't a sex-offender. Even so, that business his sister dropped about him wanting to change cells needs to be looked into. I'll speak to George Hatcher."

"Well, I suppose that gives some strength to the idea that there was a fight which delayed the murder – we *are* calling it a murder, now aren't we?" Leo looked around at the others. "Assuming you didn't want to sit with a dead body only feet away for half the night, then timing the murder to be near a time when you knew an officer would be turning up makes sense, and at that hour of the morning, taken by surprise when he was asleep, Wayne's resistance would probably have been pretty low."

"We're not officially calling it murder...," Hirst said. "...whatever we may think, and certainly not outside this room. However, it does look as if we're tending towards a murder made to look like a suicide here."

There were nods around the table.

"So, as I said, we keep these ideas to ourselves. We may only be a day or two ahead of the curve, but I'm going to have to share our concerns with Security at this point. I don't think I've any choice, and if they decide to contact the police, then it's out of our hands."

Another pause.

"Can we go any further with this line of questioning?" Hirst asked.

No one seemed sure.

"We can come back to it if anyone comes up with any other ideas." Like puzzlers, they were searching for the elusive pieces of the jigsaw that would reveal the whole picture.

"Now Leo, talk us through Hussain's visit to see Errol please." There wasn't much to tell, of course, but the others listened with interest. "Do we know if he was a regular visitor?"

"Not to my knowledge, but he wanted a private conversation so I wouldn't have thought so: the office is usually busy, and it was clear that Errol wanted to avoid seeing him... or being seen with him. He didn't want him in the office, but I forced his hand. It's also unlikely Errol visited him. He rarely left his seat in the office." He looked at McAuley and Dan.

"Never seen him on A wing," said Dan. McAuley shook his head too.

"Could you ask your colleagues. Make a joke out of it - should be easy, given how lazy Errol is - and if he has been on the wing try and find out who he saw."

"There is one other thing." Leo looked around the group. "It may not mean anything, but it was something that young Mallanaphy said to me when he came to chapel. He said that we chaplains stuck together, as if whatever he told me I'd tell the others."

"Or whatever Errol is up to – assuming he's up to anything – you're all involved." Hirst looked at his watch. "O.K. Thanks Leo. Anything else anyone? In that case

I think that's probably it for now gents." He sat back. "Thanks for coming. I'll keep you in the loop."

McAuley stopped part-way down the stairs, looked back over his shoulder and asked Leo why he thought Gov. Hirst hadn't involved the new Security Governor earlier. "Surely Gavin Moss should have been involved?"

Leo shrugged. "He'll have his reasons. Moss isn't just new to the prison, he's new to the security role. I think it's also fair to say that he's not made any friends there. According to Wikipedia," he joked, "He's a 'total bastard who is completely unprincipled and a backstabber' (citation needed)."

McAuley guffawed. "If only Wikipedia was that honest."

"You remember Kath?" Leo asked.

McAuley nodded. "She left to work at the airport."

"She was a good officer. Now, she may have been intending to go anyway, but she told people that her reason for going when she did was down to Moss's attitude. He's an empire builder and a lot of people don't trust him. Word has it that he absolutely nailed it at interview, but that he's not really followed through. He's also managed to alienate a lot of colleagues. Not a popular appointment. On top of that, Peter was Security Governor before he came here so he probably knows the job better than Gavin does. Anyway, there's a lot going on here that's just being hinted at, but if you start joining the dots you open a can of worms." There was a pause and Leo smiled. "Sorry about the mixed metaphors."

"I think we've got to avoid conspiracy theories Leo."

"But conspiracy theories are the very things we are being asked to consider."

They walked on down the stairs in silence before heading off to their afternoon duties.

Wayne Mallanaphy shouldn't really have meant so much to McAuley, but he was increasingly becoming an obsession. It was about justice.

"Shame about Wayne Massive Fanny," Wilson sniggered and McAuley came very close to losing it. Wilson saw something in McAuley's look and stepped back alarmed.

"Wilson! In here **NOW!**" The Hatchet was beetroot red. McAuley walked away leaving Wilson to his fate.

Chapter Twenty-Four

" Will you lot get out of the office! I swear to God I'm going to buy a cattle-prod!"

The Hatchet was very COVID-aware and was constantly undermined by his younger colleagues believing they were immune by virtue of their age. Dan Holdsworth had rescued two old desks destined for the bins and placed them outside the wing office where he and McAuley had adopted them. Not being in the office at this time though, was infinitely preferable to being in it where Sharon Mills was currently complaining bitterly about how all this handwashing was playing hell with her eczema.

"Aye, well, that's life that is." McAuley's comment was intended to be more of a filler of conversational gaps than anything profound. Mills pondered it for a while, nevertheless, finally nodding sagely.

"Tell me about it."

Things had quietened down and McAuley had, he hoped for the moment at least, completed the round of interviews which had followed Mallanaphy's death. He had no idea what was currently going on with the coroner, forensics or the police and had no particular desire to know. Things were out of his hands, and whatever was going on was way above his pay grade. There had been no more surreptitious meetings and he had other things to occupy his mind now.

Mallanaphy had been such a quiet lad, almost

anonymous in his attempts to be invisible. On one level it was as if he'd never been there, just a spirit, a wisp. The police were content to hold all their witness statements until the coroner had reported, and Leo had conducted a subdued funeral, a small service with a small congregation. Leo thought it unlikely that the numbers attending would have been any greater if the funeral had taken place outside of COVID restrictions. As it was, they were well short of the maximum allowed number. The hearse had just the one floral tribute, a small wreath with the word SON picked out in orange roses. It made Leo very sad to think that this boy's life had passed so anonymously and with so few people to mourn his passing, but he was cheered to know that the prison was picking up the tab for this.

It wasn't as if Mohammed Hussain was going anywhere in the near future either. Well, that wasn't strictly true. Although his sentence still had a long time to serve, he had, in fact, been transferred to another prison 'for his own safety' as Mr. Hatcher had told them during morning briefing. This had been a decision taken solely by Security, and while perfectly reasonable under the circumstances, had put Hatcher's back up because he'd not been asked to give any input, and therefore it had come as a surprise to him when Hussain's name had appeared on the transfer list. Hussain had been given an hour to pack his stuff into big plastic carry-bags and then escorted off the wing. The cell he and Mallanaphy had shared was now back in use, but the men were a deeply superstitious bunch, and no one wanted to move in, so it had been allocated to two newcomers. It took precisely seven minutes for them to be appraised of the fact that they were sharing a cursed cell.

There had been a number of COVID infections in the prison but none yet on his wing. McAuley tended to agree with Mr. Hatcher that the main problem was the staff, a significant number of whom were pretty complacent. There had been a lot of conversation, some heated, in the office about what constituted "essential" in relation to shops and travel, and on the basis of what he'd picked up from conversations, decided to put even more distance between himself and Wilson, who'd opined that the whole thing was an over-reaction; he didn't know anyone who'd had it and anyway, what if a few scrotes died in prison? He for one wouldn't mourn them.

———

In the chaplaincy meeting room, the team were deep in planning for upcoming religious festivals and how they could be managed during lockdown, although "deep in planning" seemed to mean that nothing was going to happen for most events. This was irritating Errol no end because he'd taken responsibility for liaising with outside caterers for the supply of special festival food which the kitchens couldn't manage, what with those events not generally involving soggy chips or cheese sandwiches. Leo looked at him during the meeting, considering his behaviour to be very inconsistent as Errol's general strategy was to avoid all work wherever possible. He wasn't so much work-shy as work averse. Imam Khan was adamant on one thing though. The end of Ramadan had to be marked by the feast of Eid ("Inshallah."). That was not negotiable and so Errol was given the go-ahead to order in for that event. Throughout the meeting, Errol had been dabbing beads of sweat from his forehead with a tissue which concerned Leo.

"Are you O.K?" he asked him. "You're not coming down with something are you?" By which he meant, "Is there any chance you may have COVID?"

Now that he thought about it, Errol had been on edge and twitchy recently. He simply didn't look well. Something approximating a smile crossed Errol's face. It was probably supposed to be reassuring. It was anything but.

"No, I'm fine. Really. Just a bit off colour. Something I ate."

There were murmurs of sympathy from around the room. He was making an effort to seem cooperative and affable, but his words and actions weren't matching. The problem was that having worked with liars, conmen and the downright manipulative for years, Leo's bullshit radar was now on overdrive.

If he's ill and we all get it, I'll swing for him.

But as Errol clearly wasn't about to say more, he didn't think it was worth pursuing the matter. Time would tell.

At that moment on the Health Care Wing, Paddy was opening an e-mail which caused his jaw to drop.

———

Leo went home that evening deep in thought. An idea was forming, and he couldn't quite believe what he was thinking, so he thought it again, and did so repeatedly, approaching it from a number of different directions all the way home.

Sneaky little shit! he finally conceded.

———

"You're leaving?" McAuley looked at Paddy in amazement. "By which I meant to say congratulations!"

"I know. It came out of the blue. I couldn't believe it. It's a great opportunity. I couldn't turn it down. They want me to start straight away – well next week."

"Who do you know in high places?" McAuley teased. "You got someone pulling strings for you?"

Was that a pang of jealousy he felt at the good fortune of a friend?

"It's the luck of the Irish – well, the Liverpool Irish in my case. I hadn't even applied. I was head-hunted."

Just listening to Paddy's obvious pleasure at his promotion made McAuley feel ashamed at his earlier reaction.

"I wish someone would head-hunt me. Still, a young offender's institution, eh? Bloody Hell Paddy, I'll miss you."

"Don't be wet. I'm not leaving the country."

Chapter Twenty-Five

Ramadan: how did these guys do it? No eating from dawn to sunset? That took some serious discipline. McAuley supposed that having notified the kitchen that you were observing Ramadan and then finding yourself locked up for twenty-three hours out of twenty-four, made it a bit easier in the avoiding-of-temptation area, but even so he was in awe that they did it. He couldn't imagine what it must be like when Ramadan fell during July, making the days longer and the hunger more acute. Blimey, during Lent, it was all most Christians could do to give up crisps.

Most, but not all, Muslim prisoners shared with other Muslims. What would it be like, he wondered, to be an observant Muslim sharing with a non-Muslim who ate at regular times? He knew that the Christian chaplains were particularly sensitive to their Muslim colleagues and chose not to eat in the office when the Imams were there, and he also knew that the Imams found this slightly insulting as if the sight of a pineapple yoghurt would turn them to apostasy.

Still, it would soon be Eid al-Fitr, the breaking of the fast and, McAuley wondered, the breaking of what else?

Leo was sitting in the chaplain's office pretending to be relaxed and doing a half-decent job of it. Errol was fidgety: he had the odd look of a man bracing himself for something. Imam Khan was chatting away oblivious to both of them, not actually requiring answers and not therefore noticing that none were forthcoming: today was the day the Eid food was to be delivered, no wonder Errol was stressed: getting this right was a big deal.

It was a source of some relief to Imam Khan that the holy month was nearly over, although he wouldn't have admitted it in public. Ramadan in a prison - especially a prison in lockdown - was difficult for the men, however observant (or otherwise) they were, as they were apart from their families and friends at the most significant time of the year. What was on offer behind bars was not even a pale imitation of the real thing, any more than Christmas was for the others. For prisoners, it was not only a time of piety, but a time of sadness and often of repentance borne from both, and as emotions ran high, some of the men struggled with frustration, stress and despair. Imam Khan and his colleagues had found themselves increasingly busy as Ramadan had progressed, and now they were on the verge of breathing a huge sigh of collective relief. Tomorrow it would all be over. In any other year the Eid celebrations would have involved opening the gym to all the Muslim prisoners and all the staff for the celebratory end of fast with a huge curry-fest. Instead, tomorrow the men would have their food delivered to their cells and that would be it. Not the Eid al-Fitr anyone had wanted.

Errol had arranged to meet the delivery van at 10.30. It wasn't unreasonable that Imam Khan should go too, although he didn't usually for the deliveries for other religious festivals and Errol tried to dissuade him.

"You've got far more important things to do. It's just a delivery."

"Nothing's more important than Eid," he'd replied.

Leo waited five minutes and then followed. He knew he needn't go, in fact he wasn't sure if he should, but there was a big part of him that needed to see this through. He'd had an internal dialogue going on for weeks, sometimes berating himself for prurience and telling himself that he'd done his bit and should back-off. On the other hand, he felt responsible for what was about to happen, aware that he might have to eat humble pie, and if so, that he should face up to his mistake. On the day he still hadn't resolved those feelings, but he made his decision for better or worse.

When he arrived at the vehicle entrance, the gates were already closed behind a catering van bearing the logo of a well-known local company, *Curry-in-a-Hurry (No need for you to worry)* or as Luke would insist on having it, *It doesn't taste like slurry*. Its back doors were being unlocked by two young Asian lads. Leo noted that McAuley was also there, together with the officers who were detailed to check incoming deliveries. Errol looked surprised to see Leo.

"Just thought you might need a hand," he said cheerfully.

Imam Khan looked pleased. Errol's expression was unreadable.

"Right, let's start unloading," the lead officer said.

The pallets of catering-sized packs of food were placed on the trollies, ready to be wheeled to the kitchens. "Check this one please," the officer in charge said, pointing to one pack, as he put on his disposable gloves. The Imam stood back, and Errol looked stricken.

"We don't normally do this," the Imam objected. "These are all halal and shouldn't be touched."

"Hence the gloves, Imam. We wouldn't be doing our jobs if we allowed anything through without checking." The senior officer was matter of fact, as if this was just any other day and any other load. "I'm sorry, but anything coming through's potentially a security issue, but I promise you we'll take great care and treat things respectfully."

"Even so..." Errol's tone was wheedling. He looked worried.

McAuley lifted the lid from another container and breathed in the aroma of lamb bhuna. Putting on a new sterile glove, he delved into the tub and had a good feel around. Nothing. He kept an impassive face.

"Over here Guv." This from the back of the van.

They gathered at the trolley where a box of naan breads had been opened. Nestling between the bottom two was a small zip-lock bag of pills.

"Right!" The senior officer took immediate control. "No one leaves. Please all stand over there." This to the chaplains and the two lads who came with the van. McAuley thought they looked shifty.

"Check every box and package. Leave the clean ones on the trolley and put the dodgy ones on the table here." The officers set to. Imam Khan looked heartbroken: he turned to Errol and was about to speak.

"I'd advise you to remain silent," the senior officer told him. "That goes for all of you. Do not speak to each other."

He left them, and while the other officers continued with their task, he returned to the office where he could be seen through the window talking urgently on the phone. It was only a matter of minutes before the security Governor, Gavin Moss, arrived with half a dozen other officers. He looked furious. Moss was not a tall man: he wore his hair swept back to increase the appearance of height. He looked like a middle-ranking politician and was not a man overburdened with self-doubt. New to this role and relatively new to the prison, word had it he was ambitious and that he was the sort of person who was totally focused on his own agenda, and stuff everyone else.

"What are you doing here?" he demanded, his tone harsh as he gave McAuley an irritated look. "You're not on security detail."

McAuley remembered Moss's reputation as a man who turned making enemies into an art form.

"I was just passing by, and I thought I'd offer a helping hand. There's deliveries backed up down the drive and it's quiet on my wing."

"Did you? Well, you can get back to A Wing. You're not needed here now."

Having dismissed McAuley, who took his time leaving, he turned to the officers he'd brought with him.

"Escort these two ...." Moss indicated the driver and his mate "... to the interview rooms please. Keep them separate. Do not let them talk. Chaplains with me please."

As the three chaplains followed Gov. Moss, they caught up with McAuley in the corridor. He stood back to let them pass. As they did, Leo gave him a wink, but Errol threw McAuley a look of deep animosity and that was the moment McAuley knew for sure that Errol was no mere bystander.

Gotcha, he thought, and it gave him a real sense of satisfaction. The question was no longer whether Errol was involved, but how deeply. Up until that point McAuley had been prepared to accept that he was an innocent dupe, even though Leo had been more certain. Even the high-handed way Moss had spoken to him couldn't dampen his mood as he returned to his wing.

Chapter Twenty-Six

The chaplains were escorted to the control room with its banks of CCTV monitors. The staff there looked at them with interest. Leo was pleased to see Gov. Hirst in the room, apparently going over some spreadsheets with one of the officers. Gov. O'Brien was also there.

"I don't need to tell you how serious this is," Moss began. "The police are on their way. I need you three to start writing statements about what happened, who said what to who and who did what. Clear?"

They nodded and were sat at separate tables. Imam Khan looked shell-shocked and Errol, much to Leo's surprise was shaking with suppressed anger, his face closed and hard, where Leo had expected him to be a blubbering wreck.

He's conned us all, he thought. *We've seriously underestimated him.*

"We're going to need to interview all the kitchen workers, employed staff and prisoners," O'Brien said. "Someone in there was going to handle the drugs and organise distribution." He looked at Moss. "Assuming that all the food's been checked, and photos taken..."

"Very nearly," one of the officers confirmed. "There's a lot of pills and mobile phones too."

"... what we need to do now is to send the food through, otherwise it won't be long before they realise something's wrong. Do you agree?" Moss couldn't really argue, although he looked as if he wanted to.

"We'll tell the orderlies that the van was late. They'll pass that on to the kitchen staff. Right..." to the room in general, "... I want every kitchen CCTV monitored. I want to know who handles the food, I want to see their reactions when it's unpacked, and I want the phone calls of every kitchen worker reviewed and monitored when their shift's over. Thanks everyone for your work on this. This has been a good day for us."

He set off to his office. Anyone sitting near him as he left might just have heard him mutter, "Shit's really going to hit the fan when this gets out."

The afternoon passed in a blur, interview after interview with the police and the security team.

"Regardless of what the police may decide, there may be disciplinary action," the three chaplains were told.

At some point during that long afternoon, they heard raised voices as Moss and Hirst entered into an uninhibited exchange of views in a neighbouring office. Moss could be heard shouting about being kept in the dark and how unprofessional that was. Leo couldn't hear Hirst's reply, but it sounded like an attempt to be placatory. Leo had a good idea what might be being said on both sides of the exchange. He was also now wishing he hadn't decided to see how things unfolded when the van was unpacked.

"There isn't enough evidence at this stage to arrest any staff members," Gov. Hirst told Leo on the way out at the end of the day. "The two lads who delivered the food are pleading ignorance but they're being held in custody, and the catering company are claiming to be shocked and bleating on about reputational damage. When the food was delivered to the kitchens it was put straight in the fridges, so we won't know until tomorrow who's involved there."

———

Errol's life had been marked by disappointment in one way or another. While he'd been tall and fit and good-looking, he'd never really been good enough for his overbearing father: his exam results weren't quite good enough; his efforts on the sports field not quite athletic enough; his inability to find a job and stick with it, a source of paternal contempt, and it had shaped him. His relationship history was also a source of disappointment, both to himself and his father. He'd never had any trouble attracting girlfriends: his problem had been keeping them.

In any other family he'd have been confident and self-assured, but any chance of that had been consistently mocked out of him to the extent that he'd become the invisible boy, circumspect and cautious in all his actions, almost anonymous, sticking to the shadows, particularly after his mother had left. It had hit him in his twenties that he'd never been shown respect, and that unpalatable truth had made him turn in on himself even further. The feelings that revelation stirred within him, self-pity and resentment, were an indication of how cowed he'd become. Or perhaps they were an indication of an innate weakness of character.

It would seem strange to anyone else who might be

aware of his story, that Errol Adebeyo had never taken the opportunity to reinvent himself after his father had died, never grabbed the chance of a fresh start and become what it had always been within his grasp to become, free of his past and independent.

Until now, and of course that had been forced on him.

And it had all gone horribly wrong. The very fact that it had turned sour merely reaffirmed his belief that he was cursed with the reverse Midas syndrome: everything he touched turned to shit. Yes, he was feeling particularly sorry for himself, and he'd long since lost the self-awareness that would enable him to see just how ugly self-pity was. Ironically, people like him were just the sort of people he despised.

—

McAuley's mobile rang. He liked his ringtone. It was Wallander's ringtone from the Swedish language version of the detective series and he'd gone to considerable lengths to source it. The problem was that no one else recognised it, so it had never become the witty talking point he'd hoped for. This was a number he didn't recognise, and he usually ignored those. It stopped ringing but started again almost immediately. This went on for some time until McAuley caved.

"Greg? It's Errol. Please don't hang up. Please."

What?

"Don't hang up Greg. Please. I need your help."

"Errol? What's going on? You're not exactly Mr. Popularity just now, you know."

"You think I don't know that?" It came with an edge of anger. "Look, it's a total mess. I've been set up and I need your help. Will you help me?"

"Why don't you just explain everything to the authorities then?"

"Do you think I'm stupid? I'm not getting out of this; it goes too deep. That's why I need your help."

"Why me?"

"Because I don't know who else I can trust."

"What do you think I can do?"

"Look, it's too complicated for a phone call, and I'm worried about my calls being traced. We need to meet. Second floor, main block, The Tannery, Meanwood, 2.00am. Got that?" He repeated the details and cut the call leaving McAuley looking at his phone, frowning.

Two am? Is there such a time?

Chapter Twenty-Seven

Thishis may not have been his cleverest decision. He couldn't quite believe he was doing this, and he was suspicious, but there was the nagging thought that he could help Errol, and he felt obliged to try despite his misgivings.

As far as he could see, everyone was asleep. No lights flickered behind curtains. Even so, he was cautious, and approached the block by the allotment path at the rear of the Tannery, instead of the road, nearly losing his nerve when a horse whinnied to his left. He should have known by the smell that horses were nearby, but it was a couple of minutes later, when his heart rate had returned to normal, that he tentatively set off again with his internal monologue demanding to know what the hell he thought he was doing.

He stood stock still in the shade at the edge of the building, on high alert but safe in the knowledge that he was invisible – unless someone was watching him through night-vision goggles. He stepped back further into the gloom, disturbed by that thought and irritated by his overactive imagination. He caught a whiff of cigarette smoke on the air and changed his position to get a better look at the main entrance. The red glow of the cigarette gave away the position of whoever was waiting in the entrance where he could see the road. Errol wasn't a smoker and this unexpected turn of events unnerved McAuley again. He stepped back and took out his phone, hiding it under his coat to shield its glow, and dialled the number Errol had rung him on.

You have dialled an incorrect number. Please check the number and dial again.

———

He climbed the stairs slowly. His head was fuzzy, and he didn't like the dark. Tiredness overwhelmed him. All he wanted to do was sleep. As he approached the second landing, some sixth sense told him he wasn't alone but by then it was too late. Something was pushed over his head. He took a violent shove from behind and something took his feet out from under him. He saw stars as his head hit the ground and felt the gush of blood from his broken nose. Then the kicking started, and he was sick.

———

Several hours later, Jerry Swan left his flat on the ground floor of The Tannery to head off to work at the bus depot and was irritated that someone had left their black bin out. Jerry was a rule follower, and a bin put out on the wrong day offended his sense of order. Tutting to himself, he grabbed the handles and started to move it, surprised by how heavy it was and how slippery the handles were. He stepped back and looked at his hands. For a moment he couldn't understand what he was seeing, and he looked down to see the same red stain on his uniform shirt and trousers. Knowing instinctively that he should step away, Jerry instead threw open the bin's lid - and vomited profusely over his shoes.

———

"Do you watch the local news?"

"Not usually, and certainly not if that Castle woman's presenting. Why?"

McAuley was only half listening to this exchange between Dan Holdsworth and Jimmy Marston in the queue to get in. He was tired. Common sense had won over and he'd finally arrived home from his late-night jaunt but had not slept deeply. He'd wait for Errol to get in touch again and make a judgement then. His tired brain failed to make the connection between his abortive trip to Meanwood and what Dan and Jimmy were discussing.

"I just wondered. They've found a body in a bin."

"What, a rubbish bin?"

"Yeah. Some old vagrant by the sounds of it. A local found it. Really messy by all accounts."

"Nasty," Marston winced.

"Not half. Not what you'd expect from Meanwood though. Harehills maybe, or Seacroft, but not Meanwood. Meanwood's got a Waitrose for God's sake."

McAuley missed this last bit as Mick Wilson pushed in beside him and started to talk about football, leaving McAuley to wonder about Wilson's short-term memory, that he couldn't remember their mutual loathing from one shift to the next.

———

All the police were getting from Imam Khan was what a good chaplain Errol had been, how conscientious and hard working. His was a unique viewpoint. The other chaplains, speaking freely and assured of confidentiality, had a quite different perspective, although it took the police no further forward. The Errol Adebeyo they were learning about had no friends in the prison apart from the Imam, (who it had become clear he'd been grooming), didn't socialise, gave nothing away about his personal life or background and was to all intents and purposes, completely one dimensional.

McAuley was relieved that no one asked him about Errol, but he knew it was too late now to fess-up about the phone call. He was going to keep quiet about that.

"So, Pastor Errol," Ricky Clark said to McAuley as they set off for the first-nighter's induction.

"Aye, that was a shock."

"Really? You had no idea?"

"I barely knew the man, but I've heard there was enough fentanyl in that kid's cell to start a pharmacy." A thought struck McAuley, and he stopped and held Ricky back.

"Did you suspect him?"

"I did. Not that I'd have said anything, obviously. It was when that lad was hospitalised with a fentanyl overdose. Which chaplain had been on the wing the previous night and that morning? A chaplain you never saw on the wing normally."

McAuley vaguely remembered Leo saying something about Errol's uncharacteristic volunteering to do the statutory rounds in the FNC.

"I thought about the other staff but none of them fitted," Ricky went on.

"Couldn't you have told Leo?"

"I could have, but I'm not a grass."

"Don't you trust him?"

"Of course I trust him. He's been a good friend to me. It's security I don't trust. Leo wouldn't have named me, but Security might have worked it out. Like I said, I'm not a grass. Never was, never will be. My Cat. D's coming up. I'm just keeping my head down."

"Aye, I get it." McAuley understood.

———

It was two days later and McAuley, thinking, not for the first time, about how his world had shrunk due to the pandemic, was drawing down his keys when he saw Luke gesturing him over to the visitor's area. The early morning pre-work bustle continued around them, and no one paid them any heed.

"You look a bit done in." Luke looked concerned.

"Aye, I'm jiggered. I've just had my first COVID jag." A surgery near the prison had offered what was left over at the end of the day if officers could get there within twenty minutes. "I was heading home so it was no big deal. I made it with seven minutes to spare. I just feel a bit peely-wally. Did you not fancy it yourself?"

Luke looked uncomfortable.

"What's up?"

"You know about Leo?" McAuley's raised eyebrows indicated that he didn't.

"He was escorted off the site yesterday by the Imam. Had his pass taken off him and everything. Suspended."

That only happened when things were really serious. Surely, he wasn't suspected of having been involved in what was now being called Currygate?

"What? Do you know why?"

"Not really." Luke shook his head. "The Imam was very discreet, so I doubt many people are aware it's even happened."

"You saw this?"

"Yeah, I'd left my lunch in the car and as I was coming back, I saw them. The Imam's car had the boot open so that they were shielded from view, but I definitely saw Leo hand over his pass."

"What's the rumour-mill saying?"

"Nothing so far. Like I said, it's not widely known yet. It's odd though, because that other guy's not been in either."

"What other guy?"

"The lazy one. The one that looks after the Happy-Clappies."

Things were moving too fast for McAuley to process. This made no sense.

"I'll ring him."

"You know he'll have been told not to speak to anyone at work?"

"And if that were you, would you take any notice?"

"Well, no, obviously."

"There you go then." They set off to their respective duties. At the hub, Luke turned to McAuley and said, "Look, I only mentioned it because I know he's a mate of yours, and I won't say anything about it to anyone else. What are you going to do?"

"Nothing until I've spoken to him and know what's going on. I get the feeling that if I started asking questions here it wouldn't be appreciated, so I'll be pretending to be in the dark." As he was in the dark that wouldn't prove very difficult.

In the office, McAuley walked into a conversation between Craig and Dan. "Hatcher's blood pressure's going to go through the roof."

"I can't help that," Dan shrugged. "I've got to do what's best for me and mine. Working at HMP Moorlands'll be much better for me because I live in Doncaster. The Doncaster prisons were always my first preference. I put in for a transfer ages ago."

Half listening to this exchange, McAuley wondered idly how many cups of indifferent coffee he'd drunk at this desk since he'd been assigned to A Wing.

Before any more could be said, Mr. Hatcher hurried in, looking preoccupied, clearly in a bad mood and not looking likely to involve himself in extraneous chit-chat.

"Right, let's get this meeting underway."

As the meeting wound up, Hatcher turned to McAuley. "Can I have a quick word Greg?"

"And when you've finished," Dan butted in, "Can I have a quick word with you, Boss?" McAuley mentally wished Dan good luck with that quick word.

"Yes, now bugger off the rest of you." When they were left alone in the office, Hatcher said, "Governor Moss wants to see us at two o'clock."

"What's it about?"

"No idea. Maybe you're employee of the month. I'll meet you outside his office. Don't be late."

Chapter Twenty-Eight

Over lunch McAuley rang Leo from his mobile as he sat in the car. He didn't want to use any internal phones. *Just because you're paranoid, doesn't mean they aren't out to get you,* he thought to himself, wondering who'd originally coined that truism.

"Are you doing anything this evening?" Leo asked him.

McAuley looked around the car park before he checked himself.

You're sitting in your own car. What's the matter with you man? Are you afraid it's bugged?

"Because if you're not, do you fancy meeting up for a drink at seven. How about Woodies?"

"Aye, fine by me but we're in tier two so we'll have to eat there."

Leo laughed. "Right you are. See you then. We'll save all the news until then." He sounded quite upbeat.

—

At two o'clock prompt, McAuley was knocking on the outer door of Gavin Moss's office. McAuley knew of Gavin Moss's reputation as a man it was easy to dislike. It was as if the man didn't care about being disliked he'd been told, even behaved in such a way as to encourage it.

Still, employee of the month. That would be nice.

The red "Occupied" sign changed to a green "Enter". He entered a biggish room: the furniture, nineteen-forties in style and none of it matching, was spread out as if the individual pieces had argued with each other and were no longer on speaking terms. The only surprise in the room was a large oil painting of a bucolic English landscape. It was rather nice, McAuley thought. It was a strange room, the computer the only concession to modernity, and it was occupied by a woman who might just as well have been part of the furniture, such was her look of faded anachronism, like a girl's boarding school headmistress, dressed as if the past four decades had passed her by. She had a hairstyle from another decade too, lacquered into place to within an inch of its life, sensible shoes and a white blouse that wouldn't dare to get a stain of tea or ink on it for fear of suggesting weakness. Audrey Craven, however, was far more than the sum of her parts, and there was an (as yet unsubstantiated) rumour that when she took off her glasses and shook free her hair...

This was Gov. Moss's P.A.

She smiled enigmatically and gestured him to the half open door to the adjoining office and McAuley passed from one room to the next.

Gavin Moss's office certainly seemed aspirational and a sharp contrast to the room next door. Moss had a perpetual look of disappointment about him and as McAuley entered, he was standing looking out of the window, his hands behind his back. It was, of course, a pose: the window offered nothing in the way of a view unless you considered a razor-wire topped wall a thing of aesthetic beauty. He didn't turn at once. This, McAuley intuited, was some form of power play. Make the underling wait. A pose intended to impress. Well, it failed in McAuley's view because it looked faintly silly. Moss sighed. It was a theatrical sound and probably much used, suggesting a man exasperated with his role in dealing with the lower orders.

"Gregor, take a seat please." His voice was Yorkshire but with a veneer of the posh to it. Harrogate, perhaps?

Gregor? Oh dear, his Sunday name. Was he in for a dressing down? His mind was tripping over itself to remember some offence or infraction of the regulations, he wondered if he'd let the Governor down, let the prison down but, more importantly, let himself down. He suppressed a desire to smile. Moss's face was mournful. Perhaps he went to a lot of funerals.

As he looked around, McAuley realised that they were not alone. Already seated was Scott James, the Union Rep, and hard on McAuley's heels came George Hatcher. Gov. Moss gestured them to sit, and they joined Scott James in some stylish but uncomfortable chairs. Moss, on the other hand, sat behind his large workstation. IKEA, McAuley guessed. McAuley also guessed Moss's mood: grave. Moss did another couple of rehearsed-looking set-pieces, opening a folder and looking at the paper as if deciding where to start, all very stagy, Mr. Hatcher noted afterwards.

"Thanks for coming Scott, George."

Hello? I'm here too.

"Right gentlemen, let's get started. This isn't going to be an easy meeting." He looked to his P.A. who had followed Hatcher in and seated herself behind a small desk, a tablet open, ready to take notes.

Straight in, no messing, no small talk and no tea and biscuits, McAuley reflected. *Seat-belts and hard-hats on. Here we go.*

Moss turned to McAuley, "Gregor, I've asked your line manager and union rep here today because a serious allegation has been made against you." McAuley's jaw dropped.

Scott James put a restraining hand on McAuley's arm. "What's the nature of this allegation Governor and how credible is it?"

"Well, the allegation is that Officer McAuley was directly involved in the death of Wayne Mallanaphy."

There was a moment of stunned silence, during which Audrey Craven, sitting behind and slightly to the right of Moss, gave Moss a pained look and then shook her head, almost imperceptibly, as if disappointed. George Hatcher erupted.

"That's total bollocks! The lad tried to save him." He made a gesture as if to say, "Go on. Contradict me if you can."

"Not according to the sworn testimony of Mohammed Hussain."

Hatcher rolled his eyes and snorted. "You're not seriously giving credence to anything that little shitbag says, surely?"

Moss looked at his computer screen before saying, "Let's keep things civil George. Intemperate language won't help anyone."

"But he's a compulsive liar with a history of casual

violence who's facing the probability of a further charge in relation to Mallanaphy's death, to say nothing of additional charges linked to conspiracy to smuggle drugs into this very building. He's trying to deflect attention from himself by making spurious claims against a good officer who has an unblemished record."

McAuley heard little of this. His brain seemed to be buffering, and the world around him had gone fuzzy. He blinked repeatedly in an attempt to bring his sight back from the tunnel-vision he was experiencing as the sound of his heartbeat filled his ears.

This is the body's response to shock, he thought with a strange feeling of detachment. *It's fight or flight time.*

"I'M NOT RESPONSIBLE IN ANY WAY FOR MALLANAPHY'S DEATH." McAuley wondered whose voice that was, sounding so angry. It came to him with a jolt that it was his voice, and that he had half risen from his seat.

Fight it is then.

Moss looked appealingly at Mr Hatcher, his eyes wide with shock.

"I think your officer needs to calm down."

No help came from that direction. Indeed, George Hatcher was suppressing a smile of pleasure.

McAuley's eyes flashed in challenge. "Whit is it wi' you? What needs tae be said tae me, say directly tae me!"

He was not prepared to be excluded from the discussion by being spoken about in the third person. His voice sounded harsher and more guttural. He had gone full-on

Gorbals.

He noted that Moss looked distinctly uneasy: his nostrils flared with shock and indignation.

And here's a man who doesn't take well to being answered back, Mr. Hatcher thought.

Moss was indeed startled. He had expected a more compliant McAuley. The person who'd suggested that McAuley would be a walk over was going to get a piece of his mind. He had not been prepared for an angry and increasingly aggressive Glaswegian. Moss received no supportive looks from the others and Miss Craven smiled her enigmatic smile again.

Scott James had his hand on McAuley's arm again as he slowly sat down, his eyes boring into Moss's as he met the Deputy Governor's stare with a defiant one of his own.

"Well, yes, of course no one here believes Hussain for a moment..."

Moss was flustered and had lost the initiative. His hands fluttered ineffectually as he looked to Hatcher and James for moral support. Still none was forthcoming.

"...and of course, we expect you to be completely exonerated after the enquiry..."

He was starting to regain his composure and a patronising edge had crept into his voice.

"Enquiry?" Scott James sounded incredulous. "I can't see that there's anything to be gained from an enquiry."

Whereas Hatcher had been incandescent, James was icily cool. His voice dripped with disdain.

"We already know the outcome. It will be a waste of

time and resources, and given that the outcome's beyond doubt, and the circumstances we're currently in, we can't afford to have a good officer like Greg on an open-ended suspension."

"Agreed!" Hatcher hadn't noticeably calmed down.

I'm a good officer twice. Why did no one ever tell me that before?

"Well, here's the problem." Moss was all apologetic. "My hands are tied. You see Hussain made his statement in HMP Hull and the Security Governor there involved the police. Now, I think it was a premature thing to do." He shrugged and held his hands wide, palms up. "If only my opinion had been sought first... but there you have it."

What's on show here's an object lesson in method acting, Mr. Hatcher thought. *He'll get an Oscar with that emotional range.*

Moss turned to McAuley with a look he couldn't read. "Gregor, would you mind stepping into Miss Craven's office for a while." It wasn't a question.

McAuley crossed the room with as much dignity as he could muster. At the door he turned to face a surprised looking Moss.

"I did not do this, and you know it. I don't know what's going on here, but I'll get to the bottom of it, you can be sure of that."

He turned on his heel and left. There was no parting snarky comment which surprised him because Moss gave the impression of a man who liked to have the last word. He sat in the outer office on autopilot, trying to gather his thoughts. He lent forward, his legs apart, rested his elbows on his knees and clasped his hands behind his neck.

What's just happened? I'm suspected of involvement in a murder? How could that possibly be? How could anyone think that?

As he sat there, he heard the currents of conversation coming from the next room, sometimes identifying the voices as they rose and fell, argument and counter-argument, raised voices and acrimony.

Eventually it petered out. Miss Craven returned and gave him an encouraging smile and was followed by Hatcher and James.

"Is the meeting room free Audrey?"

She looked at her desk diary, tracing the lines with her index finger.

"It is Mr. James."

He led Hatcher and McAuley across the corridor and into the conference room. Audrey Craven followed them shortly and, introducing herself with a self-deprecatory little cough, put down a tray with mugs, a plate of biscuits ("They're his favourites. He can have the cheap ones for visitors,") and a flask of coffee, then, closing the door behind her quietly, left them to it.

They stayed long enough to drink several coffees as Scott James explained to McAuley what the outcome of the meeting was, and McAuley came slowly back to life.

Moss had got his way, although McAuley hadn't seriously doubted he would.

"There'll be no escorting off the premises," Hatcher

told him. "We'll work our shift out as usual and walk out together. I've not got the car today, so you're going to give me a lift to the station, and you can give me your pass in the car. Tonight, you're going to slip on the stairs, in the bathroom, whatever - your choice – tap-dancing for all I care..."

That mental image flashed through McAuley's mind and made him smile.

"... and ring in tomorrow with a broken ankle. You'll have to stay out of circulation and not mix with anyone who works here. That shouldn't be hard under the circumstances. I'll stay in touch with you and let you know what's happening here. It goes without saying that neither of us takes this accusation seriously. Scott's got some contacts at Hull and is going to make some discreet enquiries about Hussain. Oh stop looking so bloody sorry for yourself. You know this is going to work out fine."

McAuley pondered the ethical overtones of this before deciding he didn't care.

The day ended exactly as George had planned. (He'd always think of him as George now.) The man's dour kindness and evident concern for him had touched him deeply. At the station, they'd exchanged mobile numbers and to McAuley's surprise George had given him a hug before he got out of the car, and mumbled something gruff about McAuley being a good lad.

—

He was raging. He didn't go directly home. He wanted to practice exactly what he was going to tell Mrs. Singh:

there was no way he was going to shut her out of this, but he needed to be calm to be able to do that. He sat in the park for half an hour thinking, and the more he thought about his situation, the more his mind came up with one word: shit! McAuley's respect for Her Majesty's Prison Service had been in decline for some time. Today it disappeared. Under normal circumstances he'd have hit the gym and pumped iron aimlessly until his head cleared, but this time he couldn't muster the physical or emotional energy. He'd certainly have plenty to tell Leo later.

As it happened Mrs. Singh was out: she was at Molly's baby-sitting Sammy while Molly went to pilates, which he'd completely forgotten about, but the tupperware was outside his door, so life was nearly normal. Well, that was a conversation that could wait until tomorrow.

Trying to delete feelings of anger and negativity from his internal hard-drive by concentrating on the beers he'd soon be having with Leo, he opened the front door and headed off upstairs for a shower and a quick change, only to be brought up short by Cat, who was staring at a spot on the wall with his back arched and his hackles raised.

My psychic cat has seen a ghost. Great!

223

Chapter Twenty-Nine

He was still furious about his angry exchange with Moss, even though James and Hatcher had supported him, and he kept going over it in his mind, coming up with a variety of devastating comebacks that would have had Moss begging for forgiveness. The very idea that he'd had a hand in Mallanaphy's death! Even being personally responsible for it. *Bastard! He knows I'm suspicious and that's why I'm on gardening leave. What have I blundered into?*

As he opened the door, his senses were assailed by that familiar and comforting smell that only pubs have, and it occurred to him that the makers of scented candles had missed a trick. It was a nice pub, always warm and welcoming, with a long bar and lots of discreet seating areas. It wasn't a pub where your feet stuck to the carpet. It wasn't too crowded tonight, and McAuley easily found Leo, sitting in a large armchair by the fireside, nursing a nearly full pint.

"Just arrived myself. Grab a seat."

As McAuley pulled up a chair, a cheerful young man in a corporate apron and COVID visor appeared to take his order. There was a price list for traditional ales on the table. He opted for a lager, having given up the struggle with the craft-beer mafia.

McAuley knew he wasn't the greatest at holding his booze, so he was usually fairly circumspect about drinking.

Tonight would be different.

After a few moments the waiter returned with McAuley's pint of Veltins. The first gulp went straight to his head.

I should have eaten something before I came out. Ah well, sod it!

"I could eat a scabby dog!" Mrs. Singh's meal was now in the freezer, and more than anything, McAuley fancied a steak-and-ale pie with chips.

"Before you say anything, I walked, and after the day I've had, I intend to drown my sorrows. Slàinte."

Leo held his hands up in mock surrender as McAuley clinked glasses then paused while he took another good draught.

"I guess this is like coming out for a drink with your dad."

Leo smiled. "I don't know whether to tell you to fuck off or take that as a compliment. So, you've had a tough day. Do you want to tell me your tale of woe or shall I start?"

McAuley looked stricken.

"Sorry. I'd forgotten I'm not the only one having a bad time just now."

Leo delved into his pocket for a coin, called tails and lost. As McAuley talked, Leo listened with growing disquiet, interrupting occasionally to ask perceptive questions. When he'd finished, Leo looked pensive and there was a long pause. McAuley was happy to wait. He knew there'd be a considered opinion.

"You realise Peter Hirst is the only one left?" Leo said finally. "A suspicious mind would see more than a coincidence in all this."

McAuley's suspicious mind was still playing catch up.

"O Dear God! Do I have to phone a friend?... Paddy's miraculous promotion?" Leo prompted.

"Dan's sudden transfer..." It was epiphany time. "... you and me on suspension. Oh my days! I was so busy worrying about myself I hadn't joined the dots. So, he saved the best for us?" McAuley took another forkful of pie.

"Oh, undoubtedly, and it's pure vindictiveness because we spoilt his little scam."

"His little scam? You mean he was involved?"

"Oh, absolutely. I've had a bit of time to ponder on all this as you can imagine. Look at his job. With his background in security, he's best placed to coordinate all of this, but his pettiness has exposed him."

"Go on."

"Well, getting rid of those who were involved in exposing the whole thing. I bet we'll find he had a hand in moving Paddy and Dan on. I know they weren't directly involved, but they were witnesses to Mallanaphy's death, and his death was linked to the whole business."

There was a pause while McAuley considered this.

"Anyway," Leo continued, "It's all falling apart now. They've arrested a kitchen supervisor, did you know that? Errol's gone AWOL by the way, skedaddled. No one has any idea where he is, but the police have an arrest warrant out for him, so it's just a matter of time. Trust me Greg, Moss is panicking. And you and I get suspended on the two days when Hirst and O'Brien are at a Home Office conference? Now that's not a coincidence either, and our Gavin's going to have some explaining to do tomorrow."

"How he made it to Deputy Governor, I'll never know," McAuley mumbled through a mouthful of chips.

"It might have something to do with the length of his brown nose." Now, there was a mental image it would take more than a couple of pints of German lager to dispel.

"It's all well and good being told it'll all work out and you'll be able to go back, but after this, what if I don't want to go back? I don't owe the bastards anything." He knew that was mainly bluster. It was Moss and only Moss that his anger was focused on. He gathered his thoughts. "Sorry. I'm going on and on about myself. So, what's your story Leo? Why are you suspended? Will they throw the book at you?"

"I hope not. I'm told it's very heavy." He smiled widely.

"So, what did you do?"

"Trafficking, mainly."

McAuley's eyes widened. "Tell me you're joking. Are you serious?"

"Yes, supplying too, and guilty as charged."

McAuley looked aghast.

"I'm struggling to take it seriously Greg. It appears that I'm guilty of supplying and trafficking e-cigarette liquid."

"What?"

"I always kept a little bottle I bought from the petrol

station in my key pouch, and if any of the guys were struggling, I'd give them a top up to see them through. It probably happened less than a dozen times, so I looked Moss in the eye and said it wasn't as if I'd smuggled it in in vats of curry, just to see how he'd react. He knew what I was saying alright. Anyway, they actually raided a cell that I'd been in and confiscated about two millilitres of liquid in the bottom of a bottle. They even kept it in an evidence bag. I think I was supposed to feel intimidated."

"But they're allowed to have vape-juice. It's not prohibited. They can buy it on their canteen." McAuley was incredulous.

"I know, but apparently my behaviour undermines the good order of the prison. Bending the rules makes everyone's lives a bit easier, but there's no room for that in the prison service, no compassion."

"But you and I both know officers who do the same."

"Well, I said that, of course, but they wanted me to name names. 'Have you reported these officers?'

'No. Why would I? They were acting out of compassion.'

And then Moss said to me, 'I know that some of the men like chocolate but I wouldn't buy them a Mars-bar.'

'I would', I said.

That didn't go down well. And then he asked me if I'd received payment for it. For a squirt of e-cigarette liquid! I ask you! And then, had I ever brought anything else into the prison? So I told him about the mince pies I bought for our orderlies at Christmas. He accused me of being facetious."

McAuley was having trouble taking this in.

Leo continued, "Look, they're right of course. Had I been that sort of person, I could have brought anything in in that little container. The thing is, I didn't. They also didn't like the fact that I've kept in touch with some of the chapel guys who've been released locally without clearing it with security. Apparently, I'm vulnerable to corruption. How dare they? Really, how dare they? Vulnerable to corruption! What sort of a man do they take me for? How insulting! 'So, these men' Moss asked me, 'How do they contact you?'

'By phone of course.'

'You've given prisoners your phone number?'

'No. I've given ex-prisoners my phone number.'"

"But you're a priest, not an officer." McAuley frowned. "Those rules shouldn't apply to you."

"Look Greg, they don't get chaplaincy. They don't understand us at all. Moss asked me why I spent time alone in cells with men. He wanted me to account for the time I spend there. 'What do you do when you're in a cell?' he asked. So, I told him. I told him we talked. I told him I listened. I told him that sometimes we prayed. I told him I offered encouragement. I told him that there were men who I helped with literacy, and I told him that sometimes we just drank tea and put the world to rights. He didn't get it. The Imam was very supportive throughout, though. He said the whole thing was a gross overreaction, but you know what he's like. He bends with the wind, so he'll do as he's told."

"But that makes no sense. They apply the rules here so flexibly. Look at that woman officer, Linda Whatshername. Her nephew was a prisoner here and she never declared it. The bottom line is that the men liked and trusted you because you were their advocate, and the management didn't like that. They don't do compassion. Will you appeal?"

"No, because I did what I was accused of. There's no point."

"So, what will you do?"

"It's not actually a big deal Greg. I've been thinking for some time that it's time to stop. I need to do something different."

"What? Back in a parish?"

"Sort of. There's a job advert for a priest to look after an English Language community on the continent and it comes with really nice accommodation. It's only temporary but it'll do as a stopgap. I've done holiday cover there twice now so, as it turns out, the timing's quite good wouldn't you say? One door closes and another opens. Catherine's up for it, and if not there, somewhere else."

"What about your investigation?"

"They can hold one if they like, but I'm out of there as from now, so I don't care. I'll not be going back. And do you know what really irritates me?" He didn't wait for an answer. "My lads'll be left to the tender mercies of that mad Baptist woman who plays the guitar and talks about herself all the time. And, on top of that I've already been dropped from social media by a great many colleagues I thought were friends, some of whom I've supported through tough times. People, eh? That hurt."

"I shouldn't have involved you, Leo. I'm sorry."

He looked at McAuley, already on his third pint. "Look, Greg, I don't want to guilt-trip you over this. I'll be fine – and so will you. You've got good people behind you. You know Hirst and O'Brien wouldn't have suspended you. They'd have laughed at Hussain's allegations, and I can tell you now that the police enquiry will come to nothing. The downside is that O'Brien can't reinstate you straight away: he can't rescind a suspension, not now the paperwork's gone through, but he can steer the enquiry. You know Moss can't be on it, don't you - the enquiry? The one who initiates it has to pass it on to another governor. O'Brien will either do it himself, or more likely give it to Hirst, so either way, Moss has shot himself in the foot. You'll come out of this looking better than him."

"But that's what I don't get. Moss isn't stupid. What's he playing at?"

"He wants us out of the way. Now, don't ask me why, but I think that's it – he wants us out of the way, and he wants us out of the way now."

"So, he's not bothered about the longer term?"

Leo shrugged, "Seems not."

McAuley's phone rang. The display flashed: George.

"Where are you Greg? I'm at your place and no one's there."

"I'm in Woodies with Leo."

"With Fr. Leo? That's good. Stay put. I'll be with you in... let's see... five minutes."

—

"I'm telling the truth. I had nothing to do with it." McAuley looked a bit flushed.

"I see you've already introduced yourself to the bar Son. Look, you may be many things Greg, but you're not a liar," George reassured him.

Many things? What does he mean by that? McAuley took mild umbrage.

"So..." Having heard Leo's tale, George looked at his audience and sipped his beer.

He's enjoying this, Leo thought.

The pub was getting busy now, and the multiple TVs were showing a football international, so they leaned forward to hear each other and to avoid being overheard.

"...Scott told Greg he had some contacts at Hull, and he was going to check out Hussain, but it didn't pan out quite as we'd expected."

"And?"

"Well, the Security Governor there, the one who took Hussain's statement accusing McAuley, well, let's just say Hussain was leaned on."

"Do you know this for sure?"

"It's speculation, but what Scott discovered was that the Hull Security Governor and our Security Governor are in a relationship."

Never having acquired the skill of drinking and listening at the same time, McAuley turned to look at George. He was having a little difficulty focusing as he blurted out, "You mean Moss is gay?"

"No, you dick." He turned to Leo. "How much has he had to drink? Their Security Governor's a she! You need to think more than you drink Son! And, surprise, surprise, they use the same catering company we do, so what's the betting they supply all the regional prisons? They're being fully cooperative apparently, but interestingly, a couple of their workers have been no-shows today."

"But that's at least... what... seven prisons?" Leo was frowning. "This is a big operation."

"Yes, if we assume they've got someone on the inside in all of them. They may not have, of course, but if they have, well... Anyway, Scott's rung O'Brien and Hirst, so tomorrow could be an interesting day!"

"Well, for what it's worth, Greg and I were talking about time frames, and we think Moss is playing for time. We think that might mean something's happening in the near future." Leo drained his pint.

They looked at each other, each with a variant of a perplexed look on their faces as if they were having trouble piecing it all together, which, of course, they were.

Chapter Thirty

Eventually the ringing penetrated his consciousness. "So, you're off sick? Nothing trivial, I hope."

Luke must have rung as soon as he'd heard, dragging McAuley out of his deep slumber. It would take a lot of caffeine and possibly an epidural, but he'd be alright.

"Bastard! Can't a bloke get a decent lie in?"

"I hope you're not in too little discomfort!"

"Aye well, I broke my leg. At least that's the official story."

Luke knew there was no point pushing McAuley: he'd open up in his own time. He waited.

McAuley had decided at some time in the early hours of the morning, to come clean to Luke about the whole thing: but not on the phone. Excusing himself with the lie that there was someone at the door, he invited Luke over when he finished his shift. "But you mustn't tell anyone at work that you're coming. That's really important."

"Ooh, I love a mystery. I'll bring beer." McAuley dry-heaved at the thought.

It took all the effort he could muster to drag himself out of bed and it hurt. It was one thing to tell people on an evening out that he was up for a few drinks, but quite another the next morning to be quite so blasé. Last night he hadn't cared. Although sobriety was, he felt, often overrated, this morning he cared desperately. When he belched, he could smell last night's beer. Cat sat watchfully on the bedside table, waiting for McAuley to fall asleep again, so he could launch an attack.

Instead, McAuley picked his way through last night's discarded clothes and with shaking hands, poured a pint of water, swallowed two painkillers and downed the drink in one, thought for a moment that he might throw up, didn't, and decided to brush his teeth as if somehow that might freshen him up. He was wrong about that. Forking food into Cat's bowl brought on another wave of nausea which he just managed to fight off. Cat's response to this was to fart ostentatiously, leaving an almost lethal miasma hanging in the room and McAuley left in a hurry. Toast was all he could manage. He gave up on his mug of coffee almost at once as his stomach started to churn. His shower routine, hot, then cold, revived him enough to think that getting dressed might not be a completely wasted effort, and he sank onto his sofa and began to go over last night's conversation. Those memories, much to his surprise, came back crystal clear and he felt his mood shift to a more positive outlook.

——

Mrs. Singh answered her door wearing her cooking pinny over her sari and rocking yellow marigolds.

"Gregor, Beta. You're not at work today?" She seemed to know his shift pattern and gave him a searching look. "You don't look too good. I'll put the kettle on, shall I? I have some fresh gulab jamun, but I don't suppose you'll be interested."

He ate tentatively, more out of politeness than hunger,

not quite trusting his digestive system, while Mrs. Singh busied herself in her kitchen. She was chopping a variety of herbs and dropping them into something aromatic, then dicing meat.

"Goan lamb and coconut curry for tomorrow. Now, where's my turmeric?"

It was all very companionable. When she sat opposite him with her masala chai and a chocolate digestive, McAuley took a deep breath.

"It's a long story, I'm afraid."

She reached up and touched his cheek. It was such a natural and affectionate gesture that it took his breath away.

"What do they say now? A trouble shared is a trouble halved. Is that Shakespeare or the Bible? I hope it's not too long a story. At my age you know, I could go at any time." She smiled. "So, tell me."

Mrs. Singh was an attentive listener who forgot nothing she was told. It was a singular skill.

"O.K. A while back when I was on night duty, I found a prisoner who had committed suicide, only then it turned out he may have been murdered."

Mrs. Singh, who was a great fan of crime fiction, took the tale in her stride, occasionally putting her hand to her throat as if in shock, and unconsciously playing with her necklace that had little Sikh symbols on it. She tutted disapprovingly at particular details.

"I am still listening. You carry right on." She refilled the kettle and refreshed their drinks. "So, your poor friend Leo, he's out of a job and some criminals are missing, but all the good people say that justice will be done, and you'll be proved innocent." As a summary that worked pretty well. "And Molly. Have you told her yet?"

"No. I'm going to go over there next. She's working from home."

"I'll get my coat. It's a long story and Sammy will need entertaining so don't forget your guitar. You know how much he enjoys you playing to him."

—

He'd always found it hard to share his work with Molly. The humorous elements were easy – and there were many of those, but the darker stuff, much less so. He needed to retain a professional detachment, an element of objectivity, but he'd sensed Molly's resentment when he wouldn't talk about the casual brutality and general nastiness he encountered on a regular basis. With that history in mind, the coming conversation should be interesting.

He hadn't known what to expect from Molly. He hadn't really thought about it, but he hadn't expected such an underwhelming response. It felt almost as if she was wondering why he was telling her at all. Although she listened politely and expressed sympathy, she didn't seem that engaged, and feeling a bit deflated, he finished with a rather lame, "I just thought you ought to know, that's all." Afterwards Mrs. Singh and Molly chatted happily over a cup of tea while McAuley played guess-the-nursery-rhyme with Sammy.

—

On the way back, Mrs. Singh was quite philosophical.

"It's difficult for her – for you both. You're not together in the way you once were. She's probably asking herself how involved in each other's lives you're supposed to be beyond bringing up Sammy."

McAuley dropped her off at the supermarket and, on a whim, decided to go to the gym, working on the basis that some strenuous activity and a swim would do him good. Elsbietta, the Czech receptionist flirted with him as she swiped his membership card, but he suspected that was simply a part of her friendly personality and didn't take it seriously. (As he was never to discover, she rather wished he would.) He was in no particular rush and enjoyed his work out, feeling the burn in his muscles and getting up a good sweat. With endorphins bouncing around his system, he felt energised as he packed his kit away. As he was leaving, he checked his phone. Four missed calls, all from Mrs. Singh. With a sense of foreboding, he rang her back.

"Gregor? Oh Gregor, are you all right?" She sounded barely in control. "Please come home. Something dreadful has happened. I had to call the police."

Chapter Thirty-One

He drove home in a panic, his mind working through any number of scenarios and cursing himself that he hadn't had the wit to ask for details. As he turned into the drive there were two police cars already waiting and the disturbing sight of blue and white crime scene tape across the front door. This didn't look good. He ducked under the tape and bounded up the front steps calling out for Mrs. Singh, taking the policeman at the foot of the stairs by surprise.

"Mr. McAuley?"

"Yes. Where's Mrs. Singh?"

"In her flat sir. She's fine. She's had a bit of a shock but there's a WPC with her."

"What's happened?"

"Is your flat number five sir?"

"Yes."

"Come with me please."

They climbed the stairs, McAuley with some trepidation and a sense of foreboding, wondering what awaited them and startled by sudden flashes of light. He wasn't expecting the gross sight that met them: nailed to his front door, as if crucified, was Cat. Blood had splashed the wall and dripped down the door, pooling on the laminate floor, behind a crime scene no.1 marker.

Surely the poor creature must've been dead before they put him there: he couldn't imagine Cat cooperating in any way.

Who knew such a scrawny animal could have so much blood?

"Blood must've pumped out like a geyser," the SOCO helpfully observed.

"I'd be looking for someone with multiple bites and scratches," McAuley suggested, looking away from his erstwhile pet and fighting a wave of nausea. Flashes continued to punctuate this conversation.

How many pictures does he need to take? McAuley had a rising sense of irritation.

Underneath Cat, written in what must be the poor creature's blood, were the words:

YOUR NEXT

My next what?... Ah...

His mind went into hyper-drive, full of swirling thoughts moving so fast they barely made a coherent whole as his rational brain struggled (and failed) to make sense of what he was seeing, while deciding whether or not to throw up. He was grateful that the decision was not to, but it was touch and go and he was left to reflect that although he'd disliked Cat deeply, he was both sad and angry about the poor creature's grim demise.

The door was ajar, swinging on one hinge. He looked at the officer.

"Can I go in?"

"Not yet sir. The fingerprint lady's currently in there, but I need to warn you that there's a lot of mess."

The fingerprint lady? He thought distractedly. *She'll*

not thank you for that.

"Is it OK if I go and see Mrs. Singh?"

"Of course, sir, but please don't leave the building. We'll need to take a statement from you, and your fingerprints for elimination." McAuley nodded.

Mrs. Singh rushed up to him, threw herself into his arms and burst into tears. "It was so horrible. Your poor cat." He led her to the kitchen table, and they sat down. The young WPC brought over two mugs of chai.

"Your friend has been teaching me the mysteries of Indian tea," she told him with a warm smile.

McAuley thought it would be churlish to refuse and ask for coffee, so he sipped it, trying not to look too apprehensive. Actually, much to his surprise it tasted rather good. The young officer came and sat with them, patted Mrs. Singh's hand and spoke to her in a gentle and encouraging way.

"Do you feel up to going over it again for Mr. McAuley?"

She did, and Mrs. Singh told them both how she'd come home from the Supermarket to find the front door wide open.

"And I was sure I'd locked it behind us."

She told them how she'd gone into her own flat, unpacked her shopping and made herself a drink, but then that open door was niggling at her and so she went back into the hall and stood thinking about it for a while.

"I got to wondering if there'd been a break-in, so I thought I'd just check upstairs."

She'd gone no further than the top step, seen the door with its shocking twofold message and fled back to the safety of her own flat, locking the door behind her and dialling 999.

"They came very quickly. I think they thought it was a hate crime. I may have given them that impression."

There was a knock on the door and the first officer popped his head in.

"O.K. to take your statement now sir?"

He joined them at the table and was provided with a cup of chai. McAuley clearly didn't have much to add to what Mrs. Singh had already told them about their movements.

"Do you have any hunches officer?"

"Two things spring to mind. This is clearly very personal, and I'll ask you about that in a moment."

McAuley nodded.

"It strikes me that someone could have been watching the property and took advantage when they saw you leave. I understand none of the other tenants were at home, and the house is relatively sheltered from the road. On the other hand, it may be that you were both lucky to be out and they'd come looking for you. Well, you sir, anyway."

"If that's the case, I'd like to know how they got my address."

"Now, can anyone confirm that you were at the gym?"

It was a seemingly innocuous question, but McAuley knew it was loaded. However, there was no point getting arsey about it, so he told the officer about signing in and out of the fitness centre, which seemed to satisfy him.

"We'll need a list from you. Anyone who might have a grudge against you."

"Aye, well, in that case there's something you need to know."

McAuley told him about what had been happening in the prison and the mood changed entirely. The officer made a hurried call to his station and was transferred several times. Each time he spoke he became noticeably more nervous as he was clearly speaking to someone more senior than before. McAuley felt though, that the poor man made a good job of summarising the situation. When he hung up, he said that someone else would need to interview McAuley as there seemed to be a number of complex links to other ongoing investigations, and more detailed forensic tests would need to be done on the flat.

———

It was six thirty when McAuley finally got into his flat. He wouldn't let Mrs. Singh come with him. He needed to do this alone, and as he stood in the wreckage of his sitting room surveying the damage, he understood the message he'd been delivered more keenly.

This should be my sanctuary where no one can reach me. I should be able to come home and be safe.

Aye, 'coz life's like that eh?

There was no disguising the malice and violence behind this devastation: every piece of furniture had been systematically trashed. The same was true of his bedroom although his clothes had survived, merely having been tossed around the room. The bathroom and kitchen were also disaster areas, although the porcelain had been spared. Broken crockery and glassware and scattered food littered the floor. A patina of fingerprint dust covered everything. The faint glow from the energy saving lightbulb (now without its shade) failed to lift the sense of desolation. He found a roll of black bin liners and started the task of gathering together what was beyond saving. He knew this was a displacement activity, but he had to do something. As he sifted through his belongings on the floor, somewhere in the recesses of his awareness McAuley registered how truly awful the carpet was and wondered how he'd lived with it this long.

Bastards! This is my flat. (Well, not actually mine.) This is my refuge, my safe space. How dare they?

He wanted to smash something himself. He felt rather than heard the crunching of glass and crockery underfoot as he moved around.

He picked up an old shoebox that had housed the pathetic remnants of family memorabilia and searched around for its contents, scattered around the room. As he retrieved each photo he stopped and looked at it, spending time on a picture of him as a child, in the garden at Bearsden holding an ice cream, much the same age that Sammy was now. It could have been Sammy, the same Celtic colouring, the same set to the jaw, the same dusting of freckles, the same skinny build that wouldn't fill out until well after puberty, the same lively expression of curiosity: two peas in a pod. Those precious mementos of his parents and the memories they conjured out of nowhere brought him up short and for a moment he thought he might tear up.

Apart from his large legacy he didn't have much to remember his parents by. When he'd started at university, he'd been of the mindset that keeping clutter was just maudlin, so apart from these carefully selected photos and their wedding rings, he'd decided to keep nothing and never regretted it. He felt a huge relief to discover that although the frame of his parents' wedding photo was beyond salvaging, the photo was undamaged. Until that moment he hadn't realised how important these mementos were to him. Then a thought struck him, and he searched around for a photo that had been in a frame on his sideboard: a picture of he and Molly with Sammy in happier days, by the seaside, all tanned and grinning for the camera, apparently, the ideal family unit. He remembered the occasion well.

"Greg? You in there?"

"Ah, it's yourself. In the bedroom Wee Man."

Luke came through, stepping carefully around various obstacles.

"Wow! What's happened here?"

What do you think? McAuley thought with a flash of irritation.

"What do you think?" he said in a more measured tone. "Anyway, Country Life won't be featuring us any time soon."

"What's going on?" Luke looked horrified, and then looked at McAuley's legs. "And aren't you supposed to be in plaster?"

McAuley gestured around the room listlessly.

"It'll be OK." He didn't sound as if he believed it. He gave Luke the guided tour. "They don't seem to have taken anything away for forensic testing."

"No one was hurt, Greg. I don't think they waste those sorts of resources on burglaries."

McAuley sighed. "I suppose not. If you look in that cupboard, you might just find a bottle of..."

"Gin!"

"Fancy that eh? I'm surprised that survived. Away and get me one too if you can find any glasses that aren't smashed."

He continued to root around in the wreckage for the photo and eventually found it, the glass smashed, and the picture torn beyond repair. It was a picture he should long since have removed from display, but even so...

His thoughts were interrupted by the arrival of a handleless cup of gin and then a shout from downstairs:

"Boys? Come down. There's food on the table. You can tell Luke all about it while you eat." McAuley didn't feel hungry but didn't argue, and for the fifth time that day he related the whole sorry tale, conscious that at these latter telling's there was an additional instalment to muddy the waters. It was close on nine when they'd finished, but by this retelling his shock had dissipated somewhat to be replaced by anger.

Luke though, had another piece of the jigsaw to add.

"Moss has been suspended. The senior manager's meeting was cancelled and the three governors, plus two independent observers from the Home Office had it out in O'Brien's office. They must have come up on the early train. It was all over by 11.00."

"How do you know all this?"

"Moss's P.A. She's a soft spot for me and she really dislikes Moss."

"Audrey Craven has a soft spot for you?"

"There's many a fine tune played on an old fiddle. What can I say? You've either got it or you haven't?"

"Yeah, and you'll probably have to take antibiotics for it."

McAuley tried to imagine what Miss Craven had looked like in her heyday, but struggled with the possibility that she'd actually had a heyday.

"She's leaving, by the way."

"Who? Miss Craven? The place is built around her. Why?"

"She has an elderly mother who's rather infirm. Carer's duties by all accounts. I've also heard – and you'll love this – that Errol wasn't even a proper clergyman. So much for our selection and vetting processes. Look, I'm going to ring Sonia to tell her what had happened, then we'll make a start on the mess upstairs."

Sonia had immediately told him to bring McAuley home to stay over, but he'd refused saying he didn't want to leave Mrs. Singh on her own after such an unpleasant experience and Sonia had understood. It was at that point that they realised Mrs. Singh was conspicuous by her absence. They tracked her down to McAuley's flat where she was busy sorting the salvageable from the beyond hope. The washing machine and the dishwasher were on, and some books were already back on the shelves.

"Come on, it's not that bad, is it?" ventured Luke, picking up a book from the floor and dusting it off. Mrs. Singh and McAuley looked at him as if he were mad.

"Really? Did you just get here? Did I imagine I just told you a story about a drug gang out to get me?"

"Sorry, that wasn't what I meant. Look, you had your guitar, your phone and your tablet on you. Your clothes have survived. Your computer and kit can be replaced. Not much else here is yours."

"No. It belongs to Mrs. Singh."

"Oh. Sorry, Mrs. Singh, I should've thought."

"Insurance!" she said dismissively. "Insurance will cover it."

"No." McAuley's voice was firm. "I brought this on you, and I'll pay." Mrs. Singh looked about to argue.

"He's got that voice on him Mrs. Singh, and do you see the look in his eye?" She nodded. "It's not worth arguing with him. He's decided."

"I have! Tomorrow I'm off to IKEA."

———

He slept in Mrs. Singh's spare bedroom. He was amazed by how quickly she'd rallied, particularly when she told him that she found it all rather exciting.

"I don't think you'd have said that if you'd been here when they came calling."

"Pah! We fought the Muslims during Partition." She

made sharp throat-cutting motions with her hand.

"And you were what? Three?"

"The Sikhs are a warrior people, Beta. That's how we survived."

She drew herself up to her full height and gathered her dignity around her. "You know that Singh means Lion? That's not an accident," she said.

McAuley's dreams were filled with various takes on crucifixion. He guessed his brain had been processing the events of the day and struggling with the fine line between madness and reality – or maybe the madness of reality. At one point in his fevered night-imaginings, Madam Cynthia had appeared to him asking if he had a pet and telling him his tea leaves were confused with religious imagery.

Awake at the crack of dawn, McAuley lay in bed staring at the slivers of light seeping around the curtains as he listened to the sound of other residents leaving for work.

Why did everyone feel the need to slam the front door?

Knowing there was no more chance of more sleep, he crept out of Mrs. Sing's flat and headed upstairs to his own, and before Mrs. Singh was awake, he was standing in the wreckage of his flat holding a tape measure. The look of the flat wasn't improved as the dull tones of the energy-saving light bulbs warmed up and cast jagged shadows around the rooms. It took him most of the day going backwards and forwards between home and the superstore with Sammy as his wing-man, to bring home his purchases, and much of the day for Molly and Mrs. Singh to clear up the flat. Molly was trying to make amends for her lack of interest in the early parts of McAuley's prison saga and had fully appreciated the seriousness of the latest events. That evening, after Molly and Sammy had left, Luke and Sonia joined him, and they tackled the flat packs as an effective team.

"Let's hope the cops don't come calling or we'll be in deep shit," Sonia had said because they weren't wearing face masks. They all doubted excuses would carry much weight if the police did turn up though, and they were slightly suspicious of the attitude of the man in flat three who'd given them a strange look as they'd arrived. Sonia was remarkable at self-assembly furniture whereas McAuley found the whole process deeply frustrating and lamented his lack of practical skills. They had the radio on in the background and were listening to the local station when Luke shushed them.

"... and his partner Veronica Williams, both employees of Her Majesty's Prison Service following a suspicious fire at their isolated home near Selby. A spokesperson for the Fire Service said that the fire had been quickly brought under control, but the state of the house indicated that it had been broken into and ransacked before the fire had been set. Police are asking the public to look out for the couple who might be travelling in a silver Audi S8. Police are concerned for their welfare."

"Gavin Moss. I heard her say Gavin Moss." Luke frowned.

There was a long silence. Then McAuley said quietly, "That could have been me."

Chapter Thirty-Two

Judith Hirst was a light sleeper. She put this down to being married to a man who, for all his working life, had worked shifts. As promotions came, the unsocial hours had lessened, but she had never adjusted. What had woken her? She looked at her alarm clock: 3.30. Beside her, Peter snored gently. There it was again, a noise from outside. Moving slowly, so as not to disturb her husband, she slipped out of bed and went to the window. She moved the curtain slightly and let her eyes adjust to the gloom. She wasn't sure what she'd expected to see. A fox maybe? Cats? What she hadn't expected was a figure in a hoodie standing by Peter's car. She stood mesmerised.

"Peter! Peter!" A stage whisper over her shoulder so as not to alert the man on her drive but Peter continued to snore.

Judith watched as the hooded man swung something at the driver's window to a tinkling of glass. Then he threw something in. She watched in appalled fascination as he lit a match and threw that in too. There was a woosh and the interior of the car went up in flames.

No longer concerned about whether the arsonist could hear her, she shouted to her husband, who semi-alert and dishevelled, stumbled to the window in time to see the man look up, clock them, grin, give them the middle finger and leg it.

—

The next morning McAuley was called into the police station to meet with the officer in charge of the team tasked with investigating the prison smuggling, Detective Inspector Roberts. Everyone called him Roberts. Some people called him Robert, assuming it was his first name, but no one called him by his first name because no one knew what it was.

Roberts was wearing a creased suit over a V-neck jumper and a plain shirt. His shoes were scuffed. (It was the sort of thing McAuley noticed.) There was a stain on his tie, which was, on first acquaintance, his only outstanding feature, that and his bushy eyebrows, which were much in need of the attention of a barber. He was a monochrome looking sort of a man, with the appearance of someone who was slightly unfinished, and had just walked out of a pre-colour TV programme, with the exception of his florid complexion. He had the look of a man who ate well, (or ate badly, depending on your point of view). He had the sort of face where a superior, judgemental look was perfectly at home. He was clearly not a man to tolerate fools gladly, and McAuley suspected he was the sort of man who would hold a grudge - and enjoy holding it.

The interview took place in a cramped, dingy office with old damp patches on the ceiling and a dead cactus on the windowsill. It was an office at the depressing end of generic in terms of atmosphere, with a rather dull police-dogs calendar. In an attempt to make conversation, McAuley enquired, nodding to the calendar,

"Do you like dogs, Inspector?"

"Hate the bloody things."

McAuley waited but no further elucidation was forthcoming.

Not one for social chit-chat then, our DI Roberts.

Nevertheless, he managed to give the impression of someone keen to bestow the benefit of his experience on others, whether they wanted it or not, as he repeatedly talked over McAuley.

Firstly, there was the reassurance that the Wayne Mallanaphy enquiry did not see McAuley as a person of interest, and never had. Quite the opposite: his original statement after the death had been fully accepted. Although McAuley had never doubted this, it was a huge weight off his mind.

"We have CCTV footage of Governor Williams entering Hussain's cell on a number of occasions. He's admitted falsifying his statement about your involvement under pressure from her but is sticking to the tale that Mallanaphy took his own life, but the evidence points the other way. Tissue under Mallanaphy's right index finger was a DNA match to Muhammad Hussain."

More pressingly, the police were linking the attack on McAuley's flat to the attack on Moss's house and last night's arson attack on the Hirsts. McAuley had known nothing of this event before now but was reassured that the Hirsts were fine.

"They only got the car fortunately, so it was a bit of a damp squid from the perpetrator's point of view."

Did he just say that?

"Had it not been for Mrs. Hirst disturbing their attacker though, there was the possibility that the arsonist wouldn't have stopped at the car and things would have worked out very differently. We're looking at local CCTV and may have some leads worth pursuing. Anyway, we're assuming a link between these attacks, but we need to exclude other possibilities. Do you or Millie have any enemies?"

Millie? He let that go, and thought that was a stupid question under the circumstances.

"Well, clearly. I just don't know who they'd be if we exclude this gang, and before you ask, I don't think this has anything to do with being a prison officer. I can't think of any individual prisoner who'd hold that sort of a grudge."

There was a pause while the DI digested this.

"I'm sure you're right there."

"What about Fr. Leo?" McAuley had asked with concern.

"You don't need to worry about the Revd. Thorburn. We've already interviewed him. His house is church owned and is very publicly overlooked. It also has a high standard of home security. On the other hand, as a precaution, we suggested that they go away for a while. They chose a destination, and we contacted the local police to give them a formal exemption from COVID travel restrictions and to make sure they get regular drive-bys. They left this morning. I also understand they're thinking of moving abroad in the near future for his work."

This was another huge relief for McAuley.

"As we've already advised the Hirsts, we're now

advising you to do the same Mr. McAuley. As we currently understand the situation there are a number of people involved in frustrating what's turning out to have been a large-scale drug smuggling operation within regional prisons. You, Deputy Governor Hirst and Revd. Thorburn seem to be key players and there's no doubt you're at risk. I'm not going to sugar coat this for you, because I need you to take this very seriously. We're assuming it's the same group who are after Moss and Williams, and we're also concerned for the safety of Errol Adebeyo. You're a target for thwarting them. It's as simple as that. This is a ruthless organisation and they're well out of pocket on this operation and in their view, someone has to pay, and we can't have our witnesses dropping like flies now, can we? I can't tell you what to do, of course."

"You mean I have a choice."

"You need to think very carefully what you do next Mr. McAuley. As to Moss and Williams, we think they had their cut before it all came crashing down and the last few days had been a holding operation of obstruction and misdirection from them. We think they were waiting for their payoff before disappearing. We believe they were key players but not the top dogs. We're confident that this is an Eastern European gang using local networks and your intervention has been a huge breakthrough for us. We've already arrested a number of the smaller players, but the intelligence is proving very useful. You might be interested to know that we had an officer undercover in the prison, but lockdown put paid to any further intelligence gathering."

McAuley sensed that Roberts seemed keen to be doing something else and the meeting staggered to an end.

"Well, it's been nice meeting you," McAuley offered as he left.

The DI declined to shake his hand on the grounds of possible infection, and the meeting ended rather awkwardly. It was only as he was driving away that he considered this social convention and realised that it wasn't true. It hadn't been nice meeting DI Roberts at all.

That interview gave him a lot to think about on the drive home. As he was reflecting on the interview, he remembered the dead cactus sitting on the windowsill in Roberts' office.

How do you kill a cactus?

Someone embedded in the prison?

Could that have been Errol? Would that account for his phone call? Had they blundered into his operation and put him at risk? He shuddered and turned instead to the key issue: the advice to relocate particularly occupied his mind. He wasn't going to be stubborn about this: if the Hirsts and Thorburns had heeded police advice, he was certainly going to. The question was, where was he to go? Peter and Leo may have had limited choices, but McAuley certainly didn't. In fact, with his property portfolio, he was spoilt for choice. The problem, if you could even call it a problem, was that he had only ever visited one of them, when he'd taken his then girlfriend to Malta. In the end she'd liked the house more than him, so his memory of it was somewhat tainted. As to the others, he had no idea about any of them and so had no real idea what criteria to use. He felt suddenly embarrassed that he wasn't even sure where the properties were exactly, having only thought about them, (which wasn't often), as some sort of amorphous mass: the portfolio. He'd been happy to allow the various letting agencies to maintain and rent his properties out, and had taken no interest in them at all, other than the lucrative fees he received, and which were salted away in various high-interest accounts and investments. He felt some considerable embarrassment about this unmerited, albeit taxed income, but every time he'd come to the point of deciding that he needed to review the whole situation, it had felt too complicated, and inertia had taken over. He knew that's what accountants were for, and he had an accountant, a good one, but some sort of atavistic guilt tied to the memory of his parents always sabotaged his resolve.

He arrived home to the not unwelcome presence of a police crime-prevention and security unit. Thoughts of shutting stable doors after bolted horses crossed his mind fleetingly, but he listened with interest as window locks, reinforced doors, intercom entry, motion-sensor lights (that should upset Fox) and security cameras were discussed. He took the lead officer on one side and told him to go ahead with a very comprehensive package.

"Are you the householder sir?"

He explained (with fingers crossed) that he had Mrs. Singh's authority to make such decisions, what with her being quite elderly, knowing she'd crown him one if she ever heard him describe her in those terms. He knew she was conscious of her age, and it didn't do to remind her of it. He signed the various order forms and paid-up front, deciding that he would depend on her naivety about such things to convince her that this was a free service. He would talk vaguely about government grants if she pushed him.

While McAuley didn't live a parsimonious life, his outgoings were quite modest for someone with his income. His car was new but not fancy; he liked to look smart and had a good wardrobe and there were one or two pricy colognes he liked, but other than his rent and the child maintenance he paid to Molly, he was a low spender. He had no desire to amass possessions nor to spend flamboyantly. At the same time, he knew he could afford to live far, far more extravagantly, and so the idea of presenting his credit card and taking a sizeable hit for the whole building's enhanced security didn't bother him.

"I've been told by DI Roberts that this is a priority job, so we have contractors on standby," McAuley was told. "It will be dealt with as a matter of urgency."

Deciding it was best to intercept Mrs. Singh before any work started, and head off any difficult questions, he made his way back indoors.

He'd always thought of himself as a glass-half-full sort of a person, but the successive knocks and shocks of the last few days were starting to take their toll on his equanimity. He needed to take his situation seriously, he knew, and he had every intention of doing so. On that basis he returned to the issue of temporary relocation and gave it some serious thought. Presumably, only the police knew where the Thorburns and Hirsts were, and so security was going to be important. With that thought in mind, he went down to the cellar and trawled through some of his storage boxes, finding the paperwork he was looking for after only twenty minutes. Then he picked up his phone and rang Luke.

Chapter Thirty-Three

Audrey Craven put a tray of coffee mugs and a Queen's Golden Jubilee biscuit tin down and pulled up a chair next to DI Roberts and DS Humphreys at the conference table.

"The biscuits are fresh, gentlemen. Don't hold back." She smiled encouragement. Humphreys took her at her word, ignoring Roberts' pointed cough. Miss Craven returned to her desk as if somehow, proximity to her computer gave her greater authority. It was clear to both policemen that this was Audrey Craven's fiefdom and that she managed it with anonymous efficiency, like a permanent senior civil servant, regardless of the aspirations, ambitions and policies of her transient ministers.

"Miss Craven, I understand you were Governor Moss's P.A...." Whatever else he was about to say was lost as Miss Craven began to answer the question she assumed he was asking.

"That's right, but not for long. You're probably aware that his was a fairly recent appointment."

"How did you get on with him?" Roberts followed her train of thought.

Miss Craven paused, choosing her words carefully. "I didn't find him an easy person to work with. I couldn't fault his work – and I've worked for a number of Security Governors over the years, so I know what's involved – but he didn't have... how shall I put it? He didn't have the common touch. He was not good with people."

Roberts paused to allow her to continue and was irritated when Humphreys jumped into the silence.

"In what way Miss Craven?" He offered her his most charming smile. She didn't melt.

"In so many ways, Detective Sergeant. It wasn't social ineptitude or a lack of self-awareness; he simply didn't care. He told me on his first day that he wasn't here to make friends and I have to say, that's exactly how it worked out."

"How did this manifest itself?"

She made a non-committal noise by way of comment as she chose her words.

"He was dismissive of other staff once he'd met with them, quite rude in fact," She gestured to the offices on the other side of the corridor. "And, of course, I overheard the way he talked to people; he was very confrontational and sarcastic. Patronising, sometimes. He thought he was better than everyone else. His attitude to me for instance, was very dismissive. I was his P.A. That's a role that has some status. I don't say that to blow my own trumpet, but to point out that he seemed to think I was here just to manage his diary and make coffee. It's par for the course with some men in the prison service, Detective Inspector. Middle-aged women are all but invisible, particularly in this testosterone-heavy environment. We're very easy to underestimate. Do you know he once called me his 'work wife'? I don't think he respected women at all."

"So, would you say that he'd no particular friends here?"

"I would say he was universally disliked – not only by the men, which is to be expected for a Security Governor, but by the staff too. It didn't take long for his attitude to alienate people. This is an insular place Detective Inspector, an enclosed community in more respects than the obvious. Word gets round very quickly."

"So, a bit of a wolf in cheap clothing?"

Miss Craven noted the smirk that crossed the sergeants face.

Disrespectful.

"In many ways, Detective Inspector. In many ways."

"Were you present when Governor Moss interviewed Officer McAuley?" A shift in direction.

"I was."

"What were your impressions?"

She gave the question some thought again.

"Mr. McAuley is a popular member of staff with a good reputation. What happened in that meeting was a travesty. He didn't deserve to be treated in that way. It was most unjust. I was actually embarrassed. None of Governor Moss's predecessors would have behaved in that way and it was just the same with the Reverend Thorburn."

She paused and her voice took on a tone of distaste. "Distributing e-cigarette liquid. I ask you, how pathetic is that? Pure spite and vindictiveness. Mind you, they both gave as good as they got, so he didn't have it all his own way by any means." She paused again and this time Humphreys kept quiet, busy taking notes.

"It was all a pointless charade anyway, unless the point

was to enhance his reputation, because I knew that as soon as Governor O'Brien got back, both of them would have their suspensions rescinded with no blemish on their records, as did their union rep."

"No investigation?"

"Oh yes, but they would have been completely exonerated and very quickly. In my view, the allegations were completely without foundation."

"Miss Craven, to your knowledge, did Governor Moss have any dealings with the Pentecostal Chaplain, Errol Adebeyo?"

"Well, he never came to this office. As to whether Governor Moss ever went to the chaplaincy, I don't know, you'd need to ask the Imam."

"You'll be aware that we are investigating Governor Moss over some very serious allegations. Could he have used his position here to manage a network of corrupt staff?"

She thought about it for a moment. "The role of the Security Governor inevitably involves investigating allegations of corruption against staff members. This is a department dedicated to those areas, and it's a broad remit. It would also allow for liaison with police and probation in relation to following up former prisoners, analysing intelligence about potential in-house corruption - which I must point out are often malicious allegations from disgruntled prisoners - so you could argue that all the elements are in place to misuse that information and those contacts. You could also argue that anyone who works in this department could misuse that information. Anyway, if he was involved, he didn't do it from this office; at least not while I was here."

"Well, his computer may reveal pertinent information."

"I'm not given to betting Detective Inspector, but I doubt very much whether you'll find anything incriminating. He brought a lap-top to work. Have you found that?"

They hadn't, but Roberts wasn't about to say so. "That's something we're looking into."

"Can you think of anyone who might have wished Mr. Moss harm?"

She smiled. "It would be easier for me to give you a list of those who didn't wish him harm. To be frank with you, the prison is a much better place without him. When Governor O'Brien called a staff meeting to inform us what had happened, there were no tears shed, Inspector. While it came as a shock, I think the most positive reaction was indifference. He hadn't been here long and he'd made no friends. Of course, there's been whispering in corners and in this case two and two have definitely made four: there's anger and indignation that he was corrupt, although nothing's been confirmed officially, and some staff - and some prisoners - have been making links between Moss and young Mallanaphy's death. The atmosphere's been very tense, and we could have really done with Fr. Leo's calming influence. So, there you are Gentlemen, 'good riddance' seems to be the overriding sentiment. Not exactly the obituary one would want for oneself."

Roberts was about to begin to wrap up the interview,

but Miss Craven hadn't finished.

"Of course, Fr. Leo is absolutely correct: while chaplains are highly respected by staff and prisoners, most staff only have the fuzziest idea of what chaplains do and what chaplaincy is about, but the overriding sense is that chaplains are morally above reproach. If I wanted to embed a corrupt member of staff here, it occurs to me that the chaplaincy is the best place for that, and it now turns out that Mr. Adebeyo wasn't actually a properly licensed pastor, so someone else clearly had the same idea."

"What about vetting?"

"Indeed. It does make one wonder."

As she escorted them back to the main entrance, unlocking and relocking an inordinate number of gates, she became almost chatty.

"I know this is the world you both live in so no doubt you take it all in your stride, but I find it all rather terrifying. I know that must sound odd as I work in a prison, but I have virtually no day-to-day contact with the men. I'm thinking of leaving soon actually. I've had a couple of conversations with the Governor about it."

"Not retirement surely?"

She fixed the sergeant with a sharp look.

Yes, aren't you the charmer?

"No. My mother is reaching the age where she can no longer live independently and I'm an only child. This business with Gavin Moss has just speeded the decision up for me. I'll stay long enough to induct my successor, but just between us, I know who that's likely to be, and it won't take much to bring her up to speed."

"What did you make of her Boss?" Humphreys eased the pool car out of the car park.

"I thought she was very measured, very articulate." It sounded like he was describing a suspect. "She clearly didn't like the man, but I thought she tried to be objective. I'd employ her any day." They drove in silence for a while.

"We've not found his lap-top, have we?"

"Not as far as I know."

Miss Craven washed up the mugs and returned to her office. As she powered up her computer, she thought about the two officers. The DI was old-school, and she'd liked that. She thought he was straightforward but suspected he wouldn't easily think outside the box. As to his sergeant, with his fading-matinee-idol good looks, she thought DI Roberts would do well to watch him. There was something off about him and she was a very good judge of character. It gave her food for thought.

Chapter Thirty-Four

Thankfully leaving the sound of hammering and drilling behind, McAuley made his way to Luke's, gratified to have discovered that Luke was on lates. It was an odd request he knew, but sitting on Luke's sofa he explained his reasoning. Luke asked no further questions and had no problem allowing McAuley use of his landline.

"Whatever you need Mate."

As he dialled, he had his paperwork spread out in front of him.

"Ola? Voce fala inglês?"

"But of course, sir."

He was mightily relieved.

He identified himself, answered their security questions and outlined his request. Due to COVID travel restrictions, most of their properties were currently vacant, including both of his, and the agency was using the hiatus to do some redecorating and upgrading, and there would be no problem taking one of them off the books, he was assured.

"If you would come to the office as soon as you arrive, we can let you view them both and you can make your choice."

He looked at Luke. "I know it sounds paranoid, but I didn't want that on my call history. Anyway, it'll all turn out fine."

"Don't try that false bravado crap on me, McAuley. I know you too well. You're shitting yourself – and if you're not, you should be."

"Look, I'm not going to let these people intimidate me. Well, that's not strictly true because they're already intimidating me, and next time I might not be so lucky, but you know what I mean. The police have told me to disappear for a while, so I'm going to. I'm not doing any of that, 'If I run, they've won' bollocks."

A couple of beers and a pizza later he headed for home, stopping at an electronics shop at one of those retail units down by the river where you can get pretty much anything you need – providing it's in a low rainfall year and the place hasn't been flooded, which with typical Yorkshire understatement was called 'Corner Shop.' ("We've no truck wi' definite articles or 'owt like that here Lad.") The dour owner gave him discount for a selection of burner phones and on the way out he bought The Big Issue from a lad he recognised as a former inmate.

"Don't encourage them," a fat woman said as she waddled by.

"Someone should encourage you to eat fewer chips you miserable bitch," the lad shouted after her.

She just gave him the finger without looking back. McAuley gave him a fiver.

———

He was momentarily fazed by his inability to get his front door key to work but then he noticed the shiny new five-button intercom system. Assuming correctly that Mrs Singh would be number one, he pressed the bell. She must have been standing right beside its phone because she picked up at once.

"Hello? Who is it please?"

"You know who it is. You were watching me come up the path. Can I come in?" There was a mechanical buzzing and the lock clicked. She was waiting for him in the hall.

"Isn't this fun? Look, I have your keys here."

"Have they finished?"

"Yes, it's all done. There were six of them. Lovely young men. So efficient."

Indeed, it was, and he couldn't help wondering how long it would have taken under normal circumstances. That was money well spent. She gave him a tour of the property and he was impressed.

———

McAuley spent a while reordering his books and CDs, deciding that he could do without the fun that Luke had confidently asserted the existing randomness would bring.

"After all, what's life without a challenge?"

That could be Luke's motto of course. Then he decided to relax in the dark in his sitting room, a little back from the window, overlooking the drive. Was he expecting anything to happen? Another attempt perhaps? He didn't know, but the darkness, the bottle of lager and Elgar's Cello Concerto in the background matched his mood. This was a piece of music that had the capacity to move him deeply.

His phone was on silent, and it was sometime before he realised he'd missed a call. It was an unknown number. He didn't ring back. A sort of lethargy seduced him, and he looked around at his new, improved surroundings. He actually felt at home here now, more than he ever had before he realised, surrounded by things that reflected his own taste. He felt pleased with his purchases and ironically, he began to wonder whether he should move to somewhere bigger, somewhere more grown-up than a one-bedroomed flat. He'd ask Mrs. Singh to let him have one of the bigger flats the next time one became available.

A movement caught his eye at the end of the drive. It was dark there and he couldn't quite see. He willed whoever, or whatever it was to come forward so that they'd trigger one of the new lights and he could see just what his money had bought. A couple of seconds later they came on, illuminating the garden like a night-time football fixture. Good value for money indeed. Caught in the light, but clearly not bothered by it, was a slight figure in a long-fitted coat, and a moment later his intercom buzzed.

My first visitor, he thought. His next thought was that perhaps his first thought had been the wrong first thought. He replaced it with the right thought, *That's odd. I'm not expecting anyone.*

He pressed his intercom.

"Hello. My name's Tamsin Hirst. I'm looking for Greg McAuley."

The name didn't immediately register.

"Peter and Judith's daughter. Am I at the right address?"

"Peter and Judith... PETER AND JUDITH! Come on up. Top floor."

He buzzed her in and then had a moment of doubt. All that effort to improve the security of the building and he had just invited in a total stranger because she had used a name he recognised. Still at least he now had a spy hole, bolts and a chain.

He met her at the door and was surprised by the proffered bottle of wine.

"£7.99. I'm a classy sort of a girl."

With some relief he recognised her from the photographs on Hirst's desk. Hers was a pretty face, an intelligent face with a sprinkling of freckles, framed by auburn curls. He ushered her in, took her coat and showed her into the sitting room.

"What a nice flat."

Well, it is now, isn't it? It's almost as good as a show flat.

"I'm sorry to turn up like this, I did try ringing, but I had a phone call from Mum this morning and it was all a bit garbled and rambling. Dad took over in the end, but I still only got half a tale. Anyway, I went to the house, and it was empty, (which didn't surprise me from what they said of their plans), and the drive was a mess, but someone had already taken the car away."

He thought again how quickly the combined might of the prison and police services could get things done when they put their minds to it.

"Dad mentioned you and I wheedled your address out of Uncle George, and well, here I am."

"Uncle George?"

"Well, not a real uncle, but he and Dad have worked together for decades. If I'm honest I'm slightly surprised to find you still here. I thought you'd have gone to ground too."

"Plans are in hand," he said, conscious of the enigmatic sound to that statement. She didn't press him for details.

"I've really come for answers. What can you tell me about what's been going on?"

"O.K. Shall we open this wine first?"

It actually helped to talk about what he'd now come to call 'the situation'. Not in a therapeutic sense, although there was probably an element of that, but in the sense that it helped him to clarify more the danger he was in and the risk he was taking delaying his departure. Tamsin was a good listener and held his gaze throughout. She had amber eyes, he noticed, lovely amber eyes, mesmerising amber eyes. He smiled. In contrast to the seriousness of the conversation, he felt very relaxed with her.

"So, the suicide was really a fight that had gone wrong?" she said.

He nodded while thinking, *As opposed to all the fights that went perfectly.*

"I didn't have the time to discuss this with Mum and Dad, it was all a bit of a rush, but do you think I'm in danger?"

Now there's a question!

He noticed how her slim body settled into elegant poses, much like those of a dancer.

"I'm probably not the best person to answer that but I'll give you DI Roberts' number."

He knew he was thinking out loud and his thoughts

were as much about Molly and Sammy as they were about Tamsin.

"DI Roberts says these people are dangerous and violent. They're also vindictive. Do you have somewhere you can disappear to easily?"

"Not really. I'm a junior doctor. I can't just disappear in the middle of a pandemic." She topped up their glasses. "But there is a friend I could stay with for a week or so, I guess. I could leave my car at home and travel in with her. I'm sure I could wear a hat and dark glasses."

She laughed. It was a nice laugh. The scent of her perfume was seductive, light and with a hint of citrus. He watched her lips as she sipped her wine.

Kissable lips.

Where had that come from?

He felt her knee touch his, just the lightest brush, but he was slightly surprised by the speed at which an X-rated fantasy arranged itself in his brain and he was mortified that he had to change position and cross his legs. He wondered if she was thinking the same thing of him. On balance he doubted it, but the thought cheered him no end. He felt like a teenager on his first date. He had butterflies in his stomach.

McAuley knew this conversation about personal safety was one he'd have to have with Molly too, and he was grateful to Tamsin for helping to clarify his mind. They chatted for a bit longer and McAuley found another bottle of wine. Tamsin perused his CD collection, although McAuley wasn't at all sure they were all back in the right boxes, and they chatted about music. It struck him suddenly that this was the first conversation he'd had with a woman other than Molly, Mrs. Singh or colleagues for months, and it was a conversation he was enjoying immensely.

For someone whose romantic life had been on hold (and not voluntarily) for some time, this evening was turning out to be something special, all the more so for being unexpected. There was an undercurrent here. Something was happening at a subliminal level, and it felt good. This was something he realised he'd missed. McAuley allowed himself the cheeky little fantasy that the tide might just have turned, and he felt as if the ground was shifting beneath him: conversation flowed comfortably, ranging over a number of topics, serious and funny, and they swapped stories to much amusement. McAuley was conscious of being on good form, witty and relaxed and Tamsin was equally engaging. There was a spark of amusement in her eyes as they chatted. He felt the hairs on his arms stand up as he got goose bumps.

What a shame about the timing.

⸺

Sleep had come late, long after Tamsin's breathing had become a regular but gentle rhythm. McAuley felt exhilarated and energised: what had happened had felt the most natural thing in the world and was clearly reciprocated. He turned to face her, taking care not to disturb her and lay there happily just watching her sleeping face. Her hair smelt of citrus. He was slightly embarrassed by the fact that in their haste they hadn't even closed the blinds, but the half-light of a nearly full moon allowed him the intoxicating thrill of observing this young woman as she lay facing him. He looked at her, pleased she was still sleeping. Her hair was on the pillow, spread out in a pre-Raphaelite image, and this was a moment he wanted to remember. Looking at her this way felt like a camera on a long exposure, and then she turned away from him and snuggled further under the duvet.

He lay awake for some time which was unlike him. His mind was churning with a mishmash of half-connected but delicious thoughts: he'd known her for a matter of hours, but he wanted to talk to someone and tell them what had happened and how he was feeling, and not in a sleazy or boastful way either. *Can you actually fall in love like this? Can it be this simple, this sudden? Can you really know at once?* In that moment he felt he had a glimpse of a future that might be, and he knew it was something he wanted. As they'd lain, snuggled together, and he'd peppered her face with kisses, they'd had the "When this is all over" conversation, and McAuley had been delighted by just how deeply he'd been affected by those whispered promises.

Chapter Thirty-Five

Luke's place was on the other side of the city (in one of those areas estate agents hopefully touted as the next to become up-and-coming) but easy enough to get to on the ring road. Both men thought their cars could make the journey from memory.

As soon as he told Luke about Tamsin, McAuley could have bitten his tongue off. A broad grin spread over Luke's face.

"You shagged the governor's daughter?" That's ballsy," he beamed.

"If we're being pedantic about it, Luke, he's the deputy governor."

"You shagged the deputy governor's daughter? That's ballsy."

"Don't put it like that." McAuley was irritated. "Don't take the shine off it, please. Why do you have to make it sound grubby? This was two adults who were mutually attracted and made adult decisions. I really like her, and I think the feeling's mutual. This could be something special."

He regretted mentioning anything about Tamsin's visit to Luke.

"I wonder what attracted her to the millionaire prison officer?"

"I'm not a millionaire."

"I think you'll find you are though Matey. Go on then,

how much are you worth?"

"I've no idea."

"There you go then. Only a millionaire could say that."

McAuley paused. "Anyway..."

He'd only dropped by to deliver one of the burner phones so they could keep in touch during his exile. He'd had the wit to include his spare keys too, so that Luke could move his car and look in on the flat.

"Don't forget to change the sheets."

McAuley knew there was no point in warning Luke off using his flat as a little love nest given the opportunity. McAuley was a pragmatist, and he knew Luke's odd philosophy when it came to relationships: not being married meant that Luke was single, and the fact that he was in a serious relationship didn't shake his belief in his single status for one moment.

Luke put his hand over his heart. "I promise to be a good boy." McAuley looked less than convinced.

"I'm taking Mrs. Singh to Molly's later, so I can tell them both at the same time and then I'm off."

"I shan't ask where you're going."

"Thanks, but remember I'm supposed to be off sick with a broken ankle. You could drop the occasional hint that I've gone to stay with my cousin in Aberdeen."

"You have a cousin in Aberdeen?"

"No. So, subtle hints. Can you do subtle Luke?"

He bridled slightly. "Of course I can."

"I'm sorry. It was a joke."

"Really? You need to work on them."

There was an awkward moment and then Luke beckoned him forward and hugged him.

"Take care Greg. Take care."

"I'll try – and one more thing Luke. Please don't mention me and Tamsin at work."

"Trust me."

"Ah, trust me'. My least favourite saying, especially when you say it."

"Greg, what's the definition of happiness?"

McAuley shrugged.

Luke grinned. "Insensitivity! And you, with your leg in a pot! There's no stopping you is there?"

Oh Dear God! "Look at me. Be Told! This is not a subject for gossip, OK?"

Luke looked crestfallen for a moment and then nodded. "My lips are sealed."

Chapter Thirty-Six

Given the recent break in, the conversation with Molly and Mrs. Singh was an easier one than he'd at first imagined, if rather solemn, but it left a rather bleak feeling. It was better if they didn't know where he was going, he told them as he gave Molly the third of the burner phones.

"I'm not very good at spy-type stuff" he told her, "But this sort of thing seems to work in the movies."

Mrs Singh climbed into the passenger seat and McAuley was about to drive away when he realised he'd left his jacket behind. He turned off the ignition and got out as Molly appeared at the door holding it out to him, Sammy trying to get by her to run to his dad.

It was then that the doors of a transit van parked opposite opened noisily and six men jumped out.

They didn't look like Jehovah's Witnesses.

There was no question who they were and what they wanted. Molly let out a little gasp of alarm.

"Get in the house!" McAuley shouted to Molly who, not needing to be told twice, picked Sammy up and fled back inside, slamming the door behind her, which wasn't quite what McAuley had in mind as he was halfway down the path and had thought he could have made it back in too.

The men stood menacingly at the gate, checking their options. A car started nearby. It looked for a moment like a standoff in a western, and McAuley wouldn't have been surprised if tumbleweed had blown by at that moment, but then the men started down the drive, one swinging a baseball bat.

None of them saw it coming, least of all McAuley, so it was a shock when his reversing Skoda careered at considerable speed into the posse, sending most of them stumbling forward, pinning one temporarily against the gatepost, and with a wet crunching noise, trapping another under the wheels. Mrs. Singh could just be seen peering over her shoulder from the driver's seat.

McAuley wasn't about to enquire about his health, so using the distraction to gain a moment's advantage, he took flight round the side of the house, without any clear idea where he was going, flinging bins and Sammy's tricycle in his wake and narrowly avoiding a set of aluminium ladders he'd intended to use to clear the guttering, satisfied by the sound of at least one person taking a tumble, swearing profusely and shouting in a heavy Eastern European accent. If the back door was locked, he was stuffed.

It was, but the adjacent window was open slightly. He didn't have the time to analyse the feasibility of getting in before he tore the window fully open, the strength panic had given him tearing the fitting from the frame. He was nearly in, one leg kneeling on the sill, when he was pulled violently backwards by his trailing leg.

Clinging on to the frame for dear life, he kicked out, pleased to make substantial contact and hearing a grunt, and then he was in. It gained him some respite, but not much. He looked around wildly for a weapon and picked up a bread knife from the sink and stabbed it hard into the hand of the man who was scrabbling to follow him through the window, pinning him briefly to the window frame.

As he ran into the hall, he could hear Sammy sobbing in the lounge, so he knew he had to lead the thugs away from there. He had the option of the stairs or the front door: the stairs won. McAuley was halfway up the stairs, his feet pounding on the stripped boards, when the ladder appeared at the landing window which was open ajar, and a man started to fiddle with the catch trying to open it wider. McAuley made it to the top of the stairs as the window swung open and was in time to grab the man's hair in one hand and hit him in the face hard with a heavy metal Buddha figure he'd grabbed from the little chest under the window. Then he battered the fingers of the hand that was gripping on to the sill with it and pushed the ladder away. At the same time, he heard the sound of things falling off the draining board in the kitchen, and then the back door opening and the sound of boots crunching on broken crockery.

As the ladder moved, the man's feet got tangled in it and he was left clinging on with his remaining good hand, trying to find his footing, but all he managed to do was to push the ladder away sideways with a clatter. McAuley used the Buddha again on the remaining hand and with a cry, the man disappeared from sight. McAuley just had time to turn around as four more men erupted into the hall. One, the youngest, slightly in the lead, saw McAuley, and holding the bread knife out in front of him in a bloodied hand, followed him up the stairs.

"Look what you've done you bastard. I'm going to slit your throat."

Fuck this!

McAuley swung the statuette in a ferocious arc, his arm fully extended. The lad was taken by surprise and reared back, his own momentum now his enemy: he was already unbalanced when the Buddha hit him squarely across his mouth and nose, at the very moment his feet were scrabbling for purchase on the top stair. There was a spray of blood from the blow and his head ricocheted off the wall, further unbalancing him. He was possibly already losing consciousness when he tipped backwards and tumbled down the stairs without making any attempt to stop himself, landing in a heap halfway down, trapped between the wall and the bannisters. Then, as if in slow motion like thawing snow slipping off a roof, he partially rolled down one more stair and in doing so, revealed blood pulsing from under his rib cage where the knife was embedded deep in his side.

There was a moment of stunned silence in the hall as McAuley and the other men looked from the body to each other and in the background, they could hear the frantic shouts of Molly on the phone, an edge of hysteria in her voice, and Sammy crying. They could also hear the sobbing moans of the man outside, still trapped under the wheels of McAuley's car.

"That's evened up the odds," McAuley snarled, beyond faking bravado. "Three down, three to go!"

He brandished the Buddha again and launched himself down the stairs. The oldest of the remaining group looked uncertain and started to back towards the front door, but the other two were made of sterner stuff.

"Bastard!" the stocky Eastern European shouted as he rushed the stairs. "I'm kill you!"

McAuley was already on the way down, his momentum in his favour as he shoulder-barged his assailant, an assailant who at that moment was breaking his stride to negotiate the bleeding man on the stairs. Taking the initiative, McAuley slammed the statue into the man's face, sending him careering backwards. They tumbled down together, a mass of flailing arms, knocking into the second man who had momentarily hesitated to follow his mate.

At that moment the door to the lounge flew open, and Molly hit the second man full in the face with a kettle, gouging him badly with the spout, possibly taking out an eye and splashing boiling water over his head, causing him to lose interest in the wider struggle as he clawed at his face, screaming. Molly followed up that coup by kicking the Latvian (McAuley had decided he was Latvian) several times in the head, hard.

In the meantime, Mrs. Singh had moved the car forward, releasing the man trapped beneath but in a manoeuvre that inevitably ran over him again. The man who had decided to leg it stopped to look, long enough to retch, and then he was off down the street as fast as his legs would carry him.

McAuley looked at the three men at the foot of the stairs: one bleeding profusely, one badly scalded and one probably concussed.

He stood over them, his fists balled, breathing heavily. "Here's the thing: the polis'll be here in a matter of minutes. Stay and deal with them or leave now and take them with you," he said pointing at the body in the road and his victim from the ladder who'd dragged himself, crawling, from the side of the house. "Your choice and the clock's ticking."

Molly was still brandishing her kettle and Mrs. Singh was standing at a safe distance swinging a discarded baseball bat in a belligerent fashion. She didn't give ground and there was power in her swing as the men, supporting each other, staggered past her to their transit. The Latvian came back and dragged Mrs. Singh's unlucky victim by his ankles and threw him unceremoniously into the back. He turned and glared at the little group. "I'm kill you all, you see!" He was spitting with rage and his sneer revealed a gold front tooth.

"Then you'll need to come better prepared next time, gobshite."

The man looked as if was about to come after McAuley again.

Was McAuley going to respond?

Yes. Yes, he absolutely was.

He sprinted purposefully down the path, grabbing the bat from Mrs. Singh in passing, and still high on adrenalin and beyond all reason, laid into the Latvian ferociously, forcing him to his knees. His cries of pain felt rewarding and addictive as the power of violence took over and he felt a frightening loss of self-control.

If I don't stop now, I'll kill him, the common sense voice in the back of his head warned.

McAuley stopped, turned without a backward glance, and walked away. The Latvian, blood dripping down his face, clearly thought retreat was better than retaliation and staggered to the driver's door, clutching his ribs and screaming threats over his shoulder. He heaved himself painfully into the driver's seat and drove off in the same direction as his more circumspect pal.

Rubbing his aching fingers, McAuley watched him go.

The street was silent. There were no twitching curtains and no neighbours tentatively coming to see if they could help. Of course not. There were no neighbours. There was also no sound of sirens.

McAuley looked at his hands as they began to shake.

"When will the police be here?" Molly's voice was small, and she'd started to shake too. Mrs. Singh, remarkably self-possessed, comforted Sammy.

"I don't know," McAuley looked confused. "You rang them."

"No, I didn't."

"WHAT?"

"I was ringing dad, but he didn't pick up. I was shouting at the phone."

"You were ringing your dad?"

She looked crestfallen. "I thought involving the police might make things worse after what you told us."

So you rang a funeral director instead? Aye well, might

have turned out to be appropriate.

He held her close in a hug and felt her trembling.

"Actually," he conceded, "I think you're right. Let's get inside." He shepherded them in and then started to issue orders.

"Pack a bag for you and Sammy. You'll need your passports. Mrs. Singh, could you help?" He thought at first that Molly might refuse, but after a moment, although rather on autopilot, she started to move and headed for the stairs, checking the contents of her handbag.

McAuley looked at the kitchen window. The bottom catch was gone, but the other was good enough to close the window securely. While Molly and Mrs. Singh bustled about, McAuley set about clearing up. The broken crockery from the kitchen was easy to deal with. He picked up the knife from the stairs and put it in the dishwasher together with their coffee mugs and the surviving breakfast crockery, turned it on, then mopped up the blood from the wooden stairs without much difficulty. Wiping the blood from the landing wall was more problematic but the heavy patterned paper hid the worst of what was left.

Apologising profusely to the Buddha for all the infringements of the Noble Eightfold Path he'd committed, he rinsed him under the tap, wiped him clean, replaced him on the chest and closed the landing window. Finally, he put the soiled cloths in a carrier bag. Giving the place the once over, and satisfied, he ushered them to his car, throwing Molly's bag in the boot beside his own and drove off, barely missing the only lamppost on the cul-de-sac.

If anyone had rung the police, they weren't making it a priority.

A cloud passed over the sun and all the warmth of the day disappeared.

Chapter Thirty-Seven

D S Humphreys enjoyed being behind the wheel. He was a good driver, and he knew it as he drove as fast as he dared in the half-light of the early morning, conscious of staying just below the speed limit where he anticipated speed cameras. Being pulled over by traffic cops wasn't on anyone's agenda. He tore open a chocolate bar with his teeth. No time for breakfast this morning. He munched contentedly as he drove.

They passed a fire engine heading in the opposite direction, and then ahead, they could see the blue flashing lights of emergency vehicles.

"This'll be it then," Humphreys noted unnecessarily as they were waved off the road by a pair of uniformed officers in fluorescent yellow jackets, before parking at the rear of a posse of vehicles, police cars, SOCO vans and a low-loader. They were confronted with a large, white marquee.

"I didn't know we were going to a wedding Gov," Humphreys quipped. "I'd have bought a present."

It was stupid o'clock and DI Roberts was in a foul mood. To some extent this was reassuring to those who knew him: it was an indication that the universe was on an even keel. A sunny and cheerful Roberts would have led to suspicions of alien abduction and replacement. His sergeants, Humphreys and Evans, were used to this. Their hosts from Greater Manchester Police were not, and

Evans had spent some considerable time smoothing ruffled feathers.

"It's not as if any of us wants to be out here freezing our bollocks off," a middle-aged sergeant whose name Evans hadn't caught, complained. "You're only here out of professional courtesy."

If he was about to say anything else, he thought better of it, and his mouth set in a thin line before he turned abruptly and headed off to join a small knot of his colleagues.

Evans was walking a fine line between loyalty to his DI and sympathy for their Lancashire colleagues, and he was hoping for a sudden outbreak of self-awareness from Roberts which would allow Evans to return to his normal state of happy indifference.

He wasn't holding his breath.

Evans and Humphreys were both Detective Sergeants, but they couldn't be more different in their style. Humphreys was the public face of their plain clothes unit; stylish and urbane with smart suits and hand-made shoes. Evans, on the other hand, fresh from his latest undercover operation, was used to being invisible in plain sight with ripped jeans, trainers and a range of T-shirts, tending to military camouflage. Humphreys walked with a habitual look-at-me swagger while Evans kept his head down, a head often covered by a beanie. Humphreys had the expensive haircut while Evans shaved his head. Humphreys could be an executive, Evans, a student. The thing was that they were suspicious of each other. Evans recognised Humphreys' ambition and the fact that

DI Roberts favoured him, and Humphreys was wary of Evans' informants' network in case it gave him an edge. Humphreys subtly tried to marginalise Evans and Evans knew it but kept his own counsel, quietly logging the bits of evidence that came his way until he'd have enough to act on. The reckoning, when it came, would be completely unofficial.

The day had begun badly. In truth the day had barely begun at all when they'd been rousted out of their slumbers by phone calls telling them that a car of interest to their case had been discovered on the other side of the Pennines. Humphreys had volunteered to drive, and Evans had been relegated to the back seat where he'd been able to doze for most of the journey, aided by the taciturn silence from the front, broken only by the occasional instructions from the sat-nav, which for some reason had been programmed to have an Australian voice.

That novelty had worn off very soon.

Now they were standing here on a derelict site in the half-light, fully togged up in white jump-suits facing a huge crime scene tent. This didn't bode well: crime scene tents tended to be deployed where bodies were involved, and the three Yorkshire coppers couldn't think of any other reason why one might be put up over a burnt-out car. Inside the tent, they looked at the burnt-out wreck of a high-end motor as a couple of uniforms stood on guard outside, one with a mobile pressed to her ear. Crime-scene technicians, the servants of violent crime, photographed everything and painstakingly searched the ground for clues, looking like aliens as they moved around. Roberts, dressed from the Man-at-Oxfam range in Humphreys' view, had resented giving up his ancient tweed overcoat.

No one could go near the car yet because it was still hot to the touch, hence the size of the tent, Evans realised. If you stood near enough to the wreck, you could benefit from the residual heat which still radiated from it, but you also got a strong smell of smoke, burnt plastic, melted rubber and petrol fumes. Unfortunately, it also came with a side helping of something that reminded Humphreys of barbecues, a view which he shared liberally. Evans wanted to throw open the sides of the tent because the concentration of fumes were making the atmosphere toxic.

"Good luck getting any DNA from that." Evans was right. A fire like this would have destroyed any such evidence.

The front of the car came with either an interesting or a disturbing view, depending on your own perspective: still in the driver's and front passenger's seats were two badly burnt bodies. It was not yet possible to see if there were any others in the back which might have slumped down out of sight.

Roberts was known to be queasy about dead bodies.

Now that they'd had the chance to see what they were dealing with, they were asked to leave the tent as they had nothing to contribute to the work there. They left to the distinctive pinging and ticking sounds of cooling metal and regrouped beyond the cordoned off area.

"Feeling OK?" the Manchester DI had asked Roberts

kindly, from behind a face mask. Roberts' reply was muffled by his scarf, but the tone was unmistakable. Part of Roberts' bad mood was linked to the fact that he'd not brought a COVID mask with him and had already lost the one he'd been given in the tent.

"We're outside, for fuck's sake," was what he'd actually said. Humphreys and Evans did have masks, so Roberts felt shown up, exacerbated by the fact that the Manchester team had singularly failed to offer him another one from their forensics kit. He could have asked, of course, and they'd have happily given him one.

Pride's a funny thing, Evans mused.

This guy's a congenital arsehole, the Manchester DI mused at about the same time.

Evans felt a spot of rain and looked up. Grey clouds were scudding by above. If it didn't hold off, rain would just about make their morning complete. Uniformed officers had attended with the Greater Manchester Fire and Rescue Service. Burning cars were not unusual in any big city what with joyriders, but then they'd made their grim discovery. The two bodies had looked to Evans like a cross between extras from Michael Jackson's Thriller video and a particularly bad zombie movie, with their melted features, rictus grins and scraps of clothing adhering to their frames. The skeletal remains of humans sitting on the skeletal remains of car seats. That they had once been living, breathing human beings was also debatable: one of the Manchester lads had offered the opinion that this could be an elaborate hoax. Evans was sure it wasn't, but as the fire had removed all but the vaguest appearance of humanity from the two corpses, he found it hard to feel shock or disgust. He could manage a mild sympathy but as for deeper emotions, that was as far as it went.

Humphreys was the one who drew his colleagues' attention to the car numberplates: they'd been removed but left propped up against some bricks in plain sight. That was a deliberate two fingers to the police. Whoever was responsible wanted these bodies found and identified. It was as good as a boast, and it looked very much as if Miss Craven's comment about obituaries had been prescient.

Once the numberplates had been run through the system and it was known they'd been flagged, alarm bells had rung, leading inexorably to phones ringing in Yorkshire, while the Manchester Serious Crime Squad had assembled. More experienced at dealing with violent crime that wasn't pub related than their uniformed colleagues, or perhaps inured to it, they didn't have the same horror at the scene. Theirs was a well-practiced protocol which involved the services of the on-call doctor whose job was to pronounce that life had indeed ended. He'd almost laughed out loud, was tempted to accuse them of taking the piss and was gone almost as soon as he'd arrived.

No one envied the pathologist.

Humphreys had accompanied one of the Manchester lads to a greasy spoon and returned with some very palatable coffee and bacon butties, reminding Evans how he liked to throw his money about to curry favour. They'd returned to their car for their breakfast and to wait for the wreckage to cool down sufficiently for the forensics officers to continue their examination.

Sometime later, one of the local force tapped on the window.

"They're getting ready to move the bodies..." Then after the briefest of pauses, added, "... and all that." He didn't elucidate further.

And all what? Evans decided not to pursue that thought.

Reluctantly they left the relative comfort of the car and made their way back to the centre of activity. The forensics team had gathered around the car's front doors which they'd already managed to open. Roberts was standing with his Manchester counterpart.

"Let's hope they were already dead," he commented.

Roberts was struck by this thought and was surprised it hadn't crossed his own mind.

"Doesn't bear thinking about, does it?" He shuddered involuntarily.

It looked as if they were preparing to move the bodies, so Roberts, notorious for having an uncertain stomach when it came to gore, stepped hastily away. He didn't need to see this.

"I wonder if they'll be cremated." Humphreys nodded at the car and smiled disarmingly to indicate that this was a joke. Evans thought it was rather a scary look and ignored him – along with everyone else. Humphreys looked put out.

"Too soon?"

Then, after a delay which saw the forensics team leaning into the car and conferring, they were gestured over again. Humphreys and Evans followed slightly behind, unsure whether they were included in the invitation. Humphreys, suddenly reminded of his own observations about barbecues and with visions of well-cooked meat falling away from bones, decided that discretion was the better part of valour, and stayed at the back.

What they saw confirmed that what had happened there was no accident.

Chapter Thirty-Eight

McAuley stopped about three streets away and dumped the carrier bag of blood-stained cloths in a rubbish bin that had been left out for the bin men. A quick peer inside: *not been yet.*

Then he took out one of his burner phones, took a deep breath and rang the police. He lowered the pitch of his voice and assumed his best (and very convincing) working class Yorkshire accent, playing the part of a concerned citizen and giving a brief, but heavily sanitised account of events, which included the registration number and description of the Latvian's transit van. Just before he hung up, he suggested that they checked local hospitals.

"What are we looking for?"

"I saw someone who looked badly burnt or maybe scalded, and they were carrying bodies into the van."

He heard the call handler draw breath to reply, hung up and put the phone on silent.

They were mainly quiet in the car. Sammy fell asleep fairly quickly and Molly stared out of the window, biting her lower lip. She was looking into the middle distance but without focus because she'd withdrawn into herself. The silence seemed to expand into the car until the pressure was too great.

"You have every right to be angry."

"I agree." Molly turned aside and looked out of the window, chewing a strand of hair. The conversation was over – for the moment.

McAuley desperately wanted to say something conciliatory and affirming but couldn't find the words. He said nothing because in all honesty, what could he possibly say? He'd so wanted to stay out of trouble and now trouble had come searching for him.

He turned on the radio to fill the void. It was rap. His frazzled nerves wouldn't allow him to fiddle with the tuning, so he turned it off again. Molly's continuing silence made the tension unbearable and McAuley felt waves of guilt flowing from him and waves of suppressed resentment flowing back. He studied her in the rear-view mirror. It was unlike Molly to be so quiet, indeed, uncharacteristic for one usually so animated. He knew her well enough to know that she was building up to an outburst.

Molly began to speak, stopped in mid-sentence and burst into tears. Sammy snuggled into her and held her hand.

She made a face as if McAuley had broken wind.

"This isn't happening. This sort of thing doesn't happen to people like us. Tell me this isn't happening."

"It is happening. I'm sorry. I didn't plan this. I didn't want this to happen."

He was concerned by her air of despondency.

"It never occurred to me that the job you do could put us at risk, but it's different for you. You live in that world."

There was an awkward silence in the car for a few minutes. The atmosphere was claustrophobic.

"Am I coming with you?"

Mrs. Singh's voice sounded small and tremulous.

McAuley turned to her. In her silence, he'd almost forgotten she was there, and as he hadn't given her safety a second thought, he was mortified. "Absolutely. I think you should... if you want to, that is."

"It's that or my daughter's."

She sat back, planning what she was going to take with her.

"Ring your dad again."

Molly looked dubious.

"If you don't, he'll put out a missing person's call to the police sooner or later."

She did as he asked, but again there was no answer, so she rang the office and left a rather inventive message about having a last-minute chance of a break and wasn't sure about phone reception.

"We won't have long before someone turns up," McAuley told them when they arrived at the house. "... either Roberts or more of the hired muscle, so we need to move quickly." He looked at Mrs. Singh. "Whatever you need we can buy: it's your passport that's the priority. Leave your mobile in the flat."

While Mrs. Singh gathered her bits and pieces, McAuley rang for a cab and then switched his and Molly's mobiles off, dashed upstairs and put them in his bedside dresser. When she came out, Mrs. Singh had changed her sari and was wearing a rather natty ladies-who-lunch outfit and carrying a long coat and a hat, which McAuley thought showed a considerable level of foresight.

"That's a nice coat," McAuley said, more for something to say and to break the atmosphere than to offer a compliment.

"Isn't it? It's very warm. It's got ducks in it."

They changed cabs three times, travelling separately after the first trip. At their first stop McAuley went into his bank and drew out a large sum of money, advising both the women to find a cashpoint and take out cash, but not enough to alert the bank. Then he gave them both some of his cash and told them to go separately to the ticket office, explaining which tickets to buy. When it came to her turn to pay for her ticket, Molly felt the eyes of the clerk boring into her, as if he knew all her secrets. She felt ridiculous that she couldn't meet his eye. If he knew what had happened, she doubted he'd care. Sammy took the whole thing in his stride with that unquestioning adaptability young children have.

As planned, they ignored each other on the platform and sat in different carriages. It occurred to McAuley that wearing face masks as far as CCTV coverage was concerned was a bit of a bonus, although there were few travellers.

I read too many spy novels.

McAuley held his paper cup of indifferent coffee as if his hands were cold and his life depended on it until the train reached its cruising speed.

They arrived at Luton Airport and managed to find vacancies in airport hotels, registering using false details. McAuley would have liked to have pressed on but was mindful of Sammy's tiredness. He simply wasn't sure whether a layover at an airport hotel would be sufficient misdirection, or whether the night's delay would turn out to have been a mistake. Tomorrow would tell.

———

So, Adebeyo had done as he was told, packed a bag and had been brought to this dive. Would he be here now if that little shit Dale Whatshisname had done as he'd been told? 'The powers that be' had thought the lad's arrest was a great opportunity. He'd been on the fringes of the action and had gone and got himself arrested for some trivial offence, which in Errol's view should have been a huge red flag. Still, they'd told him to slip the lad the fentanyl so that he could distribute it on the Induction Wing when he was moved out of the First Night Centre, but what had he done? He'd tried the goods and ended up in hospital and all hell had been let loose.

Errol had been as cooperative as ever and ready to ring McAuley under instruction in an attempt to draw him into a trap – but not before he'd had a good think and left a little insurance behind. He'd been there for three weeks, compliant, stressed up to the eyeballs and bored. So far so good, but no further. He'd had enough and had decided to put his own plan into action. It was certainly premature, but it was still a good plan. He'd got used to the changes of bouncer-pimps whose other job it was to keep him indoors. The guy who was on tonight had a thing for the girl in the room opposite, and Adebeyo had watched through the spyhole in his door as man-mountain followed his own timetable and paid her regular visits. Adebeyo's plan was to give him ten minutes to get into his stride and then slip out.

There was a knock at the door. He froze.

———

The next morning, they caught another cab for the twenty-odd miles to the end of the Piccadilly Line. Inside the taxi, all was calm, but under the circumstances, that meant very little. They then took the tube and finally made their way to the Eurostar Terminal at St. Pancras where they booked tickets to Brussels and tried to stay in the shadows in the passenger lounge as they checked the departure board, trying not to look like refugees, but feeling like it.

It was a little busier here and they tried a new strategy of attaching themselves to other groups, boarding with them before taking their allotted seats. Mrs. Singh had changed her coat and was now wearing a bobble hat. She was really rather enjoying herself. Sammy had swapped parents to be with McAuley today. Molly had bought him a baseball cap and a new anorak and herself a matching hat and scarf. Although he thought this was probably overkill, McAuley didn't want to pour cold water on their enthusiasm so bought a red baseball cap and a lightweight jacket. Booked to Brussels, they hunkered down for two-and three-quarter hours, feeling a growing sense of relaxation and relief as they left London behind.

Molly hadn't really allowed herself to think much during this whirlwind of escape, and at the hotel had fallen into a sleep of nervous exhaustion when she'd expected to lie awake all night fretting. She used today's journey to reflect on the events that had precipitated this flight and to try to get her head round the possibilities of what the future would hold. She wondered what on earth she was doing, but although the shock of the assault on her house had worn off, the words, "I'm kill you all", echoed loudly in her ears. Sammy seemed to have recovered from the unpleasant experience, much of which Molly reflected, he hadn't actually witnessed, and was now bursting with excitement at being on a train with his dad. She now applied herself to the problem of how she was going to explain things to her parents in a way which wouldn't panic them.

Mrs. Singh, on the other hand, was feeling more alive than she'd felt for years and was already thinking about how she was going to tell this tale to the ladies at the Gurdwara. It ought even to be enough to stem Mrs. Jethani's endless bragging about her blessed grandchildren. She gave some thought to her family and how she was going to explain her absence from home. In the end, she decided to ring them all on the nights she usually rang them, using McAuley's burner phone and claim she'd mislaid her own mobile. She'd pretend to be at home and, given how little attention they usually paid her, she'd fabricate some story or other about life in lockdown.

She was well aware that she'd possibly killed a man, but she didn't let it weigh on her conscience. She hadn't fully admitted to herself until now, how important this little broken family had become to her, and the prospect that someone would threaten to harm them was more than she could stomach, and because her actions had been unselfish and motivated by love and compassion, she had no doubt that Waheguru would forgive her. Not to forget, of course, that she was a Sikh, and regardless how old they were, Sikhs were fierce: you didn't mess with Sikhs - or those they cared about.

McAuley just wanted to relax but that wasn't going to happen. He was assuaged by guilt. Yesterday he'd been fully expecting to make this journey on his own. Why on earth had he insisted on getting Molly and Mrs. Singh together to deliver the news of his imminent departure? How self-indulgent was that? Why hadn't he left as soon as Roberts advised him to, instead of giving his enemies the chance to organise against him? Now he'd put them all in danger and he hated himself.

Guilt is a thief, he thought. *Guilt steals positive emotions and feelings and suffocates them.*

That wasn't to say that guilt is always wrong, but it tends to cling on and insinuate itself like a parasite that renders it's host incapable of rational thought and decision making, and he owed it to his reluctant companions to get this right and get them to a place of safety, so he spent the journey poring over a map of Western Europe, making it a game for Sammy's benefit and making copious notes of alternative routes and suitable stop-off points. By the time they'd reached Belgium he was happy about the next stages of their journey with the latter stages, a confident work in progress.

As planned, rather than travelling through to Brussels they left the train in Ghent, took a bus to Antwerp, sitting apart again, and booked into separate hotels. The first thing next morning McAuley found an old-fashioned barber and using style photos to guide the old boy in charge, said goodbye to his hair and beard.

They bought several changes of clothes and set off again, laying false trails and generally staying in small family-run hotels where they could pay their hotel fees in cash up-front and where they could use a range of aliases, thus avoiding the use of credit cards and passports. Visitor numbers were down because of the pandemic, so the hotels were pleased of the custom and not inclined to ask too many questions.

Alone in another strange bedroom, Molly's mind was still churning. In the immediate aftermath of the attack, she'd not, she realised, been entirely fair to McAuley. She didn't now doubt that whoever was behind it all had already known about her and Sammy, and she couldn't help wondering what would have happened if McAuley hadn't left his coat behind and had driven off. She wasn't at all convinced that she and Sammy would have been left alone, an idea that returned when she later heard what had nearly happened to the Hirsts. She also recognised McAuley's sense of guilt that they'd become involved, but she saw now that that was an inevitability one way or another, and the prospect that he might have left on his own earlier and unknowingly left them to the vengeance of the gang was a line of thought that made her shudder. These were the sort of people who would have been more than happy to have left a message for McAuley in her and Sammy's blood. She couldn't stop thinking about being held hostage and not being able to give them any information apart from the number of McAuley's burner phone, and what they would have been prepared to do to her and her son to get McAuley to turn back. Frightening as it had been at the time she reflected, she was now very pleased they'd left Yorkshire together.

McAuley's head was full of Tamsin. She haunted his sleep and shadowed his waking hours. Every thought (when he wasn't planning their protracted escape) was about that one night and what it might mean for his future.

Every day McAuley bought a British newspaper, and it was in Lyon that he came across an article that grabbed his attention:

Bodies in burnt-out car identified.
Manchester police today confirmed that the bodies found in a burnt-out car on waste ground in Urmston are those of missing senior prison officers Gavin Moss and Vanessa Williams. Police would like to speak to anyone who had contact with either of the victims in the last ten days.

Using a public phone, he rang DI Roberts.

"Where are you?" His tone was belligerent."

"And how are you DI Roberts?"

There was a pause while Roberts tried to work out whether McAuley was taking the piss. While it was true that McAuley didn't actually care, he'd been brought up to be polite. Roberts left it for the moment.

The bodies in the car were Moss and Williams, Roberts confirmed, but what the police were keeping to themselves (for operational reasons, Roberts told him) was that the bodies were chained to the steering wheel.

"Look, if they're guilty of what we suspect, I've absolutely no sympathy. I'll not be shedding any tears."

"And I shouldn't be telling you that, so that's not to be discussed with your travelling companions." McAuley thought his travelling companions were probably beyond caring.

Roberts also told him about an anonymous tip-off they'd received.

"I thought it might have been you."

"Why?"

"Because it happened near your Missus' house and she's with you, I'm guessing. How is Millie doing by the way?"

"Molly's fine, thanks."

"That's good, then." He wasn't a details man, which was unfortunate in a policeman.

He didn't sound convinced when McAuley explained that their departure had been planned, orderly and uneventful. Even so, Roberts confided that a suspicious body had been found on the York Road but with no identification. It looked as if it might have been a hit and run but cameras had clocked a Transit van in the area that could have been the Latvian's, but the film quality was too poor to read the registration number.

McAuley sighed. The U.K. was said to be the European country with the greatest CCTV coverage, but what was the use of that if the picture quality was so poor?

"It doesn't matter, they'll be false plates most likely. Anyway, your tip-off, sorry... *the* tip-off about the hospitals proved useful too, and we have a man with severe facial burns under guard in hospital. They're trying to save the sight in his left eye. Another man turned up at Casualty saying he'd fallen off scaffolding, which seeing as he couldn't remember where the scaffolding was, was clever. On the basis of what we already knew and what you told us, sorry,... what we were told, we pieced together enough to put them under pressure. They've started talking, and there's been some useful information, but we're still a long way from solving this case. We know what happened at Milly's house, but they don't seem to be able to identify their assailant. The gang-master's an Albanian who's well known to us but seems to be coated in Teflon. Nasty piece of work. We suspect he's involved in running kids across county lines."

"We'll need to see you when you get back, of course, but I can't see any charges coming your way, especially as, as you say, you'd already left, and there's not currently enough evidence to link our York Road hit-and-run to the events at Milly's, nor do I expect there to be, however likely it is. By the way, the lad with the stab wound died in the hospital. He was dumped at A&E the evening you rang, sorry,... the evening we received the call. If he'd arrived earlier, they might have saved him. Oh, and you know Adebeyo's gone to ground? So, where are you?"

Roberts tried browbeating McAuley but that didn't work either. Perhaps it was simply pre-retirement jadedness, but did Roberts really think that the hard-man act was an essential part of the job description of a senior police officer? McAuley declined to tell him where he was, but did say that wherever he was, he'd be leaving there soon, as ideas of call-tracing programmes flashed through his mind, (although why he worried, he didn't know, as surely Roberts was on his side).

"I can take care of myself," he said with more confidence than a man with a smashed up flat and a criminal gang (possibly) on his tail ought to exhibit.

There was silence on the line for a few seconds while Roberts digested this, but he wasn't about to give up so easily and gave McAuley a grilling.

"Do you have any plans?"

"Aye, but none that I'm prepared to share with you at this stage." He thought he heard the sound of a desk being thumped in the background. Later McAuley felt guilty about that. He felt that he might have been unreasonable with Roberts, but the man's attitude had got up his nose. It also occurred to him that Roberts assumed they were still in the U.K.

Albanian? Thought McAuley when he'd hung up, mentally apologising to all Latvians.

After he'd hung up, McAuley felt unsettled. As he was heading back to the hotel, he remembered having seen an INTERNET café in a side street somewhere nearby and retraced his steps carefully. It was a quiet place, and the manager, a young woman with purple and orange hair and good English, was helpful. There were about a dozen workstations, but the place was fairly quiet, the only other customers being a couple of teenage boys, nudging each other and sniggering at their screens. The door opened, and two students came in, chatting animatedly and bringing with them a scent of spring. McAuley didn't know why, but their presence seemed to offer a greater sense of security. He ordered a coffee and a croissant from the surprisingly extensive menu, paid for time on-line, logged on with a growing sense of trepidation and was surprised to find various versions of the events in Manchester on several British news outlets, although with no additional information. Unsure what the implications of this might turn out to be, he walked the streets for some time before setting off to meet the others.

———

Up until a couple of days before McAuley didn't have a clear picture of his longer-term future, (now, because circumstances had conspired against him, *their* longer-term future). The short-term picture, however, did not include travelling aimlessly around France while some extremely dodgy characters may (or may not) be following them, so having laid enough of a false trail he felt, the quartet hit the high-speed train network and headed south, still trying to give the impression of travelling separately.

Chapter Thirty-Nine

D.S. Will Humphreys was in a good mood, and he whistled contentedly to himself as the lift took him up the five floors to Errol Adebeyo's flat. His two plain clothes companions were possibly less keen on the tuneless nature of his rendition of the current No. 1. The flat had already been forensically examined from top to bottom. Now it was time to do some real detective work. Humphreys was fairly new to the team, having transferred from Nottingham about eight months earlier. He'd settled into his new role, making friends and generally making a good impression. His plan was to make himself indispensable and aim for speedy promotion.

The young uniform on the door was, in Humphrey's view, rather redundant. This was probably the most mind-numbingly boring duty an officer could be assigned to. He had an empty mug beside him.

"Mrs Axelby, the lady opposite's, been very kind," he said as Humphreys stared at it.

As his colleagues entered the flat, Humphreys slipped the lad a tenner.

"Get yourself a proper coffee and have a pee. There's a café on the corner."

He handed over his card. "Check in with us in forty minutes."

The lad grinned his gratitude and needed no further encouragement.

The building was clean and well maintained and Adebeyo's landing had a subtle smell of rose air freshener. The flat itself, while not luxurious was certainly beyond what Humphreys assumed a prison chaplain would be expected to afford without a private income. That in itself was significant. The apartment was in most respects quite anonymous, in one of those modern blocks that had sprung up behind the railway station.

All homes, however big or small had their own vibe, their own atmosphere and Humphreys stood for a few moments trying to interpret Adebeyo's apartment. What he got was a sense of absence, not of physical absence but a lack of investment, of belonging. There was little here to hint at Adebeyo's personality, very little of a personal nature at all. It was all a bit too bland for Humphreys' taste. The furniture was stylish and comfortable in the generic sort of way you get with rental properties. The sitting room had a few CDs and DVDs, some of them of a fairly hard-core nature. Humphreys didn't know much about Pentecostalism but was fairly sure this wasn't standard viewing material for its clergy. There was a huge bookshelf (with no books) and a couple of prints on the walls that you'd probably find on the walls of every other rented flat in the block. The TV remote was on the arm of the sofa and a chocolate wrapper on the little coffee table beside it. There was no balcony, Humphreys noted, so not that upmarket: it was just the wrong side of the ring road for that.

In the kitchen, the cupboards suggested a man who

ate out or bought in, and there was the packaging of a spaghetti bolognaise ready meal in the bin and a couple of empty lager cans, but little else. Not that Humphreys would criticise Adebeyo for that. In that respect, he guessed, the two men were pretty similar, both single and neither bothered about cooking in an area rammed with an endless variety of restaurants and take-aways. The fridge was virtually empty, just the congealed remains of a carton of milk, an unopened pack of ham nearing its sell-by date and two plain yogurts that it was probably best not to open.

The three policemen moved from room to room, generally duplicating each other's actions. In the bedroom Humphreys was not surprised to discover very little in the way of clothes other than socks, underwear and a T-shirt in the laundry basket. Empty wardrobes with a few mismatched hangers looking forlorn always seemed to Humphreys rather sad. Here was a modern metaphor for abandonment. In the top drawer of the bedside table was a well-worn paperback, *How to be Pentecostal* by Tony Campolo. Homework, he surmised. The bed was unmade but the quilt was neatly turned back, the bright red cover, adding a splash of colour to an otherwise neutral palette. The bedside drawers contained condoms and some interesting magazines which revealed more than Humphreys wanted to know about Adebeyo's tastes.

He rooted around the room for a bit longer, taking out drawers and checking behind and underneath them, lifting the mattress and moving the wardrobe, but there was nothing of interest here. Adebeyo had used the second bedroom as a study and again there wasn't much in it, the laptop and a few pen-drives he knew, had already been taken for analysis, although it was doubtful there'd be anything on them. Still, that was the IT Unit's problem, not his. The bathroom yielded nothing: no razor or toothbrush, just shower gel and shampoo from Boots. A white bath towel was draped over a trendy radiator but it had a damp, fusty smell that revealed Adebeyo didn't wash his towels as often as he should.

Humphreys was fairly sure Adebeyo had fled before he'd been considered a person of interest. That would have given him a small time window to organise himself and remove anything incriminating, which was why he wasn't confident about the laptop. There was something scrabbling for attention on the margins of his consciousness though, but he couldn't bring it into focus.

His phone beeped, and as he read the text from the young PC, he looked at his watch. He'd best bring the lad back: there was nothing here for them. As they left the building, Humphreys glanced up at the block, trying to get a sense of which windows belonged to Adebeyo's flat. He thought he recognised a vase on the windowsill of the sitting room of what must be the right flat, the one with the window frame that looked a bit dodgy. Again, there was that niggle, and he sent the other two back to the station as he retraced the PC's steps to the café for a coffee and a ponder, and as he did, he noticed a black off-roader with tinted windows parked just along from the entrance where it had been, he realised, when they'd arrived. He'd noticed it because those cars always irritated him. Who needs a car that size in a city? He texted the PC and asked if the window on Adebeyo's corridor overlooked the road? It did. "Keep a discreet eye on the black Toyota Land Cruiser. Text me when it leaves or if anyone gets out. If anyone from it comes into the building ring on Mrs. Axelby's door and watch through the spyhole. If anyone goes into the flat, call for back-up but don't engage."

When he got into the café, he rang the station and asked for a check on the license plates.

As he drank his builder's tea and bit into a satisfying bacon buttie, Humphreys tried to order his thoughts. Adebeyo's rent had been paid up-front for the next six months. Wherever he'd gone to ground he wouldn't have risked taking anything with him that if he were picked up, could be compromising. It wouldn't be on the laptop, he was sure of that, and they'd come up with no other properties registered in Adebeyo's name, not that that necessarily meant anything, so unless he'd destroyed anything useful to the police, it was here. Humphreys was fairly sure that Adebeyo wasn't a career criminal: everything he'd read about him so far suggested a man sucked into something beyond his control. That wasn't to say that he hadn't been a willing participant, but he wasn't a man used to the workings of the criminal mind, which was ironic considering he'd worked in a prison. His phone rang.

"I'm off duty in half an hour Sarge. I've just been told I'll not be relieved. I thought you should know."

"Is there a rear entrance or a deliveries entrance?"

The officer told him where it was, and Humphreys warned him that he was coming back in that way.

Back on the fifth floor Humphreys approached the PC again. "What's your name Pal?"

"Watson, Sarge. Paul Watson."

"Right Paul, I'm going back in the flat. Whether or not I'm done by the end of your shift I want you to leave by the main entrance as normal, but I want you to go to the corner where there's a jeweller's shop. When you turn the corner, you should still be able to see the black Toyota because the jewellers has a side window and a front window, are you with me? Stay there until I come out. If anyone leaves the car and comes into the building ring me at once."

Humphreys went back into the flat and straight to the sitting room window. Keeping behind the curtain he slowly moved the vase and turned it upside down. Nothing. He replaced it. Then on a whim he opened the window a little, the window that had looked a bit dodgy from street-level, but which looked absolutely fine from inside. Ducking down below the window, he felt around outside under the sill.

Bingo! Something was taped to the underside. He peeled it off, careful not to drop it. His phone began to ring. He shut the window. "Three big blokes are on their way in."

"Right, ring for back up and wait downstairs to meet them."

Humphreys left the flat and rung the bell of Mrs.

Axelby's door. An elderly lady answered but didn't take it off the chain. Humphreys showed her his warrant card.

"You've been very kind to my uniformed colleague. I wonder if I might come in for a second." Without hesitation the door opened fully and as it closed behind him, he heard the sound of the lift arriving. He gestured to his hostess to stay quiet and looked through her spyhole as three men arrived at the door and let themselves into Adebeyo's flat. They fiddled with the lock for a few seconds before they got the door open. He turned round to offer the old lady an explanation, but there was no sign of her. He rang Watson.

"They're on their way Sarge. I told them no blues and twos."

"Good thinking. I owe you."

It was over quickly.

The old lady's flat didn't have a view over the front of the block, so he had to wait patiently, something he wasn't good at. The lift arrived again, and he saw five officers, a mixture of uniformed and plain clothed, assemble outside Adebeyo's door, but out of sight of its spy hole. Humphreys joined them. As the suspects emerged, the officers had the element of surprise, and there was a short but surprisingly spirited fight-back with one making a break for the stairs. Humphreys set off after him, but the man had not got far because he'd met Watson coming the other way. Humphreys launched himself at the man's back and Watson, stepping smartly out of the way tripped him. They subdued him fairly easily after that. When they returned to the landing, Humphreys was amused to see

Mrs. Axelby standing in her doorway holding a mug of coffee, which she handed to him smiling.

"This has been exciting." And then turning to Watson, "Would you like a coffee Dear?"

Humphreys watched as the three goons were cuffed and escorted down the stairs. They went through the motions of posturing in what they must have hoped were macho displays of belligerence, but as Watson said later, "Being sworn at in a language you don't understand, loses something of the effect."

A small crowd had gathered to watch but drifted away when it became clear that the spectacle started and finished at the point where the men were put into separate police cars and driven off. Humphreys took Watson on one side and discreetly slipped him thirty quid, saying quietly,

"That's your overtime Paul. Thanks for what you did."

Watson looked gob smacked as he pocketed the cash. "Wow! Thanks, Sarge."

Humphreys always felt such investments were worth it. You never knew when you might want a favour in the future.

He returned to his colleagues. "I'll follow you back. My car's round the corner."

Humphreys had no intention of going straight back to HQ though. He drove as fast as he dared back to his own flat avoiding all CCTV. Once indoors he hurried to his bathroom and removed a lap-top from behind the bath panel and copied the contents of the pen-drive he'd liberated from outside Adebeyo's window, and only then did he set off back to the station, the pen-drive now in an evidence bag.

At the station it was Humphreys' good fortune that a group of drunk and aggressive football supporters had been arrested. The place was chaotic and noisy, so no one noticed Humphreys slip in and join in watching as his three suspects were processed. DI Roberts appeared at one point and congratulated him, and pleased with the affirmation, Humphreys had the good grace to big-up Watson's part in the arrest. Roberts took the hint and bustled off to give Watson a public pat on the back. While that was happening, Humphreys made a point of being seen entering the pen-drive in the evidence log.

Chapter Forty

" These people are good at covering their tracks, but this is a game-changer."

Roberts was almost salivating with excitement the next morning. His team was upbeat and self-congratulatory as they lounged in the squad room, several nursing a strong coffee and a severe hang-over: last night's celebrations had been enthusiastic.

"The information retrieved from Mr. Adebeyo's flat is potentially explosive because it names names and gives details of shipments and payments. We assume it was his insurance policy. I'm pretty sure this isn't a standard misper case anymore. He's less likely to have gone missing than to have done a runner, so kudos to Watson and Humphreys for this break-through."

Watson blushed furiously and Humphreys gave a dismissive wave and winked at the young PC. "All in a day's work Boss. All in a day's work."

"It goes without saying that there have been no calls to or from Adebeyo's phone, so the assumption is that he's using cheap disposables. Also, there's been no activity on his bank account since he went AWOL from the prison, but it's all being monitored so if he does use a cashpoint, we'll be on to him. What we really could do with knowing is where he'd go. Does anyone have any hunches on that?"

There was silence and a few shakes of the head.

"Right. Let's look into his background, see if there's

anything there. Check with the prison's HR. They might have some idea."

"The three men detained at the flat are doing the 'No comment' routine," Roberts continued. "One is from Montenegro and the others are Albanian. Whatever they have to say – or not – in the long term, they've been charged for now with breaking and entering. Other charges may follow, but they'll be in court in the morning, and we'll be asking for custodial sentences, which will give us time to carry on questioning them. Not that it matters much: they're small-fry and there are bigger fish to fry."

There was appreciative laughter at this which died away to ragged guffaws as it became clear from the perplexed look on his face that Roberts hadn't realised why what he'd just said had amused them.

"One particular name keeps popping up: Mr. Yellow."

"I've not heard that one before." Humphreys didn't look convinced. "I bet there aren't many of those in the phone book. It has to be a made-up name. A code-name maybe?"

"Who knows? It's not much to go on, is it? But we're putting the feelers out."

"Do we have a description?"

"Those that are talking say they've never met him. He always sends a heavy."

"Someone must know who he is."

"Yes, but seemingly no one we've pulled in so far. We're keeping a discreet eye on Adebeyo's flat because whoever sent them there, may not be aware yet that they weren't able to retrieve the pen-drive and so may try again. There'll be a news blackout in the short-term for obvious reasons and if there's a leak from this office, I will personally come for you! Am I clear?"

There were nods and mutters of "Yes Boss" around the room.

"We don't actually know if the pen-drive was what they were looking for, or even if they knew about it," Humphreys added. "That may just have been the luck of the draw and if so, that buys us more time to build cases against the names Adebeyo just gifted us."

"I think you're right about the names Will..." DS Evans was looking at the arrest photos of the Eastern Europeans and thinking what a dodgy trio they looked, "... but given that we'd already done a forensics sweep on the place and that they knew Paul was on duty outside and waited until they'd seen him leave, I think this was more than a quick check for any incriminating evidence Adebeyo may have left behind. I think they were after something specific."

There was a general hubbub of conversation as members of the team discussed these various viewpoints before Roberts ended the meeting and the team sloped off to their various duties. It was going to be all hands-on deck with this. Still there was always a silver lining, Humphreys thought: overtime.

Humphreys was heading back to his desk when a thought struck him. What started as a slight narrowing of the eyes morphed into a frown and then a broad grin.

Could it be that simple?

He took a staircase down and headed out across the car park to the garages. There, waiting for forensic attention was the gang's van. He slipped on the full protective gear and hoisted himself into the driver's seat, and as he had hoped, there on the dashboard was a fairly new-looking sat-nav. He switched it on, pleased that it still had battery and within minutes was returning to the squad room, a spring in his step and a tune on his lips.

He tracked down Roberts and shared his discovery.

"No way Pedro!" Roberts rubbed his hands together.

"Got to be worth a try, surely?"

Roberts agreed.

"Right, we'll need a search warrant. Come with me."

The Detective Chief Superintendent listened as Humphreys explained how the sat-nav had given up not just Adebeyo's post-code but the post-code where the van's journey had begun.

"Harrogate? And a private dwelling," the DCS mused. "Yes, leave it to me. I'll get your warrant. It's certainly worth pursuing, even if we are twelve hours behind the curve now."

Roberts and Humphreys returned to the squad room and Roberts hastily briefed his team.

"Not bad for an old thicko like me." Humphreys' attempt at self-deprecation foundered on his obvious self-belief.

"Evans! Humphreys! With me!" D S Evans gulped down the remains of his coffee, grabbed his jacket and followed Roberts' departing figure. On the corridor he passed a uniform on another call-out, in the process of putting on a stab-vest and wondered if he should bother.

"Evans. Now!"

He decided against it.

Chapter Forty-One

They drove down the leafy lane in their unmarked pool car at the head of a small convoy. It was a particularly well-heeled area with its large, detached properties set back in well maintained grounds at the end of their private drives.

"Very nice," Humphreys observed. "Well above my pay grade. Doesn't the Chief Constable live around here?" No one answered. They were too busy looking for the address.

About two thirds of the way down, Evans, sitting in the back, pointed, "That's it."

The house's electronic gates were slowly closing, and Evans pointed again, this time at a black Jaguar that had just turned into a side road ahead. There was no other moving vehicle in sight. Roberts jumped out and thrust the warrant into the hands of the plain clothes officer in the next car and told him to carry out the original raid and search.

"What are you waiting for man? A puff of white smoke?"

Roberts looked at Humphreys who, with a huge grin, set off after the black jag. Roberts had a good feeling about this: they'd been on the back foot for too long. In fact, if it hadn't been for Fr. Leo's suspicions in the prison, none of this would have come to light in the first place. But that's sometimes how things went: you played the hand you'd been dealt, even if that meant playing catch-up. They'd turned into the side road after the black jag and Roberts was willing it to make a break for it.

"Try and keep at a discreet distance. We don't want to spook him."

The Jag's driver hit the accelerator.

Humphreys hit the siren and lights and Roberts held his breath for a moment. Would the jag signal and pull over, leaving them with egg on their faces as they interviewed some poor sod going about his lawful business or would it accelerate off? All visions of an elderly couple heading off to Waitrose evaporated as the Jag took off at speed, screeched into another turning and headed for the main road, aiming, no doubt, for the A1. Roberts didn't believe he'd make it. He had to get out of Harrogate first and then negotiate the country roads between the town and the motorway.

"So much for keeping a discreet distance!" Evans muttered.

It had been a matter of seconds: had he been that fraction earlier, or they a fraction later, this suspect would have been clear and away by now. Instead, he was playing the madman on the town's roads as he overtook everything in sight, tucking in behind a Toyota and narrowly missing a pedestrian island before flooring the accelerator again. Harrogate was a quiet town; indeed, a rather sedate town and its citizens hadn't seen anything like this in a long while. They stood at the roadside gawping and a few, caught crossing the road, had to make some nifty moves to get out of the way. Roberts could see a disastrous scenario playing out in his mind, a scenario where everything went wrong, and the chase ended in a pile-up and multiple casualties.

Tension in the car was high. Were they about to get a big break? Roberts was on the radio calling for back up and interception, and Evans was thrown painfully from side to side as Humphreys bounced onto the pavement following the Jag, then jolted the car's suspension as it regained the road. The Jag's driver was good, Humphreys acknowledged, but he was better. The Jag took a chunk out of a litter bin as it sped past before returning to the road. Humphreys avoided that, and, as the engine revved, he kept the pressure up, the noise of the engine filling the car. From his position in the back, Evans had more time to observe what was happening around them and alerted the others to the lights and sirens of other cars as they joined the pursuit, while he clung on so tight his knuckles turned white.

One car, joining the chase from a side street, was just too late to get in front of the Jag, a move which might have brought the convoy to a halt and finished the whole business. Instead, they were approaching the tail-end of a procession of cars slowing at traffic lights when the Jag's driver put his fist on the horn.

Those drivers who habitually used their rear-view mirrors had already seen flashing lights, and perhaps assuming an approaching ambulance, had already had the wit to pull over. The others scattered and there was a loud metallic scraping as the Jag gouged itself down the side of a Nissan Micra, its elderly driver left clutching her pearls as she rear-ended a Vauxhall Corsa. The police car at the back of the chase, pulled over to deal with the chaos. Roberts was on the radio repeating the Jaguar's registration to Control, and Humphreys thought his quarry was losing his cool now. The traffic lights were still red against them, but the cars heading across their path had, in the main, heard the multiple sirens and were approaching the crossing cautiously. The Jag hurtled across with Humphreys in hot pursuit, leaving screeching breaks and angry horns behind them. Humphreys was a highly trained police driver. Nevertheless, Evans shut his eyes and held on for dear life. What Humphreys really wanted was a bloody great articulated lorry, a heavy load, too long for the Jag to risk passing and going at a snail's pace.

"Is this exciting enough for you Colin?"

"Well, it beats flying a desk." In fact, Evans was rather in awe of Humphreys' driving skills.

Dear God! If we've got this wrong...

As ever, fear of bad press was not far from the front of Roberts' mind, and a pile-up now would be both a disaster and a gift to the media.

On the other side of the crossing, moving more into open countryside, but with no time to admire the beautiful scenery, the Jag side-swiped a Seat people carrier, but if the Jag's driver had thought this would be an advantage, he'd reasoned without the vengeful rage of the Seat's middle-aged and apoplectic owner, who gave as good as he got and swiped the Jag back, shunting him into the line of cars coming the other way. As he fought to regain control, he scraped himself down the wings of the first three. Humphreys had little wiggle-room when it came to avoiding the resulting debris as bits of wing-mirror, door handle and bumper ricocheted towards him, the shocked faces of drivers coming the other way, virtually blurs. Evans instinctively ducked as bits of wreckage bounced off their bodywork with thuds and thwacks. The Jag juddered on, clearly damaged now and he took a corner so fast it fought to stay on the road.

"Why doesn't he give it up?" Roberts shouted over the noise of the engine. "He must know it's a lost cause now."

Evans shouted back, bracing himself against Roberts's seat. "He's got gear on him. Probably a ton. He can't afford to get caught in possession."

The car accelerated away again round a sharp bend and Humphreys floored the accelerator to keep up, his eyes all over the mirrors as he steered, but when he rounded the curve of the bend, almost on two wheels, a sign flashed by:

ROADWORKS AHEAD. REDUCE SPEED.

Finding a patch of clear road ahead, the Jag's driver did the opposite, ignoring the red light that blocked the driver's lane and hurtling into the oncoming lane, through a large pool of water, sending up a sheet of spray. The road ahead had looked clear, but his initial judgement was wrong. Lumbering towards them at its own steady pace was a steamroller, intent on flattening newly laid tarmac. Humphreys braked hard and they slewed to a halt. It was only at this point that Roberts realised how much he was sweating.

Suddenly, the Jag began to swerve and judder as the driver struggled for control.

"He's lost a tyre. Look, it's shredded." Evans was animated as the three policemen sensed the endgame approaching.

The remains of the Jag's back offside tyre disintegrated and the officers in the chasing cars could smell the burning rubber and hear the slapping sound the remaining bits made as the wheel ran on its rim, the car shuddering violently as its driver fought with the steering wheel.

It was all over. The Jag squealed to a halt and tried a three-point turn. Together with a gang of road maintenance workers, the three policemen watched as the Jag hit the orange barriers and tumbled backwards into the trench that had once been a road and was now an open maw awaiting new pipe-work. Behind them a growing line of vehicles had drawn up at the traffic lights and people had begun to get out to watch events unfold. Evans, still slightly traumatised by Humphreys' driving and hoping for a more sedate return journey, radioed for an ambulance.

Roberts and Humphreys donned their police high-viz jackets and headed for the edge of the trench. The Jag had landed at a steep angle and the driver was having trouble keeping his door open against gravity as he tumbled out into the ditch, his left foot momentarily catching in his seat belt and tipping him unceremoniously onto his back. He looked up as Roberts, Humphreys and a small group of men in hard hats peered down at him.

Evans began putting blue and white police tape across the road and trying to placate the drivers of cars who now found themselves stuck in a bottleneck.

On both sides of the accident, uniformed officers were laying out traffic cones, taking statements and supervising cars in reversing backwards to a point where they could turn round and find an alternative route.

The driver was in a sorry state with a nasty gash on the bridge of his nose and blood all over his shirt. A pair of glasses hung drunkenly from one ear. He looked to be a man in late middle age, smartly dressed like an accountant or academic. He ruined his doubtlessly expensive shoes by scrabbling out of the ditch where Evans cuffed him and Roberts began to intone,

"You do not have to say anything, but it may harm your defence..."

Humphreys made his way into the ditch and began to examine the car. The boot was flush to the ground, but scattered over the back seat were small parcels of something wrapped in cling film. Not, he assumed, the contents of a packed lunch. In the foot well of the back seats was a briefcase, its contents also scattered, bundles of high denomination notes. The stupidity of some criminals always bewildered Humphreys. Or was it arrogance rather than stupidity? Without looking round, sure of being sheltered from the others by the body of the Jag, Humphreys leaned in, picked up a bundle and slipped it in his inside pocket.

"You need to see this Boss," he then shouted to Roberts

who took a little longer getting down.

Roberts whistled as he understood what he was seeing.

"Any identification here?" Roberts asked. "He's doing 'no comment' up there."

Humphreys leaned in again and pulled out the driver's suit jacket and frisked it. The inside pocket held an Irish passport and a wallet. The passport showed the likeness of a mild-looking, nondescript man going by the name of Donal Mitchell. The wallet, however, revealed a UK photo driver's license in the name of Aled Edmonds and the address in Harrogate.

In the background they could hear the sound of another siren as the flashing lights of an ambulance appeared. Edmonds/Mitchell was hustled away by paramedics under Evans' oversight.

Roberts was inordinately pleased with himself, and his thoughts turned to how he was going to spin the press conference in such a way that he came out of it smelling of roses. It always did to be one step ahead of the press: give them something before they got to know about it and came looking with inconvenient hunches.

Chapter Forty-Two

A few days later, McAuley's little group left Lisbon on the container ship *Funchalense 7* for a two-night journey to Porto Santo. McAuley had already discovered that there was no ferry service from the mainland, which surprised him, but he was sure some freighters would carry passengers, and knowing about the absence of ferries in advance had enabled him to do some research on the alternatives: they would not fly unless they absolutely had to, because to give personal details at that late stage would undermine all the care they'd taken so far.

They were the only passengers on the ship, which was not much of a surprise, and the crew member who acted as purser told them that they'd had few passengers recently because of COVID, and they didn't get all that many at the best of times. Had they not been travelling as a party, they would have been confined to their cabins for the duration of the journey as a precaution. They were allowed to take their choice from six no-frills but identical cabins. They were well designed and functional with bunk beds, two armchairs, a writing-desk and chair, a bookshelf, adequate storage and a porthole. Each had an en-suite shower room.

McAuley's cabin overlooked the Tagus River as it flowed out to sea, and he spent some time just watching the comings and goings of commerce in *Porto de Lisboa* until a change in the tone of the engine, which he realised had been running quietly, signalled departure and with a disconcerting grinding and crashing sound (or so it seemed) the ship began to edge forward as it headed out to sea.

Sammy insisted on sharing with his dad, and of course, wanted the top bunk. The adults explored all the cabins and the cosy lounge, hunting for English language books and magazines left by previous passengers. It was a poor haul, and mainly science fiction which none of them liked. Fortunately, they'd had the wit to visit the English language section of one of Lisbon's better bookshops before they'd embarked, Mrs. Singh opting for Ian Rankin, Molly for historical romance and McAuley for a World War 1 murder mystery set in the trenches. Sammy got colouring books which delighted him. Nevertheless, the voyage was dull: they couldn't go on deck because it was a working boat and had it not been for the radio in the lounge, which seemed stuck on a station that played middle-of-the-road music, and the TV where reception which was good during the day when Sammy could watch cartoons, but bad in the evenings when the adults might have been interested in watching, McAuley was convinced they'd have caught cabin-fever.

As it was, none of the adults were good sailors and it wasn't even that rough, although there were occasions when the ship seemed to be making heavy weather as it got into deeper and less sheltered waters. Molly found it easier simply to stay in bed listening to music on her phone to stave off the nausea, although she found the ship's vibrations strangely comforting. McAuley didn't enjoy the strange and unpredictable movements of the ship and had been caught out by one particularly violent lurch and nearly found himself on the floor. Mrs. Singh remained rooted in an armchair, only moving to visit the bathroom. Still the food was good, served by a Filipino steward, and they slept well.

At Porto Santo they finally made the two-and-a-half-hour inter-island ferry crossing to their destination.

Roberts sat back from his desk and massaged his temples. Paperwork was the bane of his life, but it had to be done, and it had to be done thoroughly. He envied those officers who had a gift for language, who could put the right words into a sentence in such a way that the argument was cogent and compelling. He wasn't one of them, and it irked him that his laborious and painstaking clerical work came across as clunky and stilted. He picked up the folder in front of him and reviewed the case again as if somehow, by dint of repetition, something new would leap out from the pages.

Operation Cheetah: he'd long since given up wondering how the force came up with these names, computer generated no doubt, but the problem with Cheetahs was that they moved fast, and this cheetah was very slow. In fairness, things had gone well so far. A number of arrests had taken place, a significant quantity of drugs had been seized and some dodgy money confiscated, but the main prize had so far remained out of reach. Until the big players were brought to justice, these current signs of progress would always be just a tantalising taste of what might have been. This was, in one way or another, a stage in any investigation and it was a stage all coppers hated. At this stage in an investigation all coppers needed a break. That might come via the slog of dissecting disparate pieces of information until someone made the link that broke the case, or it might come suddenly and unexpectedly through a confession, or the breaking of an alibi. So far, the latter solution looked unlikely. The minor to middling figures they'd arrested so far were either too scared of reprisals from above or had worked on a strictly need-to-know basis and so had no names to give up. Roberts was convinced Adebeyo was the key to breaking the case, but he was in the wind. Still, the powers that be seemed pretty upbeat so far, although Roberts didn't think it would be that long before he felt them breathing down his neck again.

He threw down the folder he was working on in frustration. He needed to get out of the office and change his focus of attention. The brain was a wonderful organ and would, he believed, continue to work on the problem subconsciously. He took several surreptitious deep draws on his e-cigarette, waving the vapour away with his hand and was about to set off to the canteen for a coffee. He didn't get far before his phone rang. It was Detective Chief Superintendent Murchison's secretary asking him to drop by for an update. He knew Murchison well enough to know that 'drop by' meant 'drop everything'. He'd wanted a change of environment sure enough, but not this one. Still, Murchison's Secretary made very good coffee.

—

Errol Adebeyo stood in the centre of this bed-sit. He was deeply pissed off. This was not how it was supposed to have ended. Two more big jobs. They had promised him. Two more big jobs and then the planned exit strategy: a resignation (a new opportunity down south, he was to tell everyone), a nice speech, a few shaken hands and then out of prison chaplaincy with no suspicions or questions asked. Christmas, they'd told him. That would be the last big one. He'd have given in his notice, and to avoid suspicion they'd told him he'd leave two weeks later. And now this: on the run for God's sake! On the run and with every chance of a long prison sentence if he was caught. Out of prison chaplaincy certainly, but not out of prison, and everyone knew how convicted prison staff were treated behind bars.

Of course, there had always been the possibility that it would all go tits-up, but he had been so close to untangling himself from it all. They'd got away with it for so long perhaps they'd become complacent, but he couldn't think how. Well, he certainly hadn't been careless, but he thanked his lucky stars he'd had the foresight to get another passport. And now here he was, laying low in this dump in the Harehills suburb of Leeds, where there were many African-Caribbean faces and where his presence wouldn't attract attention. This, he'd soon realised was a complete joke as he wasn't allowed out. The only sight anyone was going to get of him was through a window.

And it was a dump. He'd worked out fairly quickly

that the other flats were used by rent-boys and hookers with comings and goings all hours of the day and night, and there had been one scary encounter with a pimp who wouldn't let him leave. He felt sick, as if the walls were closing in on him. On top of everything else was he now developing claustrophobia?

He sat on his bed wearing what he'd had on when he'd fled: trainers, jogging bottoms and a sweatshirt, his relaxation kit. Most of his other clothes were crammed into a bin liner and sat in the corner of the room waiting for him to summons the motivation to unpack them. It would be a long wait.

"Get out now. We've been busted," the phone call had said. As if he hadn't worked out they'd been busted: he'd been interviewed by prison staff and police because he'd been there when Security had searched the food for God's sake. He shivered involuntarily as he remembered the numb terror of being marched out of the delivery area. He'd wondered about that search. Was it just bad luck? Random searches weren't unknown, but festival food was usually exempt. The Imam didn't usually attend these deliveries, but it had been Ramadan, so perhaps it was to be expected, but Thorburn and his little Jock pal? No, that was suspicious. He'd passed that on in his 'debrief', but Thorburn had disappeared and McAuley hadn't turned up to the ambush he'd tried to set up.

He sat on the edge of the bed, a bed he could barely bring himself to sleep in given its former owner's life choices and tried to think positively. He'd been deeply in debt and his debt had been sold on to the gang who had made him the proverbial offer he couldn't refuse and who now owned him. Well, he was now debt-free and had a tidy little nest-egg for his fresh start: no more gambling for him. While he'd been working, he'd managed to get counselling and group therapy. He'd hit rock bottom once (and look where it had got him) so there was no way he was ever going down that route again.

Adebeyo didn't know how much he could trust those who controlled him.

Who am I kidding?

He knew exactly how much he could trust them. He was dispensable, and he knew it as he remembered with a pounding heart the execution he and a small group of other "new recruits" had been forced to watch as a warning.

A skinny pale lad was dragged in by two gorillas, snivelling and crying. It was a pathetic sight. He was a weedy specimen, probably an addict, and he looked cowed and terrified. The head honcho walked up to him, a friendly smile on his face, put an arm round his shoulders and manoeuvred him round to face the newcomers.

"We're going to put on a little show for our guests."

As the lad smiled uncertainly, the boss stepped back and punched him hard in the face, breaking his nose. The lad's head snapped back, and he dropped like a stone. He lay there, out cold for a couple of seconds before struggling to get back up, shaking his head in an effort to clear it. He was on all fours when the kicking started. Each kick was emphasised by a syllable.

"THIS. IS. WHAT. HAP. PENS. TO. GRASS. ES."

Adebeyo and the others watched in stunned shock as the lad was beaten and kicked to a pulp as he begged and sobbed for mercy, trying to crawl away. There were only so many times a head could be used like a football, but the kicking continued long after the boy stopped moving.

"Shit! Look at the state of my clothes." The psycho kicked the corpse again for good measure.

There was a sudden, strong smell of urine coming from the man next to Adebeyo, who had to drag his gaze from the pulp of the lad's face, gore everywhere, and feign indifference as the sound of boots hitting flesh echoed in his mind.

"Just in case you get any doubts about where your loyalties lie," the boss had said to them. Then he'd laughed, looked at Adebeyo and said, "You're looking a bit pale, boy."

Everyone laughed on cue – including Adebeyo. The laughter had an edge of hysteria to it.

He'd had nightmares for weeks, but it was a message that he'd got loud and clear and he'd been sure to be the most cooperative gofer possible, knowing that it had been noticed and hoping that little bit of currency would weigh in his favour when it came to it. Since then, he'd been paranoid about the chances of escaping from those who had been putting more and more pressure on him: stupid things like bringing in a phone and passing it to Hussain, the sort of thing that was so risky it could have got him instant dismissal or even arrest.

At one stage recently he'd been so stressed that he'd seriously considered going to the authorities, to the new deputy governor for security, but had been put off by his reputation and anyway, he'd have nothing to give them other than what implicated himself because he didn't know who else was involved so had no names to give up. Obviously, there were others in the prison system who were involved – clearly at least one person in the kitchen apart from Hussain, who now knew Adebeyo was part of the conspiracy, unnecessarily so, in Adebeyo's view, and it was a factor that had worried him. This was an organisation where it seemed each individual knew as few other names as possible.

The thing was, he'd had his own extraction arrangements sorted out. It was identical to the one he was ordered to follow except for one detail: timing. During this year he'd taken no leave and on Christmas Eve, he'd be out of there for good. The plan was to ring the chaplaincy office on Christmas Day during the joint carol service when he knew the call would go to voicemail, claiming some family emergency and taking the last fortnight of his notice period as leave. He'd felt sure with his new passport, that he'd be able to quietly slip away before anyone even realised he'd gone, and make it to the Caribbean somewhere. He'd fancied flying from one of the Scottish airports, or perhaps Belfast, so by the time they'd realised he'd pulled a fast one he'd have been long gone and, hopefully, untraceable. He'd fantasised about ringing from the airport. That little flourish really appealed to him.

Chapter Forty-Three

Parking his companions at a street café under an awning, McAuley crossed the square to the address where the letting agency had its offices. He was reassured to discover that the building was smart and well maintained. Putting on his mask and ignoring the sweeping staircase in favour of the ornate, gated, period lift, he travelled up to the third floor with its large windows and polished wooden doors. He was greeted warmly by the receptionist and ushered into a large and elegant open-plan office where three young people were working at computer stations. The only man in the trio stood and welcomed McAuley. He was wearing a corporate badge which announced his name to be Victor. He apologised for not shaking McAuley's hand and offered him a coffee, which he accepted as the others were enjoying theirs at the café as he could see through one of the windows.

McAuley started straight away by explaining that he and his companions had travelled for privacy and was reassured to be told that the agency did not give out client details. In fact, they would make a point of informing him if any enquiries should be made. The fact that he'd come with three guests didn't throw the letting agent at all.

"You're lucky though," Victor told him. "If you'd come any earlier, you'd have had to quarantine for a fortnight. The regional government has only just lifted that requirement."

McAuley realised that he hadn't factored that possibility into his plans.

"Anyway, you have two properties here Mr. McAuley. One is a two bedroomed seafront apartment which we had originally earmarked for you. The other is a five bedroomed quinta in *Monte*."

He gestured to the back of the building, which McAuley guessed was where the suburbs climbed the hill.

"I'll just ring our housekeeping team and make sure that the property is ready."

McAuley apologised for the inconvenience of the changed plan but was waved away with a smile. He was starting to like young Victor.

McAuley had to admit that as he'd never been here before he had no idea where *Monte* was, or indeed what a quinta was, so as they drank their coffee, the young man explained. Quinta, it turned out was the word for "estate", although here in the capital it simply meant a large house with gardens, and it was pronounced with a K, not a Q.

"But you'll be impressed Mr. McAuley. It's one of our premier properties. I would show you a photograph, but I'd rather let you see for yourself because photos don't do it justice. *Monte* is a suburb, more properly a parish, which extends along the mountainous foothills in the northeast corner of the city. It has the valley of *Ribeira de João Gomes* on one side and the river-valley of *Fundoa* on the other."

McAuley listened politely, not willing to admit that he had no idea where any of these places were.

"You get there by road or by cable-car," Victor continued. "That makes it sound a long way away, but no where's a long way away here. Anyway, if you're ready I'll take you up there."

McAuley waited with the others at the café while Victor collected a large off-roader and brought it round to meet them. The journey was fascinating. It was an urban area, yet they passed many colourful and beautifully maintained villas and plenty of gardens: it soon became clear that *Monte* was a desirable place to live, despite its winding roads and occasional hairpin bends. Victor was right: although it was high up, it wasn't that far from the city centre, and Sammy whooped with excitement as he clocked the cable car passing overhead. They'd travelled, McAuley estimated, about a mile and a half as the crow flies from the agency's offices when they drew up at the end of a small side road.

"The entrance to the botanic gardens is there." Victor pointed slightly down the hill, "As is the cable-car station, but in order to go down to the centre on that you'd have to go up first to the Monte Palace Tropical Gardens, and then down to town. It's more of a tourist thing. Locals don't use it so much. There's a bus stop there," pointing to a raised area opposite the garden entrance. "There's three or four buses will take you to and from the centre and that's much more straight forward and considerably cheaper. Now," (he gestured to the side road), "There are two properties here. Yours is on the left. Beatriz, from our housekeeping staff will meet you there. Please ring us if there's anything you need. As you know we're not terribly busy now, not like we'd normally be, so if there's any local advice you need, either ring or drop in."

He waved, reversed and was gone.

A wall, maybe ten feet high, topped with roof tiles, fronted the road. In the middle was a large arch with double wrought iron gates and in the left-hand gate, carefully disguised in the intricacy of the metalwork, was a smaller gate for people. Perhaps the gates had once opened to allow carriages to pass in and out, but now the courtyard was a chequerboard of large flagstones and gravel with a profusion of vibrant flowers and grasses, some growing in the gravel and some in large pots. Beatriz, a lady in her fifties and wearing a smart uniform, greeted them warmly. She opened the small gate for them, and they stepped into the courtyard. McAuley carried his backpack into the courtyard and looked around.

The quinta took up three sides of a square with the gated wall making the fourth. It had the roof tiles typical of the island, long, curved, interlocking but black. The walls were rendered in dove grey with white cornerstones and the doors and windows were shuttered in black. The two wings of the house were made up of ground and first floors, but the central section also had rooms in its raised attic area, and a wonderful pair of curved stairways made their elegant way up to a grand carved wooden door on the first floor, suggesting that this was an upside-down house. And so it proved to be.

Facing into the courtyard, the house had colonnaded

galleries, part walled to waist height, running all three sides of the house, making a garden walkway on the ground floor and a veranda on the first floor, heavily adorned with climbing plants.

The scent of Angels Trumpet and Jacaranda filled the air. He looked at the house, taking it all in with mixed feelings: it was as stunning as Victor had hinted and then some, and yet before today he'd had no idea of its existence. He walked around the courtyard peering in windows, smelling the flowers and running his hands over balustrades in a proprietorial way. No wonder Victor had said it was one of their most exclusive properties, and it was his, and he had just fallen in love with it.

"What do you think Molly?" McAuley had the broadest of smiles.

"It's gorgeous."

Well, at least we'll have some peace and quiet here.

Chapter Forty-Four

Three weeks later.

That had been a very profitable twenty minutes. Detective Sergeant Will Humphreys turned up his collar against the wind and lit a cigarette. Cemeteries weren't his usual haunt but on a Sunday morning he could be confident that in this little corner under a grieving angel, he'd be uninterrupted. Still, ever cautious, he'd picked up a bunch of flowers at a garage on the way. This was as good a place as any to meet informants now that the pub he liked to use was COVID-prohibited. He enjoyed working undercover and had really fallen on his feet in the drugs squad. Those raids had allowed him to indulge his taste for the white powder, little bags slipping into his pocket instead of the evidence bag.

He mulled over his conversation with the Eastern European. He'd been very tempted not to get involved: his approach had unnerved him. It was one thing to have informants, it was another to have someone know you could be bought for the right price, but with the exchange of information he felt that this piece of shit had as much to lose as him, and it was not just the valuable information that compromised him. Humphreys had recognised him, and this was not, he rationalised very quickly, a time for heroics: if this man's reputation was anything to go by, he didn't fancy his chances against him. He was the sort of man who'd think nothing of throwing acid in the faces of those who crossed him or taking a drill or a hammer to their knees, elbows, and wrists. He liked people to be a living witness to the consequences of their foolishness, and then there were also the great advantages of witness intimidation. Humphreys was unarmed, and on his own, and the Albanian, Vrioni, was known to be handy with a blade, so he did what any sensible man would do. He feigned ignorance and pocketed the money.

His informant wasn't to know that the game was up in Humphreys' opinion, or he wouldn't be hanging around like this. The drugs bust at HMP Low Moor had outed a number of staff members as corrupt. Deputy Governor Moss was dead, the faux Pentecostal Chaplain, Errol Adebeyo had fled, but others had already been charged and were in prison, and it wouldn't be long before significant arrests would be taking place in the wee small hours all over the north of England and further afield on the basis of their testimony and what had been found on Adebeyo's pen-drive.

Those early morning visits would surprise those who believed they were untouchable, the big players, and the whole edifice was about to come tumbling down. This time the Drugs Squad believed they had the evidence to net the whole gang, and Humphreys would be able to take some credit for providing extra names after today's little chat, but he couldn't understand why this guy was willing to give up so much valuable intel just to seek out information on three men's locations. This was clearly personal, but Humphreys had only been able to offer information about one of the three. Only his DI knew where the other two were, so it had been a help that his poker-playing, prison officer pal, Mick, was his way into prison gossip.

Humphreys had dropped his voice, as if somehow anxious that occupants of the nearest graves might overhear. These bits of chit-chat, together with what he knew from working the case, seemed to satisfy this thug. Humphreys knew from experience that bits of seeming hearsay could well provide a break-through.

He gave an involuntary shiver. Vrioni's smile when he'd passed over the rumour about the prison officer in hiding had been chilling. He was glad he wasn't going to be at the receiving end of this man's wrath: he was a nasty piece of work.

Humphreys was confident that Vrioni wouldn't hang around long enough to be arrested, assuming he was even on the list. And if he wasn't on the list? Humphreys wasn't about to tempt fate by throwing his name into the mix. He looked at his watch. Ten minutes before the reporter turned up. This morning was turning into a nice little earner.

—

The Albanian was a driven man, and it was vengeance that drove him. He would have liked to settle accounts with the priest and the prison governor who he held responsible for the failure of his smuggling operation, (and who knew, maybe at some point he would). In the meantime, the prospect of dealing with the third man, that disrespectful little bastard of a Scotsman was a pleasure he'd savour. He burned with indignation and humiliation whenever he thought of him, which was often, and humiliation led to a simmering anger which demanded a reckoning. It was still a source of astonishment to him that McAuley had not only dared to take him on but had comprehensively beaten him and his men in a six to one fight. How could that possibly have happened? More to the point how could the Albanian allow it to go unpunished? He'd be a laughingstock, his authority forever undermined amongst those who mattered and that was unthinkable. This was more than damage limitation now word was out about the disgrace and ignominy he'd suffered. He needed – no, demanded – blood to restore his dignity and esteem and he would have it. There was simply no line he wouldn't cross. In his line of work, reputation was everything.

And now he had a lead, albeit a slim one, and he intended to pursue it as far as he could.

—

Errol Adebeyo was in a state of panic. Last night they'd moved him to a hotel room near Manchester airport and he was now on his way to departures. They'd come for him and told him they had a job for him. He knew who 'they' were, not that he recognised any of these guys, but he knew better than to argue. They'd even told him his 'contract' still had time to run, before bundling him into a cab. You'd have thought that being near an airport would have played into his plan, but for whatever reason they'd decided to put a minder with him, one who discouraged conversation. On the plus side, they were clearly not about to permanently dispense with his services (in the short-term, at least) if

they still had work for him to do. What made him smile –
possibly the only thing – was the fact that they'd provided
him with a passport in the name of Winston Armstrong.
He now had two, and the possibility that he could make
his escape from wherever they sent him kept him clinging
on to sanity.

"We know roughly where McAuley is. Find him,"
they'd told him. "You know him. You know what he looks
like."

*Find McAuley? On an island with a population of
290,000?*

It was not up for discussion.

He had been seen to the security gate by his personal
minder who no doubt intended to hang about in the
observation lounge to make sure he actually boarded.
The only advantage he could see was that he was now
on his own which gave him some breathing space. He'd
been given a phone number, someone called Aurelio.
This contact had taken some time to organise he'd been
told and was all done by networking: contacts of contacts
and friends of friends had eventually come up with this
number. No one knew this guy's worth or pedigree, but
he'd been tasked with finding a safe house for Adebeyo
and was being paid to be his eyes and ears. Apparently, he
had passable English.

On arrival, he'd looked at the departures board and
his heart sank. It wasn't exactly an international hub, and
most of the departures that day were to U.K. airports and
were budget airline package tours. His most promising

option seemed to be to fly to Lisbon or Porto, change passports and then take his pick from a wider international selection. He'd missed those flights for today, and so, short of sleeping in the airport, which clearly wasn't buzzing when the tourist flights had left, he felt he ought to meet Aurelio and have his arrival duly reported back.

Adebeyo wondered if he was living in an alternate reality and if his situation hadn't been so serious, he might have laughed. Aurelio, the one with passable English, turned out to have almost no English, and had been clearly unhappy when he'd met him outside the airport. It was a look Adebeyo had seen many times before.

It said, 'You're black.'

Aurelio led him to the hire-car franchise and indicated that he was to rent a car in his own (well, Armstrong's) name, which seemed weird, and which rather depleted the working capital he'd been given. They drove from the airport, through streets where he saw no other black faces. They stopped briefly in a multi-storey car park while Aurelio retrieved something from a big van, and they were off again. Adebeyo wasn't used to driving on this side of the road and seriously misjudged the ticket-operated exit barrier. Being directed by a man who only used gestures and angry words that Adebeyo was clearly supposed to understand but didn't, made the journey less than idyllic and he was slightly surprised to leave the main town behind. He was even more surprised when they arrived at possibly the worst hovel it had ever been his misfortune to stay in, where Aurelio had abandoned him with one carrier bag of groceries and driven off in his hire car.

"You no go. Be back," was his parting shot but he didn't have enough English to say when.

Adebeyo sat in a threadbare armchair in the centre of the room looking anything but relaxed. He was clutching his arms across his body in a defensive pose, as if he was frightened that the walls might attack him. Had it not been for the mesmerising view from his back window and the prospect of sitting on the sliver of a rear veranda and taking in the fresh air and sunshine, he might just have topped himself. On top of that, he wasn't even sure which country he was in. Were these the Canary Islands? He put his head in his hands and wept.

Audrey Craven (not the name on her new Irish passport) removed her sunglasses and teased her fingers through her hair, appreciating the stylish new cut. This beach, in this most exclusive of exclusive Caribbean resorts was heaven. That she ought never to return to the U.K. bothered her not one bit. Life was for living, not for regrets.

Over time, she'd managed to develop a strong network using the prison's database, a database she had regular and legitimate access to. It was easy to spot who the no-hopers and liabilities were and who were the ones with nous that could be moulded into usefulness, and she had covered her tracks with great care. She'd found it easy to use middlemen: ex-cons who'd deliver a message, a warning or an occasional beating from Mr. Yellow: someone to grease palms too. She never used the same man twice, and of course she had an endless supply of ex-cons. She never met them face to face; encrypted messages on burner phones proved much easier than she'd expected. Nevertheless, she abhorred the level of violence that had taken place. She knew she couldn't have micromanaged every aspect of the operation, but the involvement of the Albanian and his crew had been a serious mistake and she felt a small prick of conscience about Errol Adebeyo. However, she balanced that against the continued wellbeing of McAuley, the Hirsts and the Thorburns on whom she wished nothing but good fortune. Neither did she feel guilt over Gavin Moss who she had despised, and the only time she ever thought about him was when she smiled to herself about the fact that he had worked in the next office without ever suspecting.

It had started as an academic exercise; a bit of fun to counter the boredom of her job until the point that she realised it would work. Then it had become Audrey's revenge after a career of being marginalised, patronised and undervalued.

Good old Audrey. She's a trooper.

So, she'd lived up to the image: a spinster who looked after her non-existent mother, discreet, unassuming, efficient, utterly reliable, and indispensable. Her assumed identity as Mr. Yellow had been a personal indulgence and a big clue for those who could see it. No one had. Of course, she'd virtually spelled out to the slow DI how it had all been done, but it had gone over his head. It was as she had always known: middle-aged women were easy to underestimate.

She thanked the waiter and watched bubbles rise in her drink, appreciating the condensation on the outside of the glass. She sat, almost contented, and with the mountains behind her, did what everyone did when they had a few moments to spare: she looked out at the shimmering sea, listening to the chatter of unfamiliar birdsong, and appreciating the warm breeze and the feel of the sun on her skin.

Characters

Prison:

Governor Declan O'Brien
Deputy Governor Peter Hirst
Deputy Governor Gavin Moss
(Deputy Governor Vanessa Williams)
Senior Officer George (The Hatchet) Hatcher
Officer Gregor McAuley
Officer Luke Quarmby
Officer Sharon Mills
Officer Dan Holdsworth
Officer Craig Heaney
Officer Tom Cooper
Officer Mick Wilson
Officer Pete Brown
Officer Maggie Fletcher
Officer Scott James
Officer Jimmy Marston
Rev. Leo Thorburn
Pastor Errol Adebeyo
Sister Mary Clodagh
Fr. Stephen
Nurse Paddy Lafferty
Imam Khan
Audrey Craven
Terry
Sprout

Bruno
Delroy
Ricky Clark
Dale Carter
Kawalski
Mohammed Hussain
Wayne Mallanaphy
Madam Cynthia

Police:

Detective Chief Superintendent Iain Murchison
Detective Chief Inspector Karen Armstrong
Detective Inspector Cuthbert Roberts
DI Sadie Brewer
Detective Sergeant Colin Evans
DS Will Humphreys
DS Gillian Baines
DS Andrew Kennedy
Detective Constable Rob Carlton
DC Don Griffiths
Police Constable Paul Watson
PC Jaitik Agarwal

Others:

Andreja Horvat
Marco Erjavec
Oskar Petek
Magda
Polina

Aaron-pronounced-Arran
Gloria Castle
Gary
Mitch
Finn
Mrs. Axelby
Kuljinder Singh
Molly Woodruff
Sammy McAuley-Woodruff
Jerry Swan
Judith Hirst
Tamsin Hirst
Sonia Green
Flamur Vrioni

Jack Parkes

Jack Parkes was born in Malta where his father was serving as a Royal Marine. He grew up on the Kent coast and North London where he attended The Ashmole School in Southgate before going to Leeds University to study Theology, and to Cambridge University for his Post Graduate Certificate in Education.

He worked as a teacher of both Religious Studies and Citizenship for Kirklees Local Education Authority and for Bradford College as a teacher trainer, before being ordained as a priest in the Anglican Church. He has since worked as a prison chaplain and a hospital chaplain. He lives in Leeds with his wife Rachel.